Praise for *Last Bite*

"Peele writes with warmth and sharp comic timing. . . . In tone and spirit, the novel recalls Fannie Flagg's *Fried Green Tomatoes at the Whistle Stop Cafe* (1987) with its bittersweet mix of mystery and humor. . . . A hearty novel layering grief and humor in a flavorful Chicago-style slice."

—***Kirkus Reviews***

"In *Last Bite*, Peele has created a cast of characters and a fast-moving plot worthy of the Windy City, her beloved hometown."

—**Stan Bunger,** author of *Mornings with Madden*

"You can almost hear the L rumbling in the distance as the smell of garlic bread wafts from a cozy kitchen window."

—**Jane Ubell-Meyer,** founder of Bedside Reading

"*Last Bite* is a delectable page-turner that left me hungry for more."

—**Michelle Cox,** author of *The Fallen Woman's Daughter*

"*Last Bite* delivers the transformative power of hope while proving laughter is indeed good medicine."

—**Sara Connell,** author of *Bringing in Finn*

Last Bite

a novel

Amy S. Peele

SHE WRITES PRESS

Published in 2026 by
She Writes Press, an imprint of The Stable Book Group

32 Court Street, Suite 2109
Brooklyn, NY 11201
https://shewritespress.com

The Library of Congress Control Number is available upon request.
ISBN: 979-8-89636-084-1
eISBN: 979-8-89636-085-8

Interior designer: Katherine Lloyd, The DESK

Printed in the United States

This book is dedicated to the vibrant city of Chicago in all her glory. It was my home in my own roaring twenties, and it was magical. Friendliest people you ever want to meet beauty and vibrancy abound. More art than you can ever hope to experience, and food that will never disappoint. And, of course, the Chicago Cubs and the friendly confines of Wrigley Field. Chicago was the place where I discovered my own path and the potential I never knew I had, and this story is dedicated to all who brave that journey.

Chapter 1

All Italians had their funerals at Rago Brothers on Western Avenue in the heart of Chicago's Little Italy. It was one of the city's first full-service funeral homes and was built in 1917 by first-generation Italian American brothers Louis and John Rago. They had organized funerals for such infamous gangsters as Al Capone and his bodyguard Frank Rio. Labor union leaders were known to have bronze caskets to the tune of ten grand. It was here that thousands of mourners prayed for their loved ones, resting their knees on one-hundred-year-old wrought iron prayer kneelers. Sun shining through the stained-glass windows cast rainbows on visitors as they moved around the outer lobby and the coffee room. Lush red carpeting lined the floor in the main room, and a black baby grand piano greeted the mourners as they chose their seats.

On this warm August day, a wave of people dressed in black funeral attire lined up to gain access. Inside the funeral home, Louie Rago, a tall, painfully thin funeral director, gently guided Angie Sortino, the forty-five-year-old widow of the deceased, away from the casket and line of mourners. He leaned in and whispered, "I thought you said hardly anyone would come. There's almost fifty people here. We'll need to move Vinnie's casket to the Florentine Room. It's a fire hazard to have this many people in a small room."

Angie had to stretch her neck to look up from her five-foot-two-inch frame. "We were only married for ten years; some of these people must have known him before then. Please don't move him. I don't have the money for the larger room. As you know, I had to put his casket on three different credit cards." She dabbed her eyes with a tissue, her hand shaking.

"I'm so sorry, Angie, the fire marshal almost shut us down last week for overcrowding. We simply must move him."

"If you must, you must." *I have no idea how I'll pay for this, or where all our money went*, she thought as she gazed over at the open casket that held her beloved husband. Vinnie's hands were crossed over each other, his Cubs 2016 World Series ring on his pinkie. It was just a year ago that his high school friend, Ralph, had gifted it to him. Of course, it was a replica, but Vinnie had treated it as if it were the real deal.

As Angie walked toward the coffee area, her twenty-year-old niece, Gina, approached. "Aunt Angie, I can't tell you how grateful I am for the chance to provide the food for Uncle Vinnie's funeral; it's my very first catering event. I didn't have much prep time, so I bought a few premade items from Jewel and Costco, but don't worry, no one will notice. I added a few fancy garnishes to the plates. I had help making homemade cookies." Gina gave Angie a gentle hug. Angie glanced to Gina's left and saw a young, fit girl with long jet-black hair standing next to her. "You remember my friend Kim from high school? We're taking an entrepreneurial course at Richard J. Daley College—the community college on Pulaski. She's going to help me with the business side of starting our catering business."

Kim held out her hand, but Angie leaned in for a hug. "Of

course I remember you, with that big smile and twinkling eyes. We're huggers in this family."

"I'm so sorry for your loss, Mrs. Sortino."

"I can't thank you both enough. Who cares where the food is from—it's here. I know this isn't the best place to kick your catering business off, but I appreciate you just taking charge. You're like a daughter to Vinnie and me, Gina. I can't think straight right now, everything happened so fast." With a sigh, Angie smiled at the girls and found a cozy high-back chair near the lobby. Sitting down, she watched Louie close the doors to the small viewing room.

Angie winced when she noticed the ladies she volunteered with from Holy Rosary, which was literally right next to Rago Brothers, all standing together by the food. She knew what they were about to do. It was a trick they all did when they went to funerals or church events. Sure enough, Ruth opened her pocketbook, which Angie knew was lined with aluminum foil, looked around, grabbed a handful of cookies, shoved them in her purse, snapped it closed, and walked away from the table.

"Oh boy." Angie whispered under her breath and looked the other way. *I can't say a word—I have frozen cookies in the freezer from the last funeral I attended.*

A blur of familiar and unfamiliar faces moved toward Angie and offered their condolences before they moved on to the table that displayed trays of food and beverages. *I never knew Vinnie had this many friends*, she thought.

Vinnie's best friend from work and second-in-command for the City of Chicago's Department of Buildings, Mario Longetti, a stout Italian, approached Angie and knelt on the floor next to her chair. "I'm so sorry, Angie. You were the love of his life; you were all he talked about most days. He made me promise him long ago, if anything ever happened to him, I would take care of you—and I will." He pulled a silver metal flask of whiskey from the inside pocket of his suit. "Take a sip; it'll settle your nerves, honey." He placed it in her hands.

Angie glanced at the flask and then took a swig. The warm, smooth liquid startled her taste buds. She shuddered as she swallowed and then looked around to see if anyone had seen her; no one seemed to notice. "That tastes like the bourbon Vinnie drank—that's some strong stuff."

Mario bent over and gave Angie a firm hug. "I remember when Vinnie introduced you to me, I told him, 'If you don't marry her, I will,'" he said, and chuckled.

"Aw, go on, Mario, you're such a tease. That said, I may need your help sorting through all his business things. I don't understand how he had a massive heart attack. He just got a clean bill of health last month."

"I don't know what to say. I guess it was just his time, sweetheart. Know that I'm here for you, Angie, whatever you need." Mario put some folded bills into her hand. "From our team at the city."

Angie looked down to see three hundred-dollar bills. "Mario, I can't take this." She tried to hand it back to him, but he shook his head. "Put it in your purse. I won't take no for an answer."

She sheepishly did as he asked, then stood and gave Mario a hug, inhaling the aroma of cigars, whiskey, and a hint of Old Spice.

Mario pointed over to a group of people clustered around the food. "The whole crew from Streets and Sanitation is here showing their respect. You remember Cookie."

Angie saw the attractive blonde looking toward Mario and giving him the stink eye, but then she smiled at Angie and waved graciously.

Angie waved back, then said, "Vinnie told me Cookie runs the show in human resources for the city. I hope she can help me with all his pension paperwork." She sighed.

A large crash originated from behind the doors of the small room where Vinnie's body was. Everyone froze.

"Uh-oh," Angie said, and walked toward the closed doors. *My Vinnie must have fallen out of his casket*, she thought.

"Everything is fine," one of the funeral parlor assistants declared from behind the door.

Angie peeked inside just as a few men were lifting a heavy crucifix that had fallen on the floor.

"Oh my!" she exclaimed and then felt a hand on her back guiding her away from the doors and closing them. Everyone's eyes were on her as she looked around the lobby.

"He's having a few last words with God," she mumbled, then chuckled to herself.

"We'll be opening the Florentine Room in a few minutes," the female assistant announced. Slowly people went back to helping themselves to the refreshments. She escorted Angie back to her chair. "How about I get you a cup of coffee and something to eat," she offered.

"That would be lovely; three creams and four sugars, just like Vinnie took his coffee," Angie instructed as she got comfortable again.

Just as the assistant returned, Louie opened the doors. "Thank you all for your patience; we'll start the service in a few minutes." He gestured for people to move through the doors, past the grand piano on the right.

Angie watched as folks moved inside and took their seats. A few elected to stand to the side of the entryway, holding their coffee and small plates filled with goodies. A tall, slender older man approached Angie and gave her a gentle hug. "I'm so sorry, Angie. I'm here for you, always."

"Oh, Ben, he loved you so much, you were like a brother to him." She leaned into him and started to sob. Ben had worked with Vinnie for twenty years in the Department of Buildings. He'd lived in the same apartment building, down the hallway, long before Angie was in the picture, and still did to this day. She took a deep breath, made herself stop crying, and whispered, "Not here, Ben; I can't lose it here."

Ben took the pressed white cotton handkerchief from his pocket and gave it to Angie. "There will be time for you to lose it."

"Is my mascara running?"

Ben leaned down, gently took the handkerchief from Angie and dabbed under her eyes, and then handed it back to her. "There you go."

Louie approached Angie once everyone was seated. "Are you ready to come in and make a few remarks?" he gently asked.

"I hate to speak in public, frightens me so. How about I tell you what I want to say and you say it," she suggested. "Maybe Ben can do it. He's known him the longest."

Louie looked over at Ben, who was shaking his head.

"Now, Angie, I'll escort you to the front of the room. I'll be right there for you."

Angie stood up quickly, holding on to Louie's arm. "Okay, Louie, I trust you. It's just so scary—but I'll do it for my Vinnie." She let out a sigh and put her coffee on the mahogany table and walked to the front of the room. Louie escorted her toward the podium and made sure she was stable on her feet.

Angie cleared her throat. "Thank you all for coming. I see some familiar faces and many I do not recognize. Welcome, everyone." Angie felt her lower lip begin to quiver uncontrollably and then tears started to stream down her cheeks. She took a deep breath, patted her eyes with Ben's handkerchief, and looked up again. When she did, she noticed the people standing in the back spitting their food into their napkins and making awful grimaces. *Oh no, the food must be bad*, she thought, but she had to put that out of her mind and get through this.

"I never loved anyone more than Vinnie. He was truly the kindest, most loving, most generous man I ever knew," Angie said, noticing a few more people spitting into their napkins, then wiping off their tongues with the napkins.

"Vinnie was the love of my life; we only met ten years ago at . . ." Before she could finish, a large group of men—some young, some older—all came walking into the room wearing Chicago Cubs World Series T-shirts singing, "Hey, hey, holy mackerel, no doubt about it, the Cubs are on the move . . ." The entire room almost got whiplash turning around.

"Oh dear!" Angie said.

Chapter 2

Louie quickly moved to the rear of the room, hushing the men and quietly guiding over ten of them to the remaining seats in the back. Angie waited until he gave her a nod, and she began again. "Thank you all for coming and welcome to our new guests—Go, Cubs." She smiled.

A man with a rather large beer belly spilling out the bottom of his Cubs T-shirt chimed in, "We loved our Vinnie. He was the ringleader at Murphy's Bleachers, like a brother—never missed a game."

"Wasn't that our Vinnie." Angie smiled in affirmation. "I sure don't need to tell anyone in here he was a die-hard Cubs fan. That's for sure."

Just as the Cubs Boys, as Angie called them, were getting settled, a cranky-looking old woman with a mangy, yapping dog on her lap steered her loud electric scooter into the back of the room. Everyone turned their heads again and stared, including Angie. *I thought Beatrice was dead!* She forced herself to feign a smile and nodded. Beatrice, Vinnie's oldest sister, was the meanest, stingiest human Angie had ever encountered. Angie had met her only once, when she and Vinnie were dating. Several years later, when Vinnie had told her Beatrice had died, he had shared that she had been mean to him since he was a child, which helped Angie understand why he didn't seem all that upset.

Louie cleared his throat. "Let's let our friend Angie here finish her comments and then we can adjourn for more refreshments." He put his hand on Angie's arm and encouraged her to finish.

Angie continued. "I'm really at a loss here. I'm sorry for the outburst, and this certainly didn't go quite as planned. Please bow your head and we'll recite the Our Father." Everyone obeyed and, just as Angie finished and was about to say "Amen," the Cubs men finished with "Go, Cubs!" Laughter filled the room, and Angie smiled.

Stepping closer to Angie, Louie said, "Thank you all for coming. Please be sure to sign the guest book and enjoy some refreshments." He escorted Angie out to the lobby, and Beatrice rolled up in her electric scooter with a small, mangy dog still sitting dutifully in her lap. "I need the key."

Angie's hands were shaking. "Key? I'm sure I don't know what you're talking about."

"The key to the storage unit," Beatrice demanded.

"I don't know anything about a storage unit or key. I'm so sorry, Beatrice, I would have called you had I known you were still above ground."

"Well, at least I know Vinnie could keep a secret. I made him promise me he wouldn't tell anyone I was alive or where I lived. I didn't need all those loser family members asking me for money." Beatrice took a bite of the cookie she was holding; Angie could see crumbs on both sides of her mouth and chocolate on her front tooth. Beatrice had certainly aged since their initial encounter years ago. Her face was full of wrinkle lines, and her disheveled hair was a mousy mixture of gray and brown.

"I guess you're right, Beatrice. He never said a word."

"Who the hell made these cookies? They taste like shit!" Beatrice yelled and spat the cookie on the floor.

Louie grabbed a napkin and bent over to clean up the mess. "Please, madam, if you'd be so kind as to use your napkin."

Angie could see Gina standing by the refreshments, her face turning redder by the minute. She—and everyone else present—had clearly heard Beatrice's comment.

Beatrice's little yapper dog barked at Louie. "Good boy, Bruno." Beatrice continued, "I gave my brother a lot of money to invest in some sports gear and he never paid me back. He did mention that if he died it would be in a storage unit and I could sell it."

Angie's mind was getting cloudier by the minute. *Sports gear? Storage unit?*

"Beatrice, how about I look around the house for this key you're talking about and give you a call," Angie offered.

"I don't have time for this nonsense. I need that key, Angie. Find it and fast! I have a driver waiting outside. Here's my card. Call me tomorrow." Beatrice thrust the card in Angie's hand and rolled away just as Gina approached Angie.

"Aunt Angie, I'm so sorry about the sweet treats; something went wrong with the recipe. There was way too much salt in the cookies, and I think the chocolate was expired. I was in such a hurry to get them all done, I hired my roommate, Thad, to bake them and I didn't supervise him. I feel awful. Will you ever forgive me?"

Kim was standing next to Gina, patting her back. "It's okay, Gina," she said. "We'll get a fresh start at our next event."

Angie pulled Gina in for a hug. "Don't worry, sweetie, that's the least of my problems. Could you and Kim please clear the rest of them and put them in the trash? So glad you're here, Kim." Gina and Kim grabbed the trays off the table and headed for the kitchen.

Connie, Vinnie's younger sister and Gina's mom, charged up to Angie. "Of all the nerve! Beatrice crashed her own brother's funeral. I'm so sorry, Angie."

Angie's legs began to wobble, and she held on to Connie's arm. "I need to sit down before I fall down."

Connie kept talking as she steered Angie to a chair. "You could have knocked me over with a feather when Beatrice rolled in; I really thought she was dead."

"Me too. Did you know anything about a storage unit that Vinnie had?" Angie asked.

"The storage unit? Well, I do recall he mentioned it in passing."

"Do you have the key? Do you know what's in it?" Angie studied Connie's face.

"This is probably not the place or time to talk about that. Let's talk tomorrow," Connie said, and then immediately walked away before Angie could object.

Angie sighed and realized she had to use the lavatory, a word that would always be in her vocabulary from her early Catholic school days. Anytime she had said the word out loud around Vinnie, he had laughed.

She moved slowly through the many people embracing her and finally made it to the bathroom. When Angie opened the door, she saw long, narrow red velvet seats with tall backs lining the walls in an L shape. Her bladder led her across the purple carpet and into one of two stalls.

Locking the stall door behind her, she let out a loud sigh and closed her eyes for a minute, trying to summon up more energy to go out and face the crowd again. *I must keep it together until I can be alone and have a long cry without worrying about my mascara running and anyone hearing me sob*, she thought. Angie was about to flush when she heard the bathroom door bang open.

"I have to have you now!" a female voice begged.

"I want you too. I've missed you so much," a man's voice responded.

"I'll put my handbag against the door so no one can enter, except you into me," the woman said, her quick breathing indicating she was ready to roll.

"I'll never make fun of you for carrying such a large purse again," the man responded.

There was a brief silence and then Angie could hear kissing and heavy breathing, a zipper and what sounded like the woman pulling up her dress.

"Do you think this sink will hold up?" she asked the man.

"You're thin; sit on the edge and lean into me. I'll push against the sink to balance."

The couple were having sex right outside her stall; she held her breath, pulled her feet up so, if they did look under the stall, they wouldn't see anything—although it was clear they were not looking in her direction. *I hope they don't break the sink*, Angie thought, just as a high heel fell onto the floor, landing slightly under the bathroom door to the stall where Angie was hiding. She glanced down: three-inch heels with a red leather bottom.

Loud sighs and groans filled the space. The sound of the ascending orgasms filled the room, and Angie took a quick breath. *They won't hear me over all that noise they're making*. After hearing a few more moans and groans, she heard a zipper and saw the man's hand grab the high heel from under her stall, noticing his shiny, manicured nails.

"You're the best lover I've ever had, Ralph. Sorry to be in such a hurry, but I need to get out of here before I am missed," the woman declared.

Angie heard the rustling of clothing and then the door open and close.

Angie found herself grinning, flushed the toilet, and peeked out of the stall to be sure no one was there. As she washed her hands, she noticed the sink was a little wobbly. She glanced at her reflection in the mirror, noticing the bags under her bloodshot green eyes and her pale complexion. She pulled her makeup bag from her purse, applied some lipstick, and rubbed some on her cheeks to add some color. She certainly didn't want to look like pale Louie, the funeral director. Angie teased her light brown hair, which had fallen flat almost immediately after she used the curling iron to add some height earlier in the morning. She glanced down at the floor before leaving and noticed what looked like a fancy tube of lipstick. She picked it up, noting the Chanel logo on the end of the square tube. Angie removed the cap and tested the color on her hand. "Color matches, it looks brand-new, I'm taking it. I'd never be able to buy this brand, especially after I pay off all these funeral debts. It's probably counter sex girl's lipstick," she murmured out loud as she placed the lipstick in her bag. She smelled the lingering sweet scent of the woman's perfume and was almost positive it was Chanel 19—her nose never failed her.

The Cubs Boys approached her and offered their condolences one by one, giving her the big bear hugs she had become accustomed to from Vinnie and his buddies. They all smelled like sausage and beer. Clearly, they had stopped at some local tavern beforehand, as was the custom, Vinnie had shared with her, when his buddies attended funerals.

Angie continued to greet each well-meaning guest, some offering their deepest condolences; others she needed to console.

A handsome man in a dark blue tailored suit approached her. He put his hand out and she reciprocated, and he gently cupped both Angie's hands in his large hands. "Hello, Angie, you may not remember me; we only met briefly a few times. I went to high school with Vinnie. We lost touch and then reconnected years ago. He and I would ditch classes and go to the afternoon Cubs games. My name is Ralph Conti." His soft smile revealed perfect white teeth, dimples, and kindness.

Angie felt his soft hands and glanced down at his manicured nails, which looked familiar, and no wedding band. She inhaled deeply and detected a hint of the perfume from the bathroom. "So nice to see you, Ralph. Thank you for coming. I believe you're the one who gave Vinnie the Cubs World Series ring."

"Indeed, I did. It was the least I could do. Vinnie was a very generous business partner; we collaborated on many city projects. He spoke so highly of you. The picture he showed me didn't do you justice; you're a very elegant and beautiful woman. You reminded me of my own wife who I lost to cancer two years ago. I'm so sorry for your loss. I know how hard it is."

Angie gazed into his rich brown eyes and let out an audible sigh. He smiled at her.

"I'm sorry for your loss too, Ralph."

"Here's my card. When things slow down, please do call me. We can meet for a cup of coffee or lunch and share Vinnie stories."

She took his card and put it in her pocketbook. "Thanks, Ralph. I'd like that." Angie noticed that Mario was glaring at her and Ralph from across the room.

After Ralph took his leave and walked toward the door, Angie watched to see if a woman followed, but saw no one.

The crowd continued to thin until it was just Connie, Gina, Kim, and Louie. Angie collapsed in the high-back chair, took her sensible pumps off, and put her feet on the ottoman. "I can't think, everything is happening so fast. This is the weirdest funeral I've ever been at."

"I must say it ranks right up there for me too," Louie commented.

Gina handed Angie a glass of water. "Here you go, Aunt Angie. You need to remember to drink a lot of water; these types of events can dehydrate the best of us."

Kim set a pitcher of water on the table next to her. "Here's some more when you need it."

"You're so thoughtful, Kim, such a help," Angie remarked.

"I'm going to go finish cleaning up. Let me know if you need anything else." Kim walked toward the kitchen.

"What a nice friend you have, Gina," Angie commented.

"I couldn't have done any of this without her," Gina shared. Angie looked around to confirm it was just her, Gina, and Connie, who was sitting in the companion high-back chair next to Angie. "You are not going to believe what happened to me in the bathroom earlier." Angie explained the brief sex interlude, and all three of them laughed.

"At least someone's getting some," Connie, who had been single a long time, declared.

"I don't know who the woman was, but the man was Ralph, that fancy pants fella."

"Sex at a funeral parlor—ew." Gina winced. "Who does that?"

Connie smiled. "You'd be surprised. I noticed that guy right away. Looked like he stepped out of *GQ*. That is one yummy-looking fella; if I were younger, thinner, and more flexible, that guy would be mine."

"Mom!" Gina yelped. They all laughed.

"When you're ready, Angie, we'll head over to Murphy's Bleachers for a little reception, then you can go home."

Angie just nodded. "Murphy's. I don't have much gas left in my tank; every bone in my forty-five-year-old body is aching," she said with a sigh. "Hmm, I guess I can go for a little while." Another long sigh.

Just as they were ready to leave, Louie pulled Angie aside and handed her an envelope. "Could you give me a call tomorrow? Two of your three credit cards were denied, and we'll need to settle your account before the end of the week for the balance." Angie raised her index and middle fingers to her temples and rubbed them, wondering, *Where did all our money go? Vinnie said we were golden.*

Chapter 3

Connie dropped off Angie in front of Murphy's Bleachers on Sheffield, literally across from none other than the friendly confines of Wrigley Field. Many die-hard Cubs fans called it home—especially her Vinnie. Murphy's had been around for over eighty years and was initially called Ernie's Bleachers until a Chicago detective, Jim Murphy, took it over.

Angie sat in the car staring; Connie's voice brought her back. "Angie, you go in and I'll find a parking space. You need to eat something. You haven't eaten all day. Sorry about Gina's disastrous nibbles at the funeral. I'm glad she kept her job at Panera." Angie got out of the car and slowly shuffled toward the front door of Murphy's. She stopped when she heard Connie's voice. "And don't worry, the reception here is on me. I called ahead and gave them my credit card and ordered some plates of brats and beer for the boys and some wings and fries for the rest of us."

Angie glanced over her shoulder. "Connie, you didn't need to do that." But Connie had already driven away.

As Angie walked through the doors, sounds of sports announcers blared from all the various mounted TVs above the long bar to her right; the smell of beer permeated the air.

Gina walked up to Angie. "Hey, Aunt Angie, we are all in the back room. What can I get you to drink?" Gina put her arm around Angie and escorted her past the long front bar, into the next room. When they got to her favorite photo of Bill Murray mounted on the right wall, Angie kissed the palm of her hand, then put it on Bill Murray's face, the most loyal Cubs fan ever, in Vinnie's opinion. They passed the plexiglass-encased kitchen, the crackle of peanut shells under their feet announcing that many had been there earlier, eating their fair share of free peanuts and throwing the shells on the floor. There was a short line of folks waiting to order brats, Polish sausage, and hot dogs. She and Gina walked directly to the long bar in the back to a familiar face that Angie recognized.

"What'll it be, my friend? So sorry about our Vinnie, he was one of my favorites. Just won't be the same without him holding court and screaming at the TV on all the away games. You want your usual, Ang?" Larry, the dark-haired, blue-eyed bartender, asked as he held out his hand to Angie. She placed her hand in his and he gave it a soft, sweet kiss.

Angie swallowed hard and mustered a smile. *The beginning of the firsts without Vinnie*, she thought. Murphy's had been his home away from home; the two of them had sometimes spent an entire day and night at the bar. If Angie got tired, she'd head home knowing Vinnie would be safe there and would always end up in a cab if he had been overserved.

Larry put a tall club soda and scotch in front of Angie. "This one is on me." He looked over at Gina. "For you?"

"I'll take a shot of Jägermeister, please. Put it on the tab under Connie Paloni; she's my mom."

The gals walked toward the back room, where there was a crowd of all the faithful Cubs Boys and Mario with mugs of beer in hand.

Angie took a long sip of her drink. "Thanks for coming today, you guys. I'm sure Vinnie is touched up there." She pointed her index finger toward the sky.

Bucky, one of Vinnie's work buddies, approached her. "He was a brother to us. You'll never know how many times he saved our asses, putting us in a cab after the game, buying drinks when some of us got laid off. Real stand-up guy." He bent down and hugged Angie with one arm. "Come sit down; we saved you a seat. We're stoked; the Cubs just beat the Cardinals in St. Louis. I hate those fucking Cardinals."

Bucky led Angie to her seat, then immediately locked into the postgame show on the TV. The rest of the fellas' gazes were glued to the screen as well. Angie took another long sip of her drink and smiled. She recalled the time Vinnie and his friends had gone to St. Louis when the Cubs played and put business cards they had made on every Cardinals fan's windshield with a printed quote, *I'd rather have a sister in a whorehouse than a brother who's a Cardinals fan.* He and his buddies laughed on the car ride all the way home to Chicago.

Gina sat down next to her aunt to listen to the recap of the game. Angie let out a huge deep breath, and felt her shoulders drop as she listened to the sound of nonstop sports announcers, interrupted with beer commercials and the atmosphere of Murphy's. Sports was a huge part of her and Vinnie's life while they were dating and their ten years of marriage. During baseball season, they spent at least three to five days at Murphy's. Their ritual on opening day was to start at Murphy's, where she enjoyed a Bloody Mary, and Vinnie always had his usual, Old Style on tap—he never drank anything else when it came to beer.

As Angie looked over her shoulder, she saw Connie, dyed blonde hair up in a bun, heading toward her carrying her usual Long Island iced tea. "Hey there, we are cabbing it home after this, so you just drink up and relax. I heard the Cubs kicked some Cardinals ass. YES!" Connie took a generous sip of her drink and sat on the barstool on the other side of Angie. All the commotion allowed Angie to sip her drink without feeling the need to say anything to anyone; she was lightheaded, like she was on another planet.

Just as Angie was catching a buzz from her drink, she spotted debonair Ralph walking toward the group with Cookie—who worked in HR at the city—following. Angie instantly thought of Ralph's manicured nails and the sound of the sex noises she'd heard in the bathroom just a few hours earlier. Angie leaned over to her niece, Gina, and whispered, "See that blonde bombshell who's walking in with Ralph?"

Gina glanced over. "Yeah, that Ralph is a handsome one. I met him a couple times when he and Uncle Vinnie stopped by Panera and grabbed a sandwich."

"Do you remember when we watched *Best in Show*, the floozy Cookie Guggleman, who had the terrier who won? I wonder if this city Cookie is anything like her, dished out like a Coke machine in her younger days?" Angie asked.

Gina let out a loud laugh. "Aunt Angie, you are too much. We'll have to watch and see."

Angie had heard a few stories that Vinnie had shared about Cookie. She had quite the reputation at Murphy's. On occasion she brought home a souvenir after a long night. She only had one requirement: They had to be a Cubs fan. *I wonder if she's the one who was in the bathroom with him?* Angie thought.

Ralph leaned toward Angie and gave her a gentle hug, and then Cookie did the same.

Angie took a deep whiff of Cookie. *Not the same perfume I smelled in the funeral parlor bathroom*, she thought.

"I'm so sorry about Vinnie, Angie. He was one hell of a guy." Cookie dabbed her eyes.

"Thanks, Cookie. You folks want a drink?"

"Sure, I'll get them. What do you want, Cookie?" Ralph asked.

"I'll have a scotch, stone sour, thanks, Ralph."

As Ralph walked away, Cookie looked at Angie and Connie. "You gals know if Ralph is seeing anyone?"

"Cookie, you are always on the lookout for a new fella," Connie declared. "I don't think he's seen anyone seriously since his wife died a couple years ago. I heard he dates around, though."

Angie smiled at Cookie. "I have no idea, honey."

Cookie put her hand on Angie's shoulder. "I'm not sure what your plans are when this all settles down, but if you need a city job, come visit me. I run human resources—don't tell my boss—and they're always looking for dependable gals like you."

"Thanks, Cookie, I may well have to take you up on that kind offer."

"I'm serious, Angie. We got a great benefits package, lots of holidays. I'm sure Vinnie filled you in, and of course, there's our pension plan, but then you'll be getting Vinnie's. You'll be set," Cookie remarked.

The Cubs Boys started hollering and clapping as they watched the game highlights. Angie watched as each of them gave Cookie a wave and then went back to watching the replay.

Ralph returned and placed a drink in front of Cookie and one in front of Angie. "Larry said this is for you, Angie." She looked toward the bar and smiled at Larry. He winked back. *What a sweet young man*, Angie thought. There had been many a night when Vinnie had been off talking baseball shop and Angie had nursed her cocktail and watched all the young girls flirting with Larry.

Ralph walked over to the boys and started a conversation with Bucky as they both gazed up at the TV screen.

After her second drink, Angie let out a sigh. "I don't want to be a party pooper, but I need to go home before I fall off this barstool and pass out. I am exhausted." She stood up.

"I'll drive you home, Aunt Angie. I have to get up early tomorrow morning; I have the early shift at Panera," Gina offered.

"Are you sure? I don't want you to leave on my account. I can hail a cab."

"No way. I'm ready to go. I was up very early this morning getting everything ready for the funeral." Gina gave her mom a quick hug goodbye.

"Please give all the fellas my best, will you, Connie? Let's talk tomorrow. Thanks for everything you've done for me during this crazy time. I could not have organized this by myself, that's for sure. And, remember, you lost a brother, so take some time for you." Angie gave Connie a hug.

"I will, but for now I'm going to drink to numb the pain. I know it's temporary. You're closer to me than my own sister ever was. Give me a call tomorrow after you've gotten some rest," Connie said.

Gina drove Angie home to her apartment, which was around the corner from Rago Brothers. Vinnie and Ben had moved into a brownstone, three-story walk-up in the neighborhood where they could afford the rent over twenty years ago. They each had their own apartment and usually carpooled to jobsites before Ben retired.

"Why didn't Kim come to Murphy's?" Angie asked as they turned down the street to Angie's apartment.

"She was tired after she cleaned up at Rago's and was heading home. She's such a great friend."

"Please give her a big thank-you for me. You know, I think she favors that young actress Awkwafina from the movie *Crazy Rich Asians*," Angie said.

"People walk up to her and tell her that a lot." As Gina pulled up to Angie's place, there was Aunt Beatrice on her electric scooter waiting outside, her ugly dog taking a dump on the small patch of lawn near the front door. A black sedan was parked out front. Angie glanced over at Gina. "I can't take her right now; drive away." Angie slid down in the passenger seat just in case Beatrice looked toward Gina's car. Gina hit the gas and steered the car toward the expressway.

"You can stay with me," Gina offered. "What does Beatrice want? We all thought she was dead and now she won't leave us alone."

"I have no idea what she's talking about," Angie said. "Some key to a storage unit that Vinnie had. He never said anything to me about it. Just keep driving, honey. We'll sort this all out later."

Chapter 4

Ralph glanced over when he heard Larry announce, "Last round!" The Cubs Boys were about the only folks left in the bar; it was an away game, so most patrons left right after the game highlights. Connie, Bucky, Cookie, and Ralph were all discussing the game and how much they missed Vinnie's commentary. Bucky threw his arm around Connie. "Won't be the same without my brother from another mother."

Connie started to tear up. "It's not real for me; I can't let it be real." She started to cry, and Bucky held her close but noticed the rest of the boys were staring toward the door, their mouths agape.

Bucky turned to see what they were looking at. "It can't be." Connie was still sobbing into his Cubs jersey. "Connie, I think you have company," he said, patting her on her back and pointing toward the front of the bar.

Connie looked up at him, black mascara lines streaming from her eyes. Then she looked over and froze.

Bill Murray, wearing worn jeans, a 2016 Cubs World Series baseball cap, and sneakers, walked up to Ralph and said, "I just heard. I'm so sorry." All the Cubs Boys were staring at him and let out a collective gasp.

"Bill, wow. I can't believe you came by. Vinnie is smiling on us from heaven right now," Ralph said.

"Larry called me, I had to. Vinnie was the only guy who knew all the Cubs stats by heart. We'd wait for you knuckleheads to leave the bar and then we'd sit and talk for hours about each player—and the coaches, of course. We called ourselves the tenth-inning scouts."

Ralph had met Bill several times through Vinnie, even got a picture taken with him. He paused and then looked over toward Connie. "Please forgive me, Bill; this is Connie Paloni, Vinnie's little sister."

Bill, removing his Cubs hat, turned backward as usual, offered her his hand. "So sorry for your loss, our loss, the Cubs' loss. They broke the die-hard fan mold when Vinnie was born."

Ralph watched as Connie wiped her eyes, which only made the black lines smear more and made it look like a Bears football player getting ready for a sunny day at Soldier Field.

"It is truly my honor; I didn't know you knew our Vinnie. I'm sure he was afraid we'd swarm you, which we would have, so probably a good thing we didn't know." Connie couldn't stop staring.

"It was an honor to have known your brother. I will truly miss him. Well, I'll leave you all to it. If there's anything you need, let Larry know. If I can help, I will. Oh, and please give his wife, Angie, my condolences; he told me she was the love of his life." Bill nodded, replacing his Cubs hat. As quickly as he had come in, he was gone.

"Bill Murray? Vinnie *knew* Bill Murray?" Connie gasped.

Ralph nodded his head. "Yes, he knew Bill Murray, all right. You could find those two hidden in a corner after any game once the crowd thinned."

Connie dabbed her eyes and looked down at the napkin with black all over it. "I must look a mess. I'm going to run to the ladies' room."

"We're going to head out, Connie. Take care of Angie and please let me know how she's doing. I know she depended on him for everything," Ralph said as he handed her his business card.

"I'll keep you posted, Ralph, thanks." Ralph watched as Connie swayed toward the bathroom.

Ralph and the Cubs Boys all staggered toward the door. "I can't believe how much fun I had; Vinnie was always begging me to come watch the game with you guys. I couldn't ever make it, my loss for sure."

As they walked outside, they were met with the omnipresent walls of Wrigley looming large, with a statue of Ernie Banks on the corner. *What a grand ballpark, the mothership of all that was baseball in Chicago, in the world*, Ralph thought.

"What are you going to do without Vinnie? He ran that Department of Buildings like a pro; no one will be able to fill his shoes." Cookie shimmied up next to him and threw her arm around him.

Ralph looked down at her. "Probably work with Mario or whoever is the next in command, no one like Vinnie, though."

Bucky leaned against the light pole outside the bar. "Didn't you and Vinnie make some deals together?" He let out a loud burp.

"We sure did, Buck." The cab pulled up, and Ralph said, "Gotta go."

"Can you drop me on your way?" Cookie stuck her head inside the car window.

"Absolutely, where do you live?" Ralph extended his hand and helped her slide in the back seat next to him.

"I live in Old Town next to Second City." Cookie slid as close as she could to Ralph.

"What do you say we stop for a nightcap at Gibsons before we part ways?" Cookie slurred. Ralph glanced over as she pushed up her breasts and unbuttoned another button on her already low-cut silk blouse. *Not a bad set*, he thought.

"Perfect. My friend is playing the piano tonight. It's where Vinnie and I would go after we closed our deals—best steaks in town."

Ralph tapped the cab driver. "Gibsons in the Gold Coast."

"Over dinner I'd love to hear about your life, how long you knew Vinnie. You must have some great stories to tell."

The cab stopped outside Gibsons where there was a line of people waiting. The doorman gave a familiar nod to Ralph as he walked inside, and Cookie followed.

"How's my favorite singer tonight?" Ralph leaned over the counter and kissed the plump cheek of the full-figured woman who had been the hostess forever.

"Give Mama some sugar, you handsome bundle of love," her rich voice announced. Peaches waddled from behind the counter and gave Ralph a full-body hug. She was as wide as she was tall, swaying in her loose dress, wearing full makeup with large, sparkly earrings accenting her pretty face.

Ralph looked over at Cookie. "You haven't been hugged until you've been hugged by Peaches, and she has the voice of Eartha Kitt." Peaches flashed her engaging smile and walked back around the glass counter.

"We're going to eat in the bar, sweetheart," Ralph said.

"Good thing, honey, because we are packed with that dermatology convention. But you know I would always find a place for you anyway, handsome," she said, winking.

Piano music found its way above the clatter of hungry diners waiting for their name to be called. Waiters dressed in waist-level, starched white coats with Gibson tie bars securing their neckties were rushing toward the main dining room. One-handed, they elegantly held huge trays carrying plates of steaks, baked potatoes, and sides above their shoulders.

Ralph walked to the right, where the bar was located, and saw his friend Dennis playing the piano and singing "Luck Be a Lady Tonight," a large crystal goblet full of cash sitting on top of the grand piano. Patrons were sitting around the piano, singing along and swaying to the music.

Ralph parted his way through the dense crowd with head nods of acknowledgment to some and a few handshakes until they got to a tall table that a young couple was just vacating.

"What will it be, Miss Cookie?" Ralph asked.

"You can just call me Cookie. I'll have a vodka martini with three olives; I need to eat something." She giggled.

Ralph motioned for one of the waitresses to come over, and she made her way through the maze of humans. The mirrored bar covered the entire wall, crystal martini glasses etched with the Gibsons' name hanging at the ready.

As soon as the waitress arrived, Cookie glanced at her. "I need some food sooner than later. Could you also bring me some bread and butter?"

"You got it." The waitress looked over at Ralph.

"Vodka martini, extra olives, for this lovely lady; dry with a twist of lemon for me. Can you bring us a menu too?" The waitress nodded and left.

Ralph looked at Cookie, who was staring into his eyes. "Your smile is delicious, and those dimples are about to drive me wild. I may just come over there and give you a big, fat kiss," she slurred.

"I'm flattered, but I think we should keep things aboveboard. You know how much work I do with the city."

Cookie grinned back and nodded. "You have no idea what secrets I know." The busboy brought the bread and butter, and Cookie immediately devoured a few pieces.

After the waitress brought their drinks and menus, they lifted their glasses. "Here's to Vinnie, one of the best guys I ever knew. Never met anyone like him and probably never will again." Ralph toasted with Cookie.

After a sip of her drink, Cookie looked over at Ralph. "You don't seem to be the type of guy who would have a friend who worked at the Chicago Department of Buildings all his life."

"What makes you say that?"

"You seem like such a highbrow, fancy gentleman. We don't usually see your type visiting his shop; the mayor's office, yes, but it's usually construction workers walking in and out of Vinnie's office."

"I never really cared about what he did, or where he worked. I judged him by his character, and Vinnie was a stand-up guy. We went to high school together and then lost touch. Of course, I ran into him at Murphy's after one of the playoff games, one of those years they almost got to the World Series; I think it was 1985."

"When they lost to the Padres," Cookie said.

"You sure know your baseball." Ralph lifted his glass and toasted her.

"Nothing like watching those fit players rounding the bases. I love men in uniform, and they have some of the tightest assess I've seen. And I know more than baseball." She fluttered her long eyelashes at him. "I've seen your name on most of Vinnie's projects, and I had to vet your company, which was squeaky clean. Otherwise, the city would never have done as much business with you as they did."

"What would you like to order? It's on me." Ralph motioned the waitress over.

"Yes, Ralph, what can I get for you?"

Ralph watched as Cookie's blue eyes gazed up over the menu and over to the waitress. "Well, if he's buying and this is social and not business, I'll take a rib eye, medium rare, baked potato with all the trimmings, and bring extra horseradish sauce."

"The lady knows what she wants," Ralph said. "I'll have my usual."

"You got it," the waitress said.

A stout man wearing a black T-shirt and business jacket approached the table. "Hi, Ralph, you're just the guy I want to see. Do you have a minute? I need to discuss an important matter."

Ralph immediately stood up. "Excuse us, Cookie, I'll be right back." He had had a few encounters with this disreputable character and didn't want to be seen with him if he could avoid it.

"No problem." She took another sip of her martini.

Ralph followed the man through the front doors and out into the street. Standing away from the long line of patrons waiting to get in, the man looked both ways to be sure no one was in earshot. "Look, I would have preferred to talk to you during business hours, but since I ran into you, why not take care of things now? We have a small problem that could turn into a big problem, and I know you don't want that." The Italian was twisting his diamond pinkie ring around his finger.

"What's the problem?"

"Your friend Vinnie, who you referred to us, hasn't paid us back a nickel yet, and the interest is mounting up. I've been calling him for over a month and no response. We may have to escalate the situation, if you know what I mean."

"Bad news on that end. Vinnie died. His funeral was today. How much was he in for with you?" Ralph asked.

"A million and half with the interest. Gambled on the Cubs again. Not a smart guy, rest his soul. We're going to go after his wife then; she must have something she can sell."

"Hold on there now, how about you and I talk tomorrow."

Ralph handed the Italian his business card. "In the meantime, please don't call his wife. Now, if you'll excuse me, I need to get back to my dinner companion."

"Okay, but just know that someone will be paying that debt sooner than later—you, his family, someone." The Italian put Ralph's card in his pocket and both men headed back into the bar. The waitress was serving their meal when Ralph arrived at the table.

"Sorry about that. Everything looks delicious."

Cookie glanced at Ralph. "I'm starving, I realized I forgot to eat today with all that was going on. I thought I could fill up on the food at the funeral, but it was horrible. How embarrassing for Angie; hopefully she didn't notice." Cookie cut a piece of her rib eye and topped it with horseradish, salt, and pepper, and took a bite. "Mmm."

Ralph started to eat his jumbo lump crab cakes. "This place never disappoints. No wonder they've been in business since 1989."

Cookie took a sip of her martini. "I met my first two husbands in this bar."

Ralph smiled. "How many husbands have you had, Cookie?"

"After my third divorce, I decided marriage wasn't for me, so I just date when I feel like it. I shop here, over at the Four Seasons, and Murphy's. I must say that I never saw you at any of those places, or I would have remembered."

Ralph smiled. "I don't have much time to dine out, but when I do I prefer Gibsons for business luncheons."

"How many wives have you had?"

"Just one, love of my life; we were high school sweethearts. I lost her to cancer about two years ago." Ralph changed the subject quickly. "So, Cookie, how do you like working for the city?"

"I love it. A cast of characters I'd never meet anywhere else, and the benefits are great. As the executive secretary to the HR director, there's always some kind of crazy show going on. I have private detectives showing up asking about different employees. Of course, I can't share any information with them, but they can be really pushy, offering me money under the table. I've never been bored, that's for sure." Cookie kept eating.

"Anyone in particular you're talking about?" Ralph asked. When Cookie raised her eyebrows, he added, "Okay, I'm wondering about Vinnie specifically."

"I'm not at liberty to say; all that stuff is confidential. Let's just say he worked for the city for a long time, I know he saw and heard all kinds of shenanigans," Cookie remarked.

They both finished their meals and Cookie asked for a to-go bag. Ralph paid the bill and walked Cookie out. He pointed across the street from Gibsons. "I live right down the street, so I'm going to head home. It was lovely to have dinner with you, Cookie. Take care." Ralph shook her hand.

"You're quite the gentleman, living in the Gold Coast, lifestyle of the rich and famous. Thank you for dinner. You should come to my office next time you're at City Hall. Maybe we could go for a cup of coffee."

"I'll be sure to do that," Ralph said. "Can I get you a cab home?"

"No thanks. I think I'll head over to the Four Seasons for a nightcap."

They walked to the corner, and Ralph turned down his street where his bathroom date from the funeral parlor would be visiting soon.

Chapter 5

Angie let her head fall back against the car's headrest and let out a quiet exhalation as Gina drove away from her apartment and Beatrice. She patted Gina's arm. "I'm sorry you had to deal with her after the rough day you had. How you doing?"

"She doesn't bother me. I'm bummed about the food at the funeral, but . . . I'll get over it. Why don't you come stay with me until Aunt Beatrice, the Wicked Witch of the West, is gone?" Gina asked.

"Are you sure I won't be putting you out? I hate to be a bother."

"My roommate, Thad, stays at his girlfriend's most of the time. You can use my room and I'll bunk in his—he's a super mellow guy."

"It will only be one night, then I can go back to my place. That's very generous of you."

"Happy to have your company. Besides, I'll need your help creating some menu options that won't poison people." They both laughed, though with a bit of a grimace.

Gina found a place across the street from her apartment on Dayton, parallel parked, and she and Angie walked toward Gina's place.

They climbed up to Gina's apartment on the second floor. Angie lagged. "I'm so exhausted, I could sleep standing up."

"I'm sure you are, Aunt Angie. I'll put some fresh sheets on the bed, and then you can sleep until you wake up."

Angie felt her eyes closing already. "What would I do without you, honey? Let's talk more in the morning." She gave Gina a hug, and the last thing she remembered was falling into Gina's bed.

The next morning, Angie awoke to the sound of a car alarm going off and sat up in bed. "Where am I?" She opened her eyes and remembered she had stayed at Gina's. And that Vinnie was dead. She lay back down, pulling the covers over her head as her mind raced: *Where is all our money? What was Beatrice doing in front of our apartment? What was this key thing she was spouting off about? And who the hell was having sex with Ralph at the funeral?*

She made her way to the bathroom and then out to the small kitchen, where she found a note from Gina. *Good morning, Aunt Angie. There's freshly brewed coffee and some eggs in the fridge. Take your time getting up—and relax. The Trib is on the table in the living room. I'll be home around three.*

Angie looked at the clock on the wall, a black cat with a tail that moved back and forth as the clock ticked; she remembered Vinnie giving Gina that old clock, which had been his mother's.

"Oh my, it's almost noon," she said, and then poured herself a cup of coffee and opened the fridge for some cream. Locating the sugar bowl, she put four heavy teaspoons in her coffee. She noticed the kitchen garbage was overflowing, so she got a paper bag from the side of the fridge and moved some of the garbage into it. As she off-loaded the garbage, she noticed Costco wrappers from the food Gina had provided at the funeral. Looking closer, Angie noticed that the expiration date was three months earlier. *I guess beggars can't be choosers, though Gina did offer to pay.*

Angie took her coffee into the living room and picked up the paper and skimmed the headlines and then turned to the obituary section, something she and Vinnie did every morning. She froze when she saw a photo of Vinnie. She placed her coffee down before she spilled it.

I never sent an obituary—it was too expensive—but someone did. Look at my handsome Vinnie; he was only fifty years old, too young. She started to cry and took a tissue to pat her eyes so she could read.

> *Vincent Carlo Sortino was born in Little Italy, Chicago, in 1968, the only son of Italian immigrant parents, Carla and Anthony Sortino, from Sicily, both deceased. He is survived by his loving wife, Angie Sortino; sister, Connie Paloni; and his beloved niece, Gina Paloni. Vinnie, as he was known to his family and close friends, graduated from St. Phillip's High School and attended Richard J. Daley Community College. He worked for the City of Chicago Department of Buildings for over twenty years, working his way up from construction worker to director of operations. He was a die-hard Cubs fan and enjoyed trips to Las Vegas.*

Angie reread the obit. *Whoever put the obit in the paper certainly knew Vinnie; maybe it was Ralph.* She refilled her coffee, then went into Gina's room, where she retrieved her phone and sat on the side of the bed. When she turned it on, bells went off announcing lots of texts and voicemails. *I'm not ready to respond to anyone right now*. She took a long, hot shower, put on Gina's robe, and returned to the kitchen.

After another cup of coffee, she stared out the kitchen window into the alley and summoned up the courage to go back into the bedroom and look at the texts and check her voicemails. There were several texts from Gina, Connie, and even Louie. There were five voicemails: a long one from Louie, three from Beatrice, and one from an unknown number.

Angie put the phone down, sat on the edge of the bed, and started to sob uncontrollably. She knew she couldn't let loose like she wanted to at the funeral and certainly not at Murphy's, but now it was safe. Grabbing a handful of tissues, she blew her nose and buried her head in her hands. "Vinnie, how will I live without you?" Her shoulders shook up and down, and she was having trouble catching her breath. She finally took a deep breath and sighed.

One foot in front of the other, she told herself. *Make a list—that always helps*. She took a pen and piece of paper off Gina's bedside table and began to write.

1. Get dressed.

2. Eat something safe.

3. Make the bed.

4. Listen to the messages and read the texts—write everything down.

5. Call the *Tribune* and find out who wrote and paid for the obit.

6. Call the bank and check the account—again—where is all our money?

7. Make some kind of plan. Can I afford the rent? How am I going to make money?

8. Find the key to the storage unit and find out what was in there—Beatrice?

9. If I must borrow money, who can I borrow it from and how much will I need?

10. OR—just pack a bag at home and leave town? Maybe get on a bus to anywhere?

She put the pen down and placed her hand over her heart. *I can only handle a list of ten things right now.*

Angie put on one of Gina's Juicy Couture sweatsuits, with the brand name written across the pants in the back. They were a little too long, as Gina was five foot seven, but she just rolled up the pants and pushed up the sleeves. She went to her list and checked off *Get dressed.* Angie took her list with her as she went to the kitchen, looked in the fridge, grabbed a few eggs, and scrambled them up and washed the pan. She ate half of the eggs, stored the rest in a container for the fridge, and then went into the bedroom and made the bed. Check and Check.

Sitting on the living room couch, she took out a pen and small pad of paper from her purse and was ready to write down who called and the message. Angie pressed the voicemail button; the first one was from Louie.

"Hello, Angie, it's Louie from Rago Brothers . . . I sure hope you got a good night's rest. I just wanted you to know someone who wishes to remain anonymous has paid all the funeral parlor bills. So, don't worry about anything. Please call me so we can discuss when you'd like to pick up Vinnie's cremains. We have a special urn your benefactor chose."

Angie let the shock of his message sink in. "Oh my. This is a miracle." She started to cry again and then hit Louie's number.

"Rago Brothers, this is Louie. How may I help you?"

"Hi, Louie, it's Angie—I just picked up your message. I am surprised and relieved, but I must ask you who paid for all of this. Whoever it is, I can't pay them back for a long time."

"The benefactor demanded their name not be used. They said that I could tell you that they were a good friend of Vinnie's and knew he would want these expenses taken care of, so it's one less thing you need to worry about. I must say I was as surprised as you are now. Can't say I've ever had this happen before, but then I've never had a funeral like Vinnie's before."

Angie took a deep breath. "I am so shocked and, of course, very grateful for their generosity. If you could let them know, I would appreciate it."

"Will do. I wonder if you would like his World Series ring to remain with him or reserve it for you?"

Angie sighed. "He never took it off, wore it every day after he got it. One of the happiest days of his life when they won the World Series. I think I'll find a perfect spot for it. Thanks for checking, Louie. You've been more than kind. When will his remains be ready?"

"Likely next Tuesday. How about I call you as soon as I know for sure."

"That would be great. Also, while I'm thinking about it, I sure hope you'll give my niece, Gina, another chance for her catering company in case any customers ask. I'll be helping her out going forward, and if you saw Vinnie's belly, you can tell I am quite a good cook, if I do say so myself." She couldn't help but smile. "Vinnie loved everything I made him, especially my homemade pasta and gravy. Secondly, would you be sure to pull out that black hair that was growing out of his chin mole at the funeral? I know that sounds funny, but I'd really appreciate it."

"No problem with that. And you just never know when we might need another caterer, Angie. You take care now and we'll be in touch."

"One more thing. I saw Vinnie's obit in the *Trib* today. I didn't put anything in—too expensive. Any idea who did?"

"I have no idea. The family always takes care of that. I can do some digging around if you'd like. I know the folks at the paper; I'll see if they can pull the order," Louie offered.

"You are a full-service funeral director, Louie. I'd appreciate it."

After Angie hung up with Louie, she heard the front door open and Gina calling out, "Hey, Aunt Angie, how are you doing?"

Angie came out of the bedroom and Gina gave her a big hug, then said, "Kinda nice to have someone to come home to, with Thad being gone so much."

Angie leaned in and held her niece tight. "This is just what the doctor ordered, honey. Why don't you change your work clothes and let me make you something to eat."

"You don't have to ask me twice; I love your cooking. I'll take a quick shower. There should be plenty of fixings in the pantry." Gina left their comfy hug and headed for the bathroom.

"I'll pour us a glass of wine and let's see if we can figure out how to help you get your catering company launched," Angie said as she made her way to the kitchen.

"That would be wonderful, Aunt Angie. I'll take all the help I can get. Hey, did you call my mom back? She's dying to tell you who stopped in at Murphy's after you left. You're not going to believe it!"

Chapter 6

Ralph's penthouse was walking distance from Gibsons. After he left Cookie, he checked his watch. It was one in the morning—*never too late for great sex.* He had been seeing Rebecca O'Brien, the alderman's wife, for the past six months after she approached him at a big city gala. He never mixed business with pleasure, but she was so stunning and persistent that he had finally let down his guard.

Once he got up to his place, he turned on the living room fireplace, creating a romantic mood, and took two Waterford crystal brandy snifters out of his glass-enclosed liquor cabinet. The doorman rang his penthouse suite announcing that his date had arrived, and Ralph instructed him to send her up.

He greeted her wearing a black silk robe loosely tied at his waist and kissed her gently on her neck. She kicked off her four-inch Louboutin heels and followed Ralph over to his plush beige couch. Ralph handed her a snifter of Remy Martin XO, picked up his snifter, and gently tapped hers and they both took a sip. "Rebecca, you took my breath away today at Rago Brothers. We need to make this permanent."They set their glasses on the end table.

He gently kissed her shoulder, unzipped her dress, removed it, and tossed it aside. He unclipped her bra, kissed her passionately, and moved her long brunette hair away from her face, revealing her pear-shaped diamond earrings.

Rebecca slid off the leather couch onto the thick, lambswool rug. "Why don't we talk about that later?" She separated his silk robe and began licking his inner thigh on one side then the other, gently touching his firm manhood with the side of her cheek. Ever so slowly, her tongue made its way deliberately.

"You are the best lover I have ever had," she whispered as she continued to caress and kiss him. Her perfect manicure displayed red nail polish.

Ralph groaned with desire. "I want you, now."

"Be patient, my love," she murmured as she continued to lick and kiss him ever so slowly.

Ralph made his way down onto the plush rug next to Rebecca, cradling her face in the cup of his two hands, and began to kiss her passionately. He removed her lace thong and then moved his fingers between her legs. Making his way slowly down, he gently kissed her breasts, her tummy, and below; Rebecca groaned with delight as he took his time leisurely exploring every inch of her.

After making love for over an hour, they embraced, the crackle of the fire soothing them.

"I'll need to leave in a bit. I'd rather stay, but I just can't, not yet." She slowly left Ralph's embrace and stood up and then put on his satin robe.

"Are we ever going to make this permanent?" Ralph sat up.

"There's an election coming up; I can't leave my husband until he's won—and he *will* win." She walked down the hall to the bathroom.

Ralph sighed. *This is too much. I can't keep doing this.*

She returned dressed, her handbag around her wrist, and tossed the robe to Ralph. "I just can't get enough of you. We'll have our day. I need you to be patient." Ralph stood up, put on his robe, and walked her to the door in silence.

She slipped on her heels and gave him a long, departing kiss. "That funeral parlor was sure fun. Twice in one day. I wish we could go for more." She blew him a kiss, stepped out into the hall, and caught the elevator down.

Chapter 7

Angie found all the fixings for a simple pasta with red sauce and garlic bread while Gina took a shower. She poured them each a glass of Vinnie's favorite Italian red wine and brought the plates out.

Gina appeared at the kitchen door. "Nothing smells as wonderful as garlic cooking. I hope I can cook as well as you do someday."

"I know you've got it in you, honey. Will you take these plates to the table? I've already set it."

Gina did as Angie asked, then sat down and waited for her aunt to join her. "Can you believe Bill Murray came to Murphy's to share his condolences for Uncle Vinnie? I had no idea they were even friends. Did you?"

Angie brought the basket of garlic bread in and sat down. "We have photos of the two of them. Vinnie would tell me Bill talked sports with him, but I figured that was when he went to the fancy sports dinners or fundraisers. I didn't know they met after the games and rehashed every inning, but I was always already home in bed by then." She took a sip of wine. "Bill Murray . . . I loved him when I watched the reruns of him on *SNL* with Gilda Radner, way before your, and even my, time.

And his movies make me laugh out loud no matter how many times I see them. How about *Stripes*?"

Angie raised her wineglass and said, "*Mangiamo*."

"*Salute*," Gina said, clinking her glass against Angie's. "I loved *Stripes* too."

As Angie remembered the time she and Vinnie had watched the movie together and belly-laughed through whole movie, the floodgates opened and tears began streaming down her cheeks.

Gina got up and put her arms around Angie. "I'm going to miss him too. Crying is a good thing—let it out."

Angie let herself cry; Gina's embrace brought her comfort. After Angie collected herself, Gina sat down and they ate in silence for a bit.

"Let's talk about your ideas for your catering company. What are you thinking in terms of recipes?"

Gina finished her wine and refilled her glass and topped off Angie's, then said, "Promise me you won't laugh or judge me."

"I promise, honey. We all have to start somewhere."

"A friend of mine gave me this cookbook that her grandma Mindy gave her; it was a fundraiser for the Arthritis Foundation. The title is *Scratch? My Ass! Store-Bought Can Be as Good as Homemade*. It's a collection of easy recipes introduced by these two women called Ethel and Blanche," Gina said.

She turned to the first page and started to read the introduction to her aunt. "Meet Ethel and Blanche. Many of you may wonder where Ethel and Blanche came from. We started out in the world's oldest profession. But as Father Time and Mother Nature came around the mountain (wearing crepe soles, the little sneaks!), we decided to semi-retire before we had to begin paying our clients what they were paying us!"

"This sounds spicy." Angie chuckled and thumbed through

the cookbook. "Very clever and fun for sure. I'll have to read the rest of this later."

"I never thought of myself as a cook, but when I started using these recipes and bringing food to parties, people were impressed. It's my go-to." Gina paused to take a bite of garlic bread. "Your garlic bread is always so crunchy and buttery. How do you get it that way?"

"I have my secrets, and you'll learn every one of them. Trick is to grate some fresh Parmigiano Reggiano on top after you've baked the bread, then stick it under the broiler for just a few minutes. Now tell me more about this cookbook you use," Angie said.

"The concept is why go to all the bother of making a dish from scratch when you can go to Jewel or a bakery, get what you want, and just transfer it into a nice bowl or platter and decorate it with a few simple items."

Angie squinted her eyes and tried to get Gina to look her straight in the eye to see if she was serious. "Can you give me an example of a dish you prepared from this cookbook?"

"Oh yeah!" Gina grinned. "I bought the potato salad from Jewel, put it in my mom's fancy ceramic bowl, cut up some parsley and sprinkled it around the edge, sliced some hard-boiled eggs, sprinkled paprika on the top, and bingo! The heads turned when I set the bowl down at the Holy Communion party."

Angie smiled. "And no one noticed?"

"Nope. Several of the wives and even one husband asked me for my recipe. Case closed."

Angie's laugh made Gina start to laugh too. "What a brilliant idea! I just wish I thought of that when I was working at La Scarola. After closing, they always offered me food to take home, but I never did. I could have transferred it to a dish and been the hit of the next church potluck."

Gina nodded and said, "Once I figured out this trick, I was a big hit at all the parties. The best part was I didn't get nervous worrying about what I was going to make. You know, not everyone can cook." Gina took another bite of her pasta.

"My first husband had to have three square meals a day, so I had to learn fast after I married him. But your uncle Vinnie loved to go out to eat; he didn't want me to slave away in the kitchen. I always made a nice Sunday supper; besides breakfast, that was the only regular homemade meal we had. He spoiled me rotten." Angie sighed. "I can't believe he's gone."

Gina leaned over and put her hand on her aunt's arm. "I'm so sorry, Aunt Angie."

Angie took the tissue from her pocket and wiped her nose.

"I don't think I know how you and Uncle Vinnie actually met."

"Well, refill that wineglass, and let's get started on that story. You'll love it." Angie cleared their plates and sat back down.

Angie took another sip of wine and then asked, "You know the Rosebud?"

"Absolutely, the one in Little Italy. There was something on the news about how the owner, Alex Dana, opened up a small lunch counter before he opened Rosebud back in the seventies, and now he has restaurants all over the Chicago area," Gina said.

"Alex took me under his wing and gave me a job after my first husband threw me out. I had never waitressed before, and he trained me like no other. I worked there for almost fifteen years, and that's where it all started. I was working a private party in the west room."

"Wow, I didn't know you were a waitress that long. I bet you saw and heard things." Gina raised her eyebrows.

"The unspoken rule of waitressing in any good Italian restaurant in Chicago, you don't see anything, you don't hear anything, you don't know anything. I found out after I left that the manager would send a person into the bar a couple days after the private parties to see if they could pry any info from the waitresses or the bartender. If you kept your mouth shut, you were good. Anyway, it was the holiday party for the managers who worked at the City of Chicago, and a few contractors who did a lot of business with the city. Very fancy hors d'oeuvres, open bar, and they could order anything they wanted on the menu rather than eat family style."

"Whenever I go to a holiday party with an open bar, I take full advantage," Gina said.

"When the City of Chicago hosts a holiday party, it goes big! Top-of-the-line booze, and price is no object. When I worked those holiday parties, I didn't get home until after three in the morning."

"I bet you fell into bed," Gina declared.

"I usually had a nightcap with the waitstaff, and the manager always paid for our cabs so we got home safe. I loved it. And the tips were huge. After working several private parties, I made enough to take a trip to Vegas."

"Sounds like it was a ball. But you still haven't told me how you met Uncle Vinnie." Gina refilled their wineglasses.

"I was working hard to pay all my bills, never got a dime from my first husband. Worked the lunch shift and then the private parties. I was carrying a tray with dishes of meatballs in red sauce. This guy was holding court with a group, all eyes on him as they listened. I went to walk around him. He was waving his arms, he didn't see me, and he hit my arm with his hand. The dishes flew up in the air; the sauce and everything got all over him, me, and everyone nearby—it was a sauce shower. One lady had on white linen. I'll never forget the look on her face. There was a loud crash, and the busboys rushed over and started cleaning everything up. Everyone in the room turned toward us and let out a gasp. I started to cry because I knew I was going to get fired." Angie took a sip of wine.

"Oh my God, what did Uncle Vinnie say? I bet he was wearing his dark blue tailored Italian suit," Gina said.

"I couldn't have told you what he was wearing; he pulled his handkerchief from his pocket and, instead of wiping the red sauce off his face, he handed it to me. I took it, wiped the sauce off my face and neck, and kept crying. The manager was there apologizing up and down."

"That Uncle Vinnie, he was a gentleman for sure. That's one of the things I most admired about him. He even opened the car door for me when I was little," Gina said.

Angie shook her head. "They just don't make them that way anymore. He made the manager get me a chair and he sat next to me. I just wanted to curl up in the corner and die. The lady with the white linen suit stormed out while everyone else was sitting down eating the first course."

"I can't even imagine how you must have felt," Gina said.

"I went to the bathroom and washed up best I could. The sauce was everywhere, including inside my bra. When I got home, I found it in my ears, hair; this had never ever happened to me."

"What happened next?" Gina leaned in.

"You have anything stronger to drink?" Angie asked as she finished her wine.

Angie watched Gina look up as if the answer was on the ceiling. "I do. I keep a bottle of Seagram's VO for Uncle Vinnie when he stops by . . . stopped by."

"Sounds perfect. Let's go sit in the living room." Angie stood up and helped Gina take the wineglasses into the kitchen.

Angie went into the small living room and saw that her cell phone was dinging and decided to turn it off. *Whoever or whatever it is can wait,* she thought to herself, and sat on the couch.

Gina came in with the VO and two glasses, poured the liquor, handed one to Angie, then sat down next to her. "Salute!"

Angie took a long sip; the rich liquid warmed her throat. "Your uncle and I would sip this at night sometimes."

Angie watched Gina take a little sip and continued her story.

"So, I'm in the restaurant bathroom talking to myself out loud: 'Everything will be okay. You'll find another job. It's not the end of the world.' I splashed water on my face and looked in the mirror and saw my mascara was all over the place. I looked like Bette Davis from the movie *What Ever Happened to Baby Jane?* without the white powder on my face."

Gina laughed. "Yikes, that's a scary look for sure."

"I took some of the soap and toilet paper, scrubbed it off, and of course, I got soap in my eyes, which burned. Finally, I was ready to walk right out the front door and catch a cab. I walked out the bathroom door, and there was Vinnie—waiting for me. I was horrified. His fancy suit and white pressed shirt were stained with red sauce; there was still some in his hair."

Angie took a deep breath as if she was reliving the entire event, and then they each took a sip of their brandy.

"He stood right in my way. I looked at him and told him I was so very sorry, that I had to leave immediately, and headed toward the door."

"I can't even image how embarrassed you must have been," Gina declared.

"I was never so humiliated. I started to cry again and walked around him. But he wouldn't let me pass. He lifted my chin and said, 'Angie, don't worry about any of this; it was my fault for throwing my arms up in the air, not yours. I made that clear to your manager, and I called my friend who owns La Scarola, and he has an opening. So don't give that manager a second thought. You're a good waitress; a pretty lady like you shouldn't be crying. Let me buy you a drink.'"

"What did you do?" Gina asked.

"I just stood there and looked at him. He was so kind and handsome. He led me to a booth in the back. I said, 'I don't even know your name. I should be buying you a drink for all the trouble I caused.'

"Then he leaned over and touched my hand and said, 'Oh, I have a feeling you'll be buying me more than a drink. I think we'll be spending lots of time together.' I got goose bumps all over, and I knew I had met the one." Angie felt the edges of her mouth reach for her ears. "It was a crazy, magical moment."

She watched Gina gazing at her. "That is the silliest, most romantic story I've heard in a long time."

"Enough about me. Let's talk about how we can make you the best caterer in the funeral business. Let's get in our pajamas, have another nightcap, and brainstorm."

"I would love that!" Gina said and made her way to her bedroom.

Angie reached for her cell. When she turned it on, there were eight new voicemails, five of them from Beatrice, two from Mario, and one from a number she didn't recognize. She went into Gina's bathroom and put on a pair of Gina's pajamas. Thankfully, Gina wore loose ones so they fit fine—a little long, but good around her tummy.

She started to listen to one of her voicemails. "Hi, Angie, this is Ralph; I saw you at Vinnie's funeral. Would you please call me as soon as you get this message? I want to make sure you're safe and find out where you're staying." *Why is he worried about my safety?* she wondered.

She turned the phone off again and went into the living room where Gina had a big down comforter on the couch. Gina patted the place right next to her.

"Come on over, get warm, and let's talk about my catering company. You know how it's exclusively for funeral parlors?" Gina asked, and Angie nodded. "Well, Kim and I have decided on the name. What do you think about 'Last Bite'?"

Chapter 8

After Ralph left Angie the message, he started to figure out a way he could help her pay off Vinnie's debt. Thinking of the man who confronted him at Gibsons, he thought, *These are not people to mess with.* It was the least he could do after all the business Vinnie had thrown his way over the years. Ralph had gotten very rich by reinvesting his share, while Vinnie made one bad gambling decision after another. Angie was a sweet, innocent woman; she was too trusting and a little naive from what Vinnie had told him. She was blindly loyal. He dialed Mario, Vinnie's second-in-command at the city. Mario picked up on the first ring. "This is Mario Longetti."

"Hi, Mario, this is Ralph Conti, a very old friend of Vinnie Sortino."

"Yeah, I know who you are. What do you want? I'm pretty busy." Ralph could hear his thick Chicago—with a splash of Italian—accent.

"I'm concerned about his wife, Angie. She may be in harm's way. I was hoping we could meet and talk about how we could protect her," Ralph explained.

"I'm not sure I know what you're talking about, my friend. I promised Vinnie, if anything happened to him, I would keep a close eye on her, and that's exactly what I plan to do. I don't need any help from you. They don't make that kind of woman anymore. Innocent to a fault, doesn't ask any questions and takes good care of her man, if you know what I mean." Mario chuckled.

"I couldn't agree with you more, Mario. How about we meet at Lou Mitchell's for breakfast tomorrow morning? I can give you the rundown."

"I can meet with you, Ralph, but I'm certain I can take care of the little lady. I'll be there at seven thirty sharp, but I need to get to a jobsite immediately afterward."

"Thanks, Mario, see you then."

The next call Ralph made was to Rebecca. Even though he enjoyed their wild sex, having an affair with a married woman, especially an alderman's wife, was too risky—and getting riskier. He was determined to end their affair.

The call went directly to voicemail. "Hi, Rebecca, it's Ralph. I really need to talk to you as soon as possible. Give me a quick call when you get a chance."

Ralph owned one of the most successful development companies in the Midwest. As was usual in his workday, he spent the entire day at his office meeting with investors and tracking the various projects his firm had under construction in Chicago. After work, he grabbed a light dinner, and it was after nine when he headed home and took a hot shower. As he got into bed, his house phone rang.

"Mr. Conti, I have a lady down here who would like to come up to see you," the doorman announced.

"Send her up." *I'm sure it's Rebecca coming for a late booty call. Maybe just one more time*, he thought. Ralph got out of bed, put on his silk robe, and went to the double doors in the entryway. The elevator bell rang as he opened his front door, and a tall blonde exited the elevator—none other than Cookie Cunningham.

"Hello there, handsome, looks like you've been expecting me." Cookie batted her long eyelashes and walked into the foyer. "Now this is what I call class. I just came from work, and before I go meet a friend for a cocktail, I need a few minutes of your time." She leaned into his neck. "You smell delicious."

Ralph backed away and closed the doors behind her. "Well, hello, Cookie, I wasn't expecting to see you tonight. I was just about to hit the hay."

Cookie walked into the well-appointed, oval living room with a bay window overlooking Lake Michigan. "I can see the Drake Hotel from here; I love their high tea."

"May I get you a nightcap?" Ralph asked.

"Only if you'll join me." She glanced at his collection and pointed at the Remy Martin Louis XIII.

"Absolutely." *This woman knows her cognac.* He nodded and poured each of them a finger and handed her the Baccarat tumbler.

"Please, have a seat. What brings you here so late? I'm surprised you know where I live."

"Oh, Ralphie boy, you must remember the forms you had to fill out when you were pitching the city on all those contracts. It's all in HR, and I have access to *so* much information."

"Ah, yes, that makes sense. So, tell me, what can I do for you?" Ralph could hear his mobile ringing repeatedly in the other room.

"Do you need to get that?" Cookie asked.

"I do. I'll be right back, please excuse me." Ralph went into the kitchen where he kept his cell charged and could see it was Rebecca. "Hi there, thanks for calling me back so late. Can I call you back?"

"You don't have to. I'm having my driver drop me in front in five minutes. I need to see you." She hung up.

How am I going to get Cookie out of here before Rebecca arrives? Then he remembered that his building had two separate elevators. He would deal with that shortly. In the meantime, he walked calmly back into the living room where Cookie was studying the framed photos of Ralph posing with various famous people.

"Love Bill Murray. How cool was that when he showed up at Murphy's?" Cookie asked.

"What a great guy," Ralph said.

"Looks like you and the Daley family were close, by the looks of you with the dad and his son."

"I've always had a close relationship with all the Chicago mayors, given all the projects we've built over the years." He was talking faster than he normally would.

Before Cookie could comment on another photo, Ralph jumped in, "Cookie, I must apologize but I need to end our visit. That call was from a close friend who needs me, and I must leave momentarily. I am so sorry. Maybe we can meet later this week for a coffee or a cocktail." *I can't have her run into the alderman's wife coming to my place for a booty call*, he thought. *It would be all over City Hall in the morning.*

Cookie polished off the rest of the cognac. "I must say this is the fastest I've ever finished a fancy brandy. I hate to waste it."

"Cookie," Ralph said, more loudly and firmly than he usually spoke, feeling beads of sweat beginning to form on his forehead. "We will have to talk tomorrow; please don't think me rude, but you really need to go now. I am so sorry. This isn't my usual behavior."

His heart was pounding faster and faster as he escorted her to the door just as his house phone rang; he knew it was the doorman announcing the arrival of Rebecca. Cookie knew who Rebecca was, so he couldn't risk them passing in the hall or downstairs. The phone kept ringing.

"Good night, Cookie." Ralph opened the front door; the phone continued to ring in the background.

Before he shut the door, Cookie blurted out, "We do need to talk sooner than later. There are some complications at the city regarding Vinnie that will affect Angie. They must be resolved immediately." Cookie handed him her business card. "Call me tomorrow—first thing. I'm concerned about Angie and, just between you and me, I don't trust Mario."

"I promise, I'll call you in the morning, Cookie. Thank you for stopping by." Ralph closed the door and rushed over to pick up the phone. "Hello!"

"Your guest is starting to cause a scene in the lobby. She is demanding we let her up now."

"Would you please escort her to the service elevator? Make some excuse. I'll meet her there. It's important that these two women do not cross paths."

"I understand, sir."

Ralph wiped the sweat from his brow, quickly went into his bedroom and threw on a polo shirt and pants. Then he said out loud, "It has to end. Things are getting complicated."

He met her at the service elevator. Rebecca looked beautiful as usual, sporting a tight pair of pants and a low-cut blouse exposing her man-made breasts and cleavage, which he always had a hard time taking his eyes and hands off.

"You called, sweetheart, I am here." Rebecca slid her hand around his neck and drew him in for a passionate kiss, which he enjoyed.

After their lips parted, he gestured for her to come in. He spotted Cookie's snifter, the edge smeared with her lipstick, the same time Rebecca did. "Looks like I'm not the first female visitor tonight. Good thing we aren't exclusive or I'd be a little jealous." She threw her purse on the couch and slipped off her high heels.

Ralph took the glass to the kitchen. "Would you like a glass of wine?"

"I'll have whatever you served what's her name with the cheap pink lipstick, not even the color of the season." She followed him into the kitchen and put her hands around his waist from behind. "My husband is out of town for a week on business. I think we should have a slumber party." She pulled off her top, tossing it on the carpet, exposing a black lace bra.

Staring at her voluptuousness, Ralph caught his breath, saying, "I hate to disappoint, but I have an early morning meeting." He handed her a glass of cognac.

Rebecca took the cognac and walked into the living room. "That's not what I want to hear, Ralph. Reschedule your meeting for me; I never ask you to do much." She placed the glass on the end table, slipped her pants off, and walked toward him. "Come here and tell me why you look so troubled. I'm sure I can take your mind off whatever it is." While she kissed his neck, her hand slid to his zipper and she slowly pulled it down.

The smell of her expensive perfume always disarmed him. Ralph could feel his resolve waning; she had such an amazing body.

"You know I would love nothing better than to have you right now. I want you all the time, not just our random get-togethers. I just don't feel right being the other man. If that's not possible, then we need to end this." He blurted it out, his heart racing.

Rebecca removed her hand from inside his pants and stepped back. "What the fuck are you talking about! This has been working just fine for me. I'll be the one who decides when this is over, not you. And it's not over."

Ralph swallowed hard. "Rebecca, we need to discuss this civilly. It's only a matter of time before we get caught, and I can't risk that and neither can you. I need to keep my connection with the city clean, and if we're discovered, everything will go south, and that just cannot happen."

Rebecca sat down on the couch, crossed her long, curvaceous legs, and took a sip of her cognac and stared at the fire.

It took everything he had not to take her into his bedroom. "Please don't be angry, Rebecca."

It was a standoff. The longer Rebecca was silent, the longer he took in her sensuous body, and he knew he couldn't resist her. This had to be the last time.

She finally leaned over and whispered in his ear, "I'll be in the bedroom waiting for you." She unfastened her bra, let it drop to the floor, and walked slowly toward his bedroom.

Chapter 9

Early the next morning, Gina offered to take her aunt to her apartment. "You can't keep wearing that Juicy sweatsuit around the house. My stoner roommate, Thad, won't be able to resist you much longer. Good thing he stays at his girlfriend's most of the time." They both chuckled.

"You're right, I don't know how *any* man can resist me," Angie said.

They both left Gina's apartment building and Gina drove her run-down Subaru sedan into a parking space near Vinnie's apartment. She took her aunt's hand as they walked to the entry. "I'm here for you."

"Thanks, I couldn't do this without you." Angie squeezed her niece's hand.

"In my wish of all wishes, I wish Vinnie would be sitting in his easy chair waiting for me to cook him dinner." Angie covered her mouth with a handkerchief and started to sob. "This will be the first time I walk through the door knowing my husband won't be coming home."

Gina could see Angie's hands shaking and gently took the keys from her, opened the door to the apartment building, and helped her aunt step up onto the tiled floor of the entryway.

Gina skimmed the old brass mailboxes that lined the right wall and found the name Sortino. Finding the mailbox key on the key ring, she opened the mailbox, which was full of cards addressed to Angie.

"You take them home and open them, Gina. I just don't think I can right now," Angie whispered.

Gina placed the cards into her purse and put her arm around her aunt's waist as they slowly ascended the stairs. The echo of their footsteps reverberated, filling the space around them. Gina noticed she was holding her breath and forced herself to exhale deeply.

As Gina recalled what had happened less than a week earlier, it felt like a time warp. Time was moving faster in one way and in slow motion in the other. Angie had not yet come home after she received the call from the emergency room that Vinnie had had a massive heart attack and was rushed from the jobsite to the emergency room. She remembered the call from her aunt summoning her to the hospital. "He's gone, sweetheart. Get your mom and come meet me. *Now*," Angie had sobbed into the phone. Everything had happened so fast—funeral arrangements, decisions about what he should wear at the wake.

Gina and Connie knew that Angie could not handle these decisions. She stayed at Connie's, so Gina and her mom took care of everything, including coming to the apartment to get clothes for Vinnie and toiletries and a funeral outfit for Angie.

As they continued to walk up the stairs, Gina glanced over at her aunt. "We'll get through this together." Gina was doing everything in her power not to break down. *I have to be strong for her*, Gina thought. As they approached the apartment front door, Ben—Angie and Vinnie's neighbor down the hall—stepped out and walked toward them. "Oh, Angie, let's get you inside. I am so sorry." He walked over to Angie and wrapped his long, thin arms around her.

"Thanks, Ben, he loved you so much. I was so comforted you were at his funeral," Angie mumbled as she sank into him and sobbed.

Ben was part of their family; he had lived down the hall from Uncle Vinnie ever since Gina could remember and long before Angie was on the scene. Ben worked for the city of Chicago for over forty years, retired, and was always coaching Vinnie on how to navigate the city systems in order to survive. Gina grinned when she remembered that Vinnie would always give Ben a hard time for being what he called a "loser" White Sox fan.

Gina watched Angie lean into Ben's warm embrace, stepped around them, and walked into Vinnie's apartment. She looked at the familiar, cozy living room, the crocheted red, white, and blue blankets that Angie made draped over the La-Z-Boy loungers with a shared table in the middle. Gina had watched more baseball games and Disney movies than she could count there. This was her safe home, away from the loud arguments of her parents. The wall opposite the loungers was the shrine, as they all referred to it. The World Series flag was displayed above the huge TV, solid evidence that the Cubs indeed did win in 2016 after 108 years, along with framed photos of Vinnie with Bill Murray, Aunt Angie, and Vinnie at game seven in Cleveland.

Gina walked into the kitchen. Two stained coffee cups, spoons, and crusty plates were still in the sink. She was about to check the fridge when Ben called out, "Hey, Gina honey, can you help me get our gal to her chair?"

Gina glanced over and could see Aunt Angie leaning on Ben, her knees buckling. Running over, she put her arm around her aunt and she and Ben got Angie to the chair.

"I can't stay here—I just can't," Angie sobbed.

"It's okay, I'll pack some things and we'll go back to my place. Ben, you want to take her down to your apartment?"

"Sure. Angie, are you able to stand up and walk with us?"

Ben and Gina walked Angie down the hall into Ben's living room and made her comfortable on his couch. Ben sat next to her and put his arm around her, and Angie leaned into him.

Gina lightly touched her aunt's shoulder. "I'll go pack your bag, then lock up and come back. Sound good?"

Angie slowly nodded her head.

As Gina was walking toward the apartment, a stout, gray-haired man approached her. "Aren't you Angie's niece?"

"Yes, I am."

"Your aunt is so proud of you. She's shown me pictures from time to time and so did your uncle. By the way, I haven't seen anyone around. Everything okay? I'm Gus, the building manager."

Gina's heart sank. "I'm sorry to tell you, my uncle Vinnie died. We just had his funeral."

Gus gasped. "I am so sorry. I hadn't heard. Where's Angie?"

Gina pointed down the hall. "At Ben's. I'm packing her some clothes and we're heading back to my place. It's been a nightmare."

Gus just shook his head. "I won't bother you right now, but would you ask Angie to call me or maybe you could call me tomorrow? There seems to be a hiccup with the last two months' rent payments. I'm sure it's nothing, but I need to get it handled. The owners have been calling and wanting to know where the rent money is. They are very strict. I'll let them know what happened, but they're all about keeping their apartment buildings full and generating revenue."

Gina swallowed hard, then said, "I understand, Gus. I'll call you tomorrow after I've had some time to speak with Angie. Can you give me your number?"

She walked inside the apartment and Gus followed, taking a pen from his shirt pocket protector and rummaging around for a piece of paper. He scribbled down his name and number and handed the wrinkled piece of paper to Gina. "Thanks, Gina. Let me know if there is anything I can do. I'll do my best to buy you all some time to sort things out."

"I appreciate that, Gus. I know Angie will too."

Gus left and Gina went into Angie and Vinnie's bedroom, opening the closet door to look for a suitcase or bag to pack Angie's things. When she saw all of Vinnie's clothes hanging, she fell to the floor and broke down crying.

"Why! Why did this have to happen?" All the memories of her uncle Vinnie, her godfather, came flooding into her mind. She couldn't believe this. Last week he was alive, joking, giving her bear hugs. Now he's gone. She buried her face in her hands and cried.

Gina finally stood up and looked in the closet, moving her hands through his ironed shirts and pants. The smell of his cologne brought back all the long hugs over the years. No one made her feel safer than her uncle. *He taught me how to keep score at Wrigley when I was five. He's the reason I'll always be a Cubs fan.* She let her tears keep coming.

Gina found a small suitcase on the closet floor, placed it on the end of the bed, and started packing. She mindlessly selected an assortment of blouses, slacks, and a few dresses, folded them and put them in the suitcase. She opened the top dresser drawer that had all of Uncle Vinnie's pressed handkerchiefs, cuff links, and other personal items neatly organized. Gina knew Aunt Angie prided herself on taking great care with all of his things and ironing his clothes. Gina remembered how he would ask her aunt, "Are we Vegas ready, sweetheart?" and Angie would say, "Always, my love, let's go!" and indeed there were times when they did just that. Connie, the family travel agent, would get them a cheap package, and off they'd go.

Gina opened Angie's dresser drawer. A recent *Cosmopolitan* magazine promising tried-and-true ways to keep your man was tucked beneath the underwear. That made her smile. She packed the rest of the items, including several pairs of her aunt's pajamas. There was a folder marked PRIVATE in bold letters at the bottom of Angie's underwear drawer. Gina put that with Angie's things. She really wanted to look inside but would never breach her aunt's privacy. She closed the suitcase, locked the apartment door, and went down to Ben's place. Before knocking she took a long, deep breath, told herself, *Stay strong for your aunt*, and tapped on his door.

Ben opened it. "Come on in, would you like a cup of tea? I made one for Angie."

Gina put the suitcase down and went into the kitchen where Angie was sitting at the small Formica table. "No thanks, Ben, I need to get my aunt home and then get to work." She looked over at Angie. "Are you okay to walk downstairs?"

Angie placed the teacup in its saucer and stood up. "I'm better now. Thank you, Ben, for all your kindness. Thanks for being my family; it means the world to me." She gave him a hug.

"Vinnie was like a brother to me. I'll water the plants and take in your mail until you're ready to come back. You promise me you'll take extra special care of yourself now." Angie nodded. Ben walked them out to Gina's car. He opened the door and made sure Angie got in comfortably.

Gina placed the suitcase in the back seat. "Oh—you'll need her keys," she realized and said to Ben.

"Vinnie and I had each other's keys for years. I'll just need the mailbox key."

Gina took the mailbox key off the key ring and handed it over to him. Ben opened the car door for Gina; she slipped behind the driver's seat. Ben bent down and looked over at Angie. "You call me anytime, day or night."

"Ben, do you know anything about a storage unit Vinnie had? Beatrice is hounding me for the key, and I have no idea what she's talking about." Angie wiped her eyes.

Ben ran his fingers through his hair. "That Beatrice, you can always count on her stirring things up. I'll deal with her. Let's talk about that later; you need to get some rest and take care of yourself."

Gina started the car and Ben tapped the roof. "Be safe."

Chapter 10

Ralph awoke, turned to his side, and put his hand on the silky skin of Rebecca's bottom. She was sleeping soundly as they had made love well into the early morning hours. *This was wonderful while it lasted*, he thought as he slipped out of bed, glancing at the clock. It was six thirty, and he had to meet Mario at Lou Mitchell's, where many important business decisions were made over a huge breakfast.

After showering, he left a note for Rebecca, letting her know that he had had a wonderful evening but that they still needed to talk. The relationship he wanted to be in was with someone who wasn't married, someone he could take to the galas he attended and even travel with at some point. While he knew he could never replace Alice, he hoped someday he could find a companion who had some of her qualities. Rebecca had been fun. But he was getting the idea that she wasn't exactly faithful companion material. No judgment—he was a willing party in their arrangement. He couldn't help thinking that Alice wouldn't approve of his compromising ethics, not to mention the risks of their affair affecting his business if anyone found out.

As he walked to the elevator, tears started to stream down his face, his legs weakened, and he had to sit down on a chair for fear that he would collapse on the floor. He buried his face in his hands and began to sob. This had happened several times after Alice's death, and he had hoped that, with time, the intensity of his tears might have disappeared or at least lessened, but he knew by now that grief had its own timeline and that he had no control over when or where it might emerge. *Just let it out*, a voice inside him said gently. *Let it out. It's okay, Ralph.*

When he was finally able to take a deep breath and blow his nose, he knew this wave of weeping had run its course. Thankfully, Eunice had coached him on how to manage these waves of grief when he broke down in front of her at the office over a year ago. He sat for a few more minutes, continuing to focus on his breathing, until he was ready to stand up.

His doorman had a cab waiting for him downstairs. "Lou Mitchell's on Jackson," the doorman instructed the driver.

As the cabbie pulled away, he glanced back at Ralph. "Love Lou Mitchell's. Been going there for years before I start my morning shift. You know that place has been around for over ninety years."

"That's the word on the street." Ralph already knew this; he nodded and started reading his *Wall Street Journal.*

Once inside, he saw Lou, the owner, speaking to several businesswomen in line for a table. "Good morning, you beautiful ladies, would you like a sweet treat while you're waiting?" He held out one basket with small-sized boxes of Milk Duds and another with hot donut holes. Ralph watched as they smiled and declined his offer. Lou recognized Ralph right away. He held out both options and Ralph chose the warm donut hole, popped it into his mouth, and followed Lou to a booth. Peggy, his favorite waitress, approached holding a stainless steel coffeepot. "Hello, handsome. Coffee?"

Ralph smiled. "You bet, Peggy. You look fabulous as always."

"I know you're full of shit, but I'll take that. Waiting for someone?" Peggy poured his coffee.

Ralph could see Mario approaching the booth. "Here he is." Mario looked disheveled; part of his comb-over was sticking up and his lower shirt button was undone, exposing his beer belly.

Peggy turned the other cup over and poured some coffee for Mario as he slid in, opposite Ralph. "I'll be back in a minute for your order," she said.

"Thanks for meeting me, Mario. I know you must be busy taking care of everything now that Vinnie's gone." He took a sip of his coffee.

"It's a shitstorm as always at the city. Vinnie was not good with paperwork, and now I have to manage all his jobs, complete that backlog, and keep things moving. I don't need to tell you the city never stops."

Mario's eyes were bloodshot with heavy bags under them. Vinnie had mentioned that Mario liked to knock back a few—or frequently more than a few—every night after work, and he looked the part.

"I'm not here to talk about all my jobs with the city," Ralph said. "I'm here to talk about Angie. She's in real danger."

Peggy was back, standing at their table. "What'll it be?"

"I'll have two eggs over easy, bacon, and rye toast," Ralph ordered.

"I'll have the three-cheese bacon omelet and an English muffin, extra strawberry jelly." Mario glanced at her and then took a big slurp of his coffee.

"You got it." She refreshed their coffee, headed to the kitchen, and yelled out the order.

Mario snapped at Ralph, "I don't know what deal you made with Vinnie, but consider any past agreements, and I mean any, null and void. As far as Angie goes, I don't need your help watching over her. Vinnie was clear with me that if anything happened to him, I was to take, I think the word he used was 'exceptional,' care of her, or he would come back from the dead and cut off my balls with a butter knife."

Ralph wondered why Mario was so aggravated with him, but he wasn't going to react. "Good to hear that he was that specific. Then you know the mob is after her for his unpaid gambling debt, correct?"

Ralph leaned back as Peggy placed a small skillet in front of each of them. "Enjoy," she said as she refreshed their coffee.

"I did know he was into the mob but wasn't aware they were going after poor Angie. When did this happen? We just buried the guy, for Christ's sake." Mario slathered jelly on his English muffin and took a big bite, followed by a forkful of his omelet, oozing cheese.

"I was approached by one of their thugs the night of his funeral when I was having a late dinner with Cookie at Gibsons." Ralph dipped his rye toast into his eggs and took a bite.

Mario's face turned red and he slammed his fist on the table. "What the hell were you doing out with Cookie?"

Ralph watched the vein on Mario's neck pulsating. Mario reached for his pack of Pall Malls tucked in his shirt pocket and then stopped. "I forgot, no smoking in here. That's bullshit," Mario said.

"I agree. Nothing like a good smoke with your breakfast," Ralph said.

"Anyway," Ralph continued, "me and Cookie had some drinks at Vinnie's reception at Murphy's, had a lovely time. I didn't know she as much as ran the city HR department. A fountain of information."

"What did you talk about?" Mario kept eating.

"Nothing important, really. I hadn't realized she reviewed the paperwork for all the developers who work on city jobs, and my company is one of the biggest. They make you disclose everything, including personal information as well as past tax forms. She's quite a character." Ralph watched Mario as he used the last of his muffin to clean the skillet of all the tidbits.

"Well, stay away from her and Angie. I can handle this mob thing. I don't need your help." Mario stood up. "I've got to go to the jobsite. I'm sure you can afford breakfast."

"Happy to pay. But before you go, did you know Vinnie was into the mob for a million and half?"

Mario stopped and gaped at Ralph. "That much?"

"Yeah, and if they don't get it soon, they threatened to go after Angie and, by the looks of things, she doesn't have a pot to piss in." Ralph put cash on the table and walked out with Mario.

A line of cabs waited out front. Mario lit a cigarette, hopped in the cab, and looked out the open window. "I'll handle this, Ralph. Mind your own fucking business. You have no idea what Vinnie was into. I'm in charge now, and if I hear of you talking to either Angie or Cookie, your contracts with the city are canceled!" The cab pulled away.

When Ralph's cell rang, he heard a familiar voice. "Ralph, this is Cookie. I need to see you now. There's some weird shit going on and I don't want to get mixed up in it."

"Okay, can you tell me what's going on?"

"I'm not saying anything on the phone. Meet me at the Half Shell on Diversey at noon."

"Okay, Cookie, see you then. Be careful."

When Ralph arrived at his office, his executive secretary, Eunice, intercepted him. She motioned him with her index finger to follow her into her office and closed the door. Eunice had been with Ralph for over twenty years, always wearing her graying hair in a tight bun, her trim frame professionally dressed, her eyeglasses hanging from her neck on a chain for immediate access. Ralph knew Eunice prided herself on keeping the office atmosphere extremely professional, which was why Ralph loved her.

"What's going on?"

Looking up from her short frame at Ralph, she remained calm. "Rebecca, Alderman O'Brien's wife, is in your office and she has demanded I close your office blinds, order a bottle of Dom Pérignon, which I won't do, and let you know she's waiting for you. This is very unprofessional. You know we don't do those kinds of things here, but I didn't want to ask her to leave until I spoke with you in person."

"I'll take care of this, Eunice. As always, I appreciate your sensitivity and support." As Ralph walked to his office, he thought, *If Eunice knew what I was doing to Rebecca last night, she would have a heart attack on the spot.*

Ralph opened his office door and immediately closed it as Rebecca was sitting on his desk, in her white, lacy lingerie and nothing else. "Rebecca, this is so inappropriate. Not in my place of business."

She tilted her head. "What's the matter, Ralphie, you don't like what you see? I bought these just for you." She reached around and unsnapped her bra and let her pert breasts fall out, nipples hard.

Ralph moved his gaze away from her and walked toward his office door. "You have crossed the line. I need you to leave *right now.*"

"Come on, Ralph—you know you want this." She pointed to her breasts and walked over to him.

He stepped away. "I'm not kidding, Rebecca. Put your clothes on and get out. This is unacceptable behavior."

Rebecca studied his face, then gathered her clothes and put them on. She walked over to him and put her finger in between his lips. "I just can't get my fill of you, and when I want something, I usually get it. I'm not used to being turned down."

"Well, not in my place of business you don't." He opened his office door.

"I'll see you tonight—your place. I must run, lunch plans."

"I won't be home tonight."

She stopped and turned her head. "Where will you be? I'll meet you there."

"Business meeting in Oakbrook with some nervous investors, so it will run very late."

"Your loss. I'll see you tomorrow," she retorted and left.

That's not going to happen, he thought. He walked around to his desk and sat down and opened his email and went to work.

After Rebecca left, Eunice popped her head into his office. "Everything all right?"

"All good."

He returned phone calls and emails until it was time to go meet Cookie for lunch. He walked into the Half Shell and noticed her sitting at a booth near the back. He studied her face as he walked toward the booth. Her mouth turned down, she was tapping her fingers on the table. He sat down. "You don't look too happy. What's going on?"

The waitress came and they ordered lunch. Cookie continued, "After we left Gibsons, I went to the Four Seasons to meet a retired baseball player. As we were going up to his room, the ruffian who pulled you outside when we were at Gibsons stopped me. He threatened me and said if someone doesn't pay Vinnie's gambling debt, he's going after me. What the fuck? I have no idea why he was coming after me. He also threatened to go after Angie. Said he was going to get that money—one way or another."

As Cookie wrung her hands, Ralph said, "That's the same thing he told me. I met with Mario for breakfast this morning and told him about my encounter with the mafioso dude and that you and I had dinner at Gibsons. Mario demanded I have no contact with you or Angie, said he would handle things."

"Well, fuck Mario. He called my office early this morning and made me pull all Vinnie's pension paperwork and make a copy to put on his desk. Which is none of his business, but he was so angry that I got scared and did it. I have no idea what's going on here, but I'm really concerned about Angie. Mario said we needed to change Vinnie's pension beneficiary to him. Said Vinnie had told him to manage the pension money since Angie doesn't have any money sense. I told Mario that's illegal; his response was not if no one knows about it. Make it happen or you'll be sorry."

"Does he have something on you?"

"I don't know you well enough to tell you that, but Vinnie and I have been working at City Hall for a long time, and he has discovered a few things about me that could cause me to lose my job." Ralph decided to leave it alone.

The waitress placed their Caesar salads in front of them, ground some black pepper, and left. Ralph looked at Cookie again. "Angie is in danger. Vinnie left a huge debt with the mob; I know Angie has no money. I can't pay it, and Mario says he'll take care of it. Not sure what that means—maybe he's thinking of using Vinnie's pension."

As he dug into his salad, Cookie said, "I invited Angie to lunch this week so we could discuss Vinnie's pension. I'm hoping to get her a job with the city once I know what she can do. I'm not going to let Mario steal her pension if I can help it. That said, Mario could have me fired. He knows the higher-ups, and I can't afford to lose my job. I've got a mortgage to pay."

After a few bites, Cookie cleared her throat. "If I'm not mistaken, I think I saw Rebecca walking into your building after we left Gibsons. That woman is trouble. I have witnessed her telling outright lies to her husband about a city employee, and they were fired on the spot. I'm sure she can make up all kinds of lies about you, and poof! No more city jobs for you."

Ralph put his fork down and looked at Cookie. "I appreciate the info."

"Just saying, if anything is going on, you should be careful."

"I appreciate your concern, Cookie." Ralph already knew he had to end it with Rebecca immediately. *I am not going to let that woman take me and my business down.*

Cookie wiped her mouth and stood up. "I need to get back to the office. Things are spiraling out of control. The city attorneys are doing an audit on all of Vinnie's jobs before they recommend a replacement to the mayor. Mario thinks he's a shoo-in, but I don't. I'm guessing they'll pull all your paperwork too. Hope your house is in order, Ralph." She left a twenty on the table. As she headed toward the door, she glanced over her shoulder. "And no matter what, we have to take care of Angie. Vinnie may have made mistakes, but he was a good guy. Always so nice to me. And, boy, did he love his Angie. We owe Vinnie to take good care of her."

Ralph threw two more twenties on the table, which more than covered the bill. "I agree. Angie has no idea what's happening. She shouldn't have to pay for Vinnie's sins. How about I meet you at City Hall so I can review all my projects before the lawyers comb over all the records?"

"You need to come over tomorrow before noon," Cookie responded.

"I'll be there at nine."

Cookie hopped into a cab and gave Ralph a thumbs-up.

It was clear to Ralph that Mario was not going to help him at all, and, after his talk with Cookie, Mario was likely going to take advantage of Angie. Ralph called Ben, who he knew was a stand-up guy who cared about Angie. Ben picked right up. "Hey, Ralph, what's up?"

"I'm concerned about Angie. Okay I swing by your place in a bit?"

"Sure, no problem; I'm home. That poor woman almost collapsed when her niece brought her here. Angie couldn't stay in their apartment, too busted up over Vinnie. That was love those two had. She had to sit in mine while Gina was packing some of her things."

"I'm on my way." Ralph put his hand out to hail a cab. "See you soon."

Ralph had enjoyed Ben's company with Vinnie over the years. Ralph had also offered Ben investment advice from time to time, and Ben had done very well by it. It made for a trusting relationship. Too bad Vinnie hadn't done the same.

Ralph rang the buzzer and Ben let him in. Ralph went up the stairs and down to Ben's apartment, Ben received him out in the hall, and they went inside and sat down.

"Can I get you anything?" Ben offered.

"No, I can't stay long, but I need to talk to you about Mario and Angie. Glad you were available."

"No problem. Now that I'm retired, I have all the time in the world. Is Mario giving you the runaround? He's good at that. I saw him in action over the years when I worked at the city. He was gunning for Vinnie's job from the start, but the higher-ups knew Vinnie had more street smarts, even if Mario had a degree."

"Mario is running off at the mouth about how he'll manage Angie's money and that Vinnie made him promise to do that if he died," Ralph began.

"That's bullshit! Vinnie had zero trust in Mario. You know the old saying 'Keep your friends close but your enemies closer'? Mario was no friend of Vinnie's. Vinnie always knew if anything happened to him, I would take care of Angie, and that's what I plan to do," Ben said.

Ralph continued. "I just had lunch with Cookie, and she shared some disturbing news: Mario is making her change the name of Vinnie's beneficiary on his pension to him. He wants Cookie to remove Angie's name."

Ben sat back and crossed his legs. "I'm not surprised Mario is pulling this crap. Jesus, Vinnie's barely gone. Looks like I'll need to drop by HR tomorrow and visit with Cookie. She's a straight-up gal. I know between the two of us, we can iron things out while still allowing Mario to think he's running the show. That said, there's one big problem I can't help with."

"The gambling debt?" Ralph asked.

"They already came by my place threatening me. I told them I had no idea what the hell they were talking about. Which is partially true. I knew Vinnie gambled, but I didn't know how much and who he owed. He kept his own counsel there."

Ralph stood up. "I need to head to the office. Would you let me know how your visit goes with Cookie? I'll give Angie a call later this afternoon."

Ben followed him out into the hall. "Vinnie was a couple months behind in their rent, so I paid that and the next two months until Angie can figure out what she can afford."

The two men shook hands. "You're a good man, Ben."

Ben smiled. "They're family. I wouldn't have it any other way."

Outside, Ralph hailed a cab and headed back to his office. He called Angie on the way and got her voicemail.

"Hi, Angie. It's Ralph again. Would you please give me a call when you have a chance? I just had a nice visit with Ben, and we'd like to help you out until all the pension paperwork gets done at the city, since it can take a while. I look forward to hearing from you and scheduling our lunch when you're up for it. Take care, Angie. These are tough times, I know."

Chapter 11

Angie awoke to the sound of her cell ringing and the smell of Gina's roommate, Thad, enjoying his morning joint. Very different from her floral-scented air freshener at home. She glanced at the clock. It was ten in the morning. She never slept this late. She slowly sat up and remembered the whiskey she and Gina sipped into the wee hours of the morning. Rubbing her head, she got out of bed and made her way to the bathroom. Thad was sitting on the couch. "Hey, dude," Thad said through a smoky haze.

Angie shook her head. "Good morning to you too." She closed the bathroom door and looked in the mirror. *No more of this monkey business. You've got to straighten up and figure out where all the money went—you're all alone now—it's just you—no more Vinnie to take care of you.* Her tears mingled with the shower water; she toweled off and got ready for her day. When she walked out of the bedroom, Thad had disappeared, leaving half of a joint in the ashtray with a note: *Going to Subway for a sandwich. Help yourself.* Angie had never tried marijuana but had smelled her fair share of it over the years. Whenever Gina smoked it with her pals, the scent embedded itself deep in her clothes.

After several cups of coffee and a piece of toast, Angie sat at the small kitchen table with a pad of paper, listened to all the voicemails, and wrote everything down. *I have never been so popular for all the wrong reasons,* she thought. She couldn't keep staying at Gina's tiny apartment, and she wasn't wild about Thad as a roommate. But he helped pay the rent, did Gina's dishes, and had a girlfriend who he stayed with most nights.

Angie decided to call Cookie's personal line at City Hall. She needed to find out how much Vinnie's pension would be and then decide if she needed to get a job to supplement her income.

When Cookie picked up, Angie said, "Hi, Cookie, it's Angie, Vinnie Sortino's wife. I was hoping I could come down today to file any paperwork necessary for his pension."

There was a slight pause on the other end. "Angie—yes, of course. I'm glad you called."

Angie heard Cookie clear her throat. "How about you come down around three this afternoon; we're on the eleventh floor. Can't miss us. When you get off the elevator, we're on the right."

"Great, that will work, Cookie. Do I need to bring any paperwork?"

"Just Vinnie's death certificate and your proof of identification. That should do it."

"You had mentioned you might be able to get me a job if I needed one. Would it be possible to talk about that too?"

"We can absolutely talk about a possible job here at the city once I understand what your skills are. Do you have a résumé?"

I've never had a résumé. "I haven't worked since shortly after I met Vinnie over ten years ago. I was a waitress before that—a pretty good one, if I say so myself."

"We don't have any restaurants, but we do have some food inspector positions that might be a good fit—or some receptionist jobs. We'll talk more when you get here; I have to run. See you at three." Cookie hung up.

Angie browsed through all the clothes Gina had packed for her and chose a simple and sensible dress with a colorful silk scarf, hose, and pumps. She had plenty of time, so she called Gus, her landlord, back. He picked up right away.

"Hi, Gus, this is Angie Sortino. You left me a message about our apartment."

"Angie, I'm so sorry for your loss. How are you doing?"

"Doing the best I can. I'm heading downtown to City Hall today to fill out paperwork and look for a job. Everything is happening so fast—I'm staying with my niece Gina for a while until I sort things out."

"I saw Gina when you came to pick up some things. What a great young gal she is—I feel like I got to see her grow up, she came around to your place so often." He paused. "The reason I called is to let you know there is no rush moving out. Your rent is paid up for the next couple months."

"Who paid my rent?" Angie asked.

"They asked me not to say—just a friend. Once things settle down you can let me know if you plan to stay or move."

"Was it Ben?" Angie checked her makeup in the hallway mirror while she waited for a response.

She heard Gus clear his throat.

"I won't push you on it, but I'm pretty sure it was him." Angie could hear jingling from Gus's big set of keys he always kept attached to his pants. She guessed he was walking as he was speaking to her.

"I promised not to tell," Gus said.

"You're a good secret keeper. I'll have to move, Gus. I'm not sure what Vinnie's pension is going to be and what kind of job I can get, but I know it won't be enough to pay the rent on our big place and live. Why don't you plan on me leaving end of next month. I'll need a little more time before I can go and stay there by myself," Angie said.

"No rush, Angie. If there is anything I can help you with, just let me know. I'll start saving moving boxes for you. We have someone moving in on the first floor. Packing boxes can be very expensive."

"You're the best, Gus. I'll be in touch soon. Take care." Angie ended the call, looked at the other messages and was not in the mood to call Beatrice back about some stupid key to a storage unit she knew nothing about. She put on her coat and gloves and headed out. She decided to leave early; City Hall was a big place. She wanted to allow time to get lost. She boarded the local bus downtown to LaSalle.

Angie held her purse on her lap and gazed at all the people on the bus. Thankfully, it was after the morning rush hour, so it wasn't crowded. A group of high schoolers were all laughing and yelling. A couple in their mid-forties, Angie's age, were sitting together, holding hands and looking out the window. *How sweet*, Angie thought, *Vinnie liked to hold my hand. Always the romantic.* Tears rolled down her cheeks; she took a tissue from her purse and gently wiped her eyes. Hopefully, her mascara wasn't running.

Angie disembarked and walked to the entryway of Chicago City Hall, where she'd been only a few times with Vinnie. Before entering, she gazed way up at the tall windows trimmed in brass and framed with white marble. A wide band of brass with ornate designs separated the high windows from the revolving doors. Angie stood as tall as her five-foot-two frame would allow. *Best foot forward*, she thought, and walked through the doors. The long, arched hallway had old-fashioned streetlight fixtures radiating pink light that lit each side of the hallway, and larger fixtures emanating white light hung from the ceiling. She approached the man at the main desk. "What floor is human resources on? You have quite a grand place to work."

"It's on the eleventh floor; take the elevators on your left. And, yes, this building is a beauty. Makes coming to work a pleasure, although it does get cold during the winter with the revolving doors."

"I bet you have to wear long underwear!" Angie chuckled and proceeded toward the elevators. She noticed Chicago policemen standing on the other side of the elevator banks she was going to take. *Looks like serious business over there*, she thought as she entered an open elevator and hit eleven. Angie walked out of the elevator, turning down the hall into the human resources office. No one was at the desk so she hit the bell. A young man came out. "May I help you?"

"I have an appointment with Cookie."

"Please have a seat. I'll go get her."

Angie looked around the front of the office at all the brochures inviting folks to join the City of Chicago team. She picked up a brochure and had started to read it when Cookie came out.

"Hi, Angie. Would you please follow me?"

Cookie seemed distant and very businesslike, not the friendly gal Angie had met at Murphy's and spoken with over the phone. She followed Cookie back into the office area and into Cookie's well-appointed office with a view of downtown Chicago and Lake Michigan.

"You have such a beautiful office."

"Thank you. It was a long time coming. I spend a lot of time here so it's nice to have a view. Please sit." Cookie sat behind her oak desk, opened a file, and looked over at Angie. "I'm sorry we have to do business and paperwork. I'm just so sorry about Vinnie. Seems rude to ask for documents and all . . . I've been going through Vinnie's employment file, and I'm going to need some time to summarize all his outstanding vacation time so we can issue you a check for that. Did you bring his death certificate?"

Angie opened her purse, pulled out the death certificate, and slid it over. "Here you go, a whole life and all that is left is a single piece of paper." Angie shook her head and glanced out the window to distract herself; she didn't want to start crying.

"I'll need to keep this. I'm assuming you received several of these from the funeral parlor, as you'll be needing them to close out or reconcile all his accounts."

Angie nodded. "Yes, Louie was very thoughtful about those things, thank goodness."

Angie watched as Cookie reviewed Vinnie's file. "Do you have any idea how long it will take for me to start receiving his pension?"

Cookie cleared her throat. "It won't happen right away, so I think you should expect it to take at least several months. Things move slowly here—on a good day."

"Maybe I can fill out an application while I'm here today. You mentioned that there may be some receptionist openings and possibly a food inspector position." Angie's shoulders slumped as she felt her hopes dwindling.

"Yes, we do have quite a few open positions. How about we go downstairs and have a cup of coffee and talk about your background. That will help me know what direction to go." Cookie stood up and motioned for Angie to follow her out. As they were waiting for the elevator, the doors opened and Mario strutted out and came to a halt.

"Cookie, I was just coming up to see you. We need to finalize that paperwork we talked about—it's urgent." He looked at Angie. "Hi, honey. How are you doing?" He leaned over and gave her a hug.

"I'm as good as I can be right now."

"I need to take Angie downstairs now; I'll be back in about a half hour. I'll come find you. Are you going to be in your office?" Cookie asked.

"Yes, but not for long. I need to get back out to a jobsite, so if you could shake a leg, I'd appreciate it." He looked over at Angie. "I'm only a phone call away, so don't hesitate to call me—anytime." Mario walked toward his office; the Department of Buildings was down the hall from HR.

Cookie and Angie caught the next elevator and walked outside and across the street to a coffee shop, where Cookie bought two cups of coffee, and the two sat down. As Angie put her cream and sugars into her coffee, Cookie began. "What type of skills do you have, Angie? I know you said you haven't worked for over ten years and before that you were a waitress. How long were you a waitress?"

Angie stirred her coffee and looked over at Cookie. "I worked mostly in Italian restaurants for about fifteen years. I was working as a waitress when I met Vinnie, and beyond, but he soon insisted I quit. He wanted to take care of me, and truth be told, my legs were getting tired."

"Do you have any office experience at all?" Cookie inquired.

"Not really. I did help the hostess when we got really busy, but that was as close as I ever got to desk work." Angie sipped her coffee.

"When you get home tonight, go online and see what positions might interest you and what you think you're qualified for. Then go ahead and put in your application—we do that all online now."

"I'm not that great on the computer, but my niece can help me. I really appreciate anything you can do to help me secure a job, any job." Angie couldn't hold back the tears. "I hate to tell you this, but I have no money. All our accounts are overdrawn. I don't know where it went. I had to use our credit cards for the funeral, and most were denied." Angie took a tissue out of her purse, wiped her eyes, and blew her nose. "I trusted Vinnie to take care of everything. I feel so stupid."

Cookie reached over and patted Angie's arm. "There, there, we'll figure this out, honey. I'll get you something. I can't believe Vinnie left you penniless, you poor thing." Cookie finished her coffee and stood up. "If you have a high school diploma, we'll find you something. Sorry to rush, but I better get back to work. Mario has a hot temper. If he doesn't get what he wants fast, he'll complain to my boss."

Angie stood up and followed Cookie outside. "I'm embarrassed to tell you that I didn't finish high school. My mom got sick and my dad made me get a job to help at home. I finally got my GED when I turned twenty."

"Angie, you'd be surprised how many people work at City Hall who only have a GED."

"Good to know I have company." Angie felt a little lightness replace the tightness in her chest.

Cookie and Angie walked back to City Hall. Just as they were about to go their separate ways, Ralph walked out of the building and shortly thereafter Rebecca followed.

"Fancy meeting you two here," Ralph said as he turned toward Angie. "This is Alderman O'Brien's wife, Rebecca. She owns a very successful real estate business."

"Nice to meet you, Angie. I was just visiting with my husband—such a busy man. He's running for reelection." Angie noticed the fancy diamond earrings, ring, and necklace Rebecca was wearing. *This woman doesn't have to worry about money, that's for sure.*

"Lovely to meet you too. I believe you were at my late husband's funeral, but I don't believe we were formally introduced.

I love the lipstick you're wearing, and your perfume smells very familiar. What's it called?" Angie asked.

"It's Jardin d'Amalfi. I must go. I have an appointment. Oh, and I'm so sorry for your loss, Angie," Rebecca said with a dismissive look. Angie knew that Rebecca didn't care about Vinnie—or her, for that matter.

Angie glanced over and caught Ralph looking at Cookie. "Cookie, thanks for meeting me earlier this morning and reviewing all my projects." He glanced over at Angie. "You're just who I need to talk to. Do you have a few minutes?"

Cookie interrupted before Angie could respond, "I must run. Talk to you tomorrow, Angie. Nice to see you as always, Ralph." Cookie winked at him.

"Nice to see you too, Cookie," Ralph responded, and looked over at Rebecca. "Rebecca, I'm so glad we ran into each other. Please give your husband my best. I know he'll win."

"That's what we're all counting on," Rebecca replied.

Rebecca looked down her nose at Angie as she walked away. Angie smelled the scent that Rebecca was wearing. *That was Ralph's bathroom date, all right*, she thought, and then turned to Ralph. "I'm so sorry I haven't returned your phone calls, but I have some time now. Where would you like to talk?"

Ralph checked his watch. "Well, it's almost five. Would you like to join me for a glass of wine and some appetizers?"

Angie thought about it. "Why not?"

"May I escort you?" he asked, offering his arm to Angie.

Angie put her arm on his and was surprised to find her whole body tingled immediately. She couldn't help noticing what a gentleman Ralph was. And handsome too . . . but her heart was still with Vinnie.

Chapter 12

Gina had been at work since six in the morning, and it was now ten. She washed her hands and looked over at her boss at Panera. "I'm taking my break." Her boss gave her the thumbs-up. Gina walked outside and found a quiet place to call her mom; they talked almost every day—sometimes two to three times.

"Hi, sweetheart, how's work?" Connie asked.

"Same day, same orders, same people. I can't wait till I have my own catering company so I don't have to work here. If one more customer asks me what my favorite thing to eat is, I'm going to scream."

"What's going on? You sound tired and tense."

"Since Aunt Angie is living with me, for now I've been sleeping in Thad's room, a lumpy single bed with a *Star Wars* comforter. No wonder he sleeps over at his girlfriend's—so not sleeping so well. He still comes over during the afternoons to get high and watch his Spanish telenovelas. Some people have Glade air freshener; we have eau de marijuana."

"How's Angie coping with all of this?"

"Well, she's getting familiar with the smell of pot, but she is in bad shape, Mom. When I took her over to their place, she almost collapsed on the floor. Ben and I had to help her walk down to his place. She's heartbroken and broke too."

"I can have her come stay with me, if that helps. I'm never home. My travel agency is crazy busy, so I'm at the office until ten most nights. Great, cheap deals to Vegas right now—Vinnie would be all over them."

Gina interrupted, "I don't mind having her stay at my place. She offered to help Kim and me with our catering company, but I'm going to need some start-up money. I barely make my rent now. Thankfully, Thad is being cool, since he's paying part of it. I can't ask Angie for money. I have to figure out about how much I'll need to buy cooking equipment, get a website . . . so many things."

"Oh, Gina, you're a good daughter. I'll transfer a couple thousand dollars into your checking account, no worries. My business is booming. Since Uncle Vinnie is the one who gave me the start-up money, the least I can do is help. How's school?"

"It's hard but good, almost finished with all the business courses. Kim and I are applying for our food service sanitation certification through the Department of Public Health, and then we have to get a business license. It's a lot, but I know together we can get this new catering company off the ground."

"You and Kim can do anything you set your minds to; you were both top of your high school class. She was such a doll to help with the funeral. You both have a ways to go with the food, but with Angie's help, you'll get there."

"We're almost done with school; we should hear back from the city on our license, and then we can get off to a fast start. I'm an okay cook and Kim's much better. Aunt Angie said she'll teach me everything she knows. I don't need to tell you what a great cook she is. I feel lucky that she's living with me, and I told her she's going to be a partner just like Kim and me.

We're going to start practicing simple dishes this week. I found a fun cookbook a friend gave me from her grandma Mindy. It's called *Scratch? My Ass! Store-Bought Can Be as Good as Homemade*. It was published in 1984 by two women named Ethel and Blanche. It's hysterical."

Her mom laughed. "You don't have to tell me; I was at the women's smoker in Bridgeport, where the idea got started."

"What's a women's smoker?"

"It's fashioned after men's smokers. In some of the Catholic churches, the guys would get together, play poker down in the church basement, and donate the winnings back to the church. They'd smoke cigars and sip their beverage of choice, no women allowed."

Gina laughed. "So this Blanche made one just for women?"

"Yup. She and her friend Ethel created a women-only club and had several events at the local Bridgeport VFW; the only men allowed were the ones who served them. Drinks were like ninety cents, and they had great food and entertainment. They donated the profits to the Arthritis Foundation. The event sold out, and Ethel and Blanche invited the women to submit their favorite simple recipes—thus was born Ethel and Blanche's cookbook."

"What a fun idea. Are they still having these smokers?" Gina asked.

"Not anymore. But what you really need to know is that Ethel and Blanche are fictitious names. The two gals who started it worked together, and one of them moved to the West Coast after the second fundraiser."

Before Gina could ask another question, her boss walked outside and was pointing at his wristwatch. She could see there was a long line of customers. "Gotta go, Mom. I'll call you soon. You keep killing it at your agency." Gina walked toward the door.

"I'll call you tonight. Give Angie a hug from me—she took such good care of my brother. Talk soon."

As Gina got behind the counter, she remembered when her mom opened her own travel agency over fifteen years ago. *Wonder Travel. Did you ever "wonder" what it was like to fly to Europe or Mexico? Wonder no more, we have a deal for you.* It took off, right away. Uncle Vinnie told everyone at the city to use her and they sure did. She booked at least six Vegas trips a year just for him and Angie. Her mom made enough to pay the bills and support them since her dad took off.

Gina's thoughts were interrupted. "What's your favorite? So much to choose from," a customer asked.

Gina finished her shift and drove home. When she got to her apartment door, there was a bouquet of flowers sitting there. She picked it up and walked into her apartment; the scent of garlic and butter greeted her. "Something smells good, and look, someone sent you flowers, Aunt Angie. Do you have a secret admirer?" She placed the flowers on the table.

"Welcome home, honey. I made us dinner. Go get comfortable and let's have a glass of wine—lots to talk about."

Gina grinned and gave her a big, long hug. "I'm so glad you're here. It's nice to come home to dinner cooking and you. Let me change real quick."

When Gina came back in her comfortable clothes, Angie handed her a glass of wine, and they sat at the kitchen table admiring the flower arrangement.

"Well, open the card. This looks like an expensive arrangement. They're from Fleur de Lis, ooh là là."

Gina watched her open the card and read it. "It was lovely spending time with you, Angie. Some fresh flowers to brighten up your day. Ralph."

"These are beautiful. White orchids and white roses," Angie said.

Gina leaned over and took a whiff. "These smell divine. That Ralph is very thoughtful."

Angie took a sip of her wine. "He is. In fact, I had a drink with him earlier."

"Look at you, going to City Hall and drinks afterward. Wasn't he the one from the funeral, looked like a *GQ* model?" Gina asked.

"That's the guy. He and Vinnie went to high school together. They lost touch and then reconnected and worked on projects with the city. We shared a glass of wine and appetizers. He's such a gentleman, manicured fingers, dressed so elegantly. He opened doors for me, even hailed a cab when it was time to leave." Angie smiled.

Gina noticed a little twinkle in her aunt's eyes when she talked about Ralph. "He must like you if he sent you flowers. What did you talk about?"

"I started to tear up when we started to talk about Vinnie. Ralph gave me his linen handkerchief. I need to wash it; my makeup is on it. He did share that he was the one who put Vinnie's obit in the *Tribune*, which was very thoughtful. Such a kind man; he understood what I was going through, as he lost his wife to cancer two years ago."

"I'm glad you have someone who understands what it's like to lose a spouse," Gina said.

Angie continued, "I also solved part of the mystery of the bathroom sex at the funeral parlor."

"Do tell—I can't wait." Gina leaned in and took a sip of wine.

Angie recapped running into Ralph outside City Hall and how Rebecca had come out several minutes later. "Cookie was clearly flirting with Ralph. When Rebecca was getting ready to walk away, I smelled the perfume, dead ringer from the bathroom at Rago Brothers. I asked her what the scent was, and she looked down her nose and told me. I never heard of it, but I'm sure it's expensive. It was her for sure. There was clearly some chemistry between Ralph and Rebecca, even though they both tried to pretend there wasn't." Angie winked.

Gina chuckled. "Case closed. You are something else. What did Ralph want with you?"

"He wanted to see how I was getting along. Asked me some questions about Vinnie's pension. I'm not sure how he knows anything about that, but he offered to help me expedite it since he knows the inside of City Hall. Said he'd call Cookie to check on the status of it but wouldn't do that without my permission. Of course, I said yes. He invited me to dinner next week," Angie said.

"That was generous of him. Where are you going?" Gina asked.

"One of his favorite places is Gibsons. I've never been, but I hear it's quite the fancy place. I told him I'd call him once I know my schedule. I hope I can get a job soon so I can at least pay you for food and rent here." Angie tapped her fingers on the table.

"You don't have to worry about that," Gina said, looking into Angie's eyes.

"Well, I can't mooch off my niece forever. I have to stand on my own two feet. I need to go over to our apartment and start packing. I can't afford that place. Thankfully, my rent is covered for the next couple months; I know Ben paid it, but he won't admit it. I need to make sure the place is spotless so I can get our security deposit back. I'll need every nickel I can get until I start earning a regular paycheck." Angie folded her arms across her chest.

Gina could see the dark circles under her aunt's eyes, and she was biting her lower lip. She reached over and put her hand on

Angie's arm. "Just so we're clear, you are not paying me any rent or giving me grocery money. I ate at your place more times than I can remember. Let me take care of you for a change. I talked to my mom today and she said she'll help you pack up the apartment, just let her know when."

Angie put her hand over Gina's hand. "You are such a sweetheart. I'm lucky to have you and your mom in my life. I don't know what I'd do without you."

"You'll never have to find out. You're stuck with us."

"Let's eat before the food gets cold. And I want to talk about your catering business; I have some ideas," Angie said.

Over a simple dinner of pasta, garlic bread, and red wine, Gina and Angie started to list all the things they needed to do to get their catering business off the ground. Gina jotted down notes.

"You'll have to register the business with the city. Are you going with Last Bite?" Angie asked.

"I think it's perfect since I'm targeting funeral homes; I should add churches and temples to my outreach as well. But first, will you help me with a list of easy finger foods I can make and then market?" Gina asked.

"Absolutely. We can take some ideas from the old cookbook you found. We can also go online and see what other catering companies are offering and get a sense of what people are charging. We want to start simple at first," Angie offered.

"I spoke with Kim, and she and I are going to block out the next couple weekends and go to as many funerals as we can. Nobody knows everyone who attends, and we want to see what people are eating," Gina shared.

"I can ask my church if you can come to our services. Some folks are having a celebration of life; maybe you can get some good ideas there. Do you have a black outfit you can wear? That still seems to be the dress code on record."

"Yes, Kim and I both have black outfits. I'm excited about doing the research. Uncle Vinnie's is the first funeral I've been to, so I have no idea what they are all like. I forgot to ask you how your visit to City Hall went?"

Angie refilled their wineglasses and cleared the table. "I have to go online and fill out my application. I have no idea how to use a computer; Vinnie didn't think I needed one. Honestly, you're probably the only reason I know how to use a cell phone. Can you help me with my application?"

"No problem. Did Cookie say if she has any openings?" Gina asked.

"She said she may have some food inspector positions open. She wants a list of all the restaurants I worked at, and I'm hoping you can type that up for me."

"I can do that super quick. When did Cookie say you'll start getting Uncle Vinnie's pension?" Her aunt let out a deep breath.

"She really didn't say when, but I did everything but beg her for a job, so I can let you and Thad enjoy your apartment without an old lady hanging around. Ya never know, you might have a gentleman come calling."

"Oh, don't worry about that. Too busy. We have a business to start. I hope you can stay for a while. You're a full partner and we need you. I invited Kim over tomorrow to start writing our business plan. She's bringing some of her tried-and-true appetizers over for us to sample."

"That sounds fun; I can't wait to taste her treats. From what I remember when you were both in high school, her parents came here from China before Kim was born. I bet she'll have some authentic, tasty morsels. How about I write down my job information so you can type it up and then send it off to Cookie before we hit the hay."

There was a knock at the door early the next morning, and Gina opened the door to Kim who was carrying large shopping bags. "Come on in, looks like you cleaned out Jewel."

"Actually, I've been cooking, and I want you and Aunt Angie to taste some of my new creations. I just need to heat them up." Gina grabbed one of Kim's bags and they both went to the kitchen to prepare a tasting platter.

Kim put various dumplings and fried appetizers on a cookie sheet and placed them in the oven just as Angie walked into the kitchen in her robe.

"Good morning, my talented chefs. What is that wonderful smell?"

Gina hugged Angie. "Good morning to you. I've made coffee and we are preparing samples for you to taste."

"Let me wake up, and then my palate is at your beck and call." Angie poured herself coffee and added her cream and sugars. "May I ask what we'll be tasting this morning?"

"I've made some bite-size treats from my grandmother's private recipes. I was baking till late last night," Kim replied.

"Well, bring them on. I am so proud of both of you for pursuing your dreams, and I promise I will do everything in my power to help you succeed." Angie sat down at the kitchen table, took a sip of her coffee, and put her napkin on her lap.

Kim and Gina watched as Angie tasted each bite, not saying a word. Finally, Gina broke the silence. "So, what do you think?"

"I think you don't need my help; these are delicious. Combining ginger with chestnuts and garlic spinach in a wonton is brilliant. These will disappear in a minute; that sesame dipping sauce is delightful."

Gina smiled at Kim and gave her a thumbs-up.

"However, if you make these all by hand, you will never recoup the cost. If you have a client where money is not an issue, then I'd go for it."

"My great aunt and grandmother love to make these, and they don't mind making as many as we want. We could freeze them," Kim offered.

"Then let's add them to our menu. I bet no other catering company has talent like that," Angie said.

"We could have several menu options, depending on the client's budget," Gina said.

"Good, then let's get started with a list of comfort foods I make, low-cost but soothing to the soul. Those and a few of Kim's grandma's delights would be great. We're going to need to turn a profit sooner than later. You don't want to work at Panera the rest of your life, do you, honey?" Angie gently touched Gina's cheek.

"I can't get out of there fast enough."

"Let's kick things off. I'll call my friend Louie at Rago Brothers and schedule a tasting. If he likes what we offer, then he can give us a reference. His family has been in the funeral business forever, so his word carries a lot of weight. When I pick up Vinnie's ashes . . ." Angie paused and stared down at the floor, collecting herself. "Anyway, I can get them when we go for the tasting. When do you think you'll be ready?" Angie asked.

"In one week, if we spend every hour preparing between now and then," Gina said.

After Gina supplied their new team cheer, all three women put their right arm out in front of them—their hands touching in the middle as if they were on a sports team. "One—two—three!" they all screamed and then put their arms up in the air. "Team Last Bite!"

Angie rinsed out her dishes. "I'm going to get dressed and pop down to City Hall to check in with Cookie. If I go in person, she'll get that I'm serious about employment ASAP."

"I think you should call her first. She may have meetings," Gina suggested.

"Nope. I need her to see how serious I am about working and about getting my husband's pension. I'm not letting those fancy City Hall folks push me around." With that, Angie headed off to get ready for the day.

Gina shrugged and glanced over at Kim. "Don't be messing with my aunt when she means business."

"I hear you," Kim said.

"Let's write up a draft of all the appetizers we have so far, and then we can create a sample menu for Rago's," Gina suggested.

"No problem. And, Gina, I am so excited to be launching this business with you. I have a good feeling about it and us working together." Kim hugged her.

Gina hugged her back. "I think we're going to make an awesome team."

Gina's cell rang. "Hey, Mom."

"How's my favorite daughter?"

"I'm your *only* daughter."

"I know," she giggled, "but you're still my favorite. How are things going?"

Gina walked into her bedroom so she could speak to her mom privately. "Things are ramping up with our catering company. I am so excited I can't stand it. I am going to need that loan you offered to get the business off the ground. We'll pay you back once business starts booming. Wait till you taste Kim's appetizers; Angie said they were delicious, and you know she's a truth teller when it comes to food."

"I sure do. I remember when she sent back her entrée at Spiaggia, Vinnie's eyes about popped out of his head; his neck and face got beet red. Even if they comp you a meal, it should be cooked, right? But she was right, the pork was raw, and both of them would have gotten food poisoning. How much are you thinking, honey?"

Gina paused. "Kim and I are finalizing our business plan this afternoon and presenting it to our class tomorrow night. Our best guess is between five and ten thousand dollars each. Kim has about ten thousand saved from working in her family's store in Chinatown and all the odd jobs she's done over the years, and her family is hopefully helping her. I'd need to kick in my ten. As you know, I have no savings."

"Jeez, that's a lot of money, honey, but I should be able to make it happen."

"Kim and I are cooking all day. Call me later. I've never asked you for money before. It feels scary to ask now. This is my dream." Gina ended the call.

When Gina walked into the kitchen, she was greeted with a sweet scent. "What the hell are you baking? My mouth is watering." She glanced over at Kim and the tiny oven covered with small cookies topped with slivers of almonds.

"Close your eyes and open your mouth." Kim popped a cookie into Gina's mouth. "What do you taste? Keep your eyes closed."

"I taste almonds, crunchy, sweet yumminess. More, please." She opened her eyes and Kim had the biggest grin.

"This is one of our family's oldest recipes. Almond cookies. You can't find them like this anymore. This will be one of our signature cookies. No one will be spitting these out." They both laughed, recalling all the folks at Vinnie's funeral who spat out the nasty cookies they had made in a hurry.

Kim cleared her throat and looked directly into Gina's eyes. "I'm really nervous about this whole thing, but if anyone can do it, we can."

Gina looked at Kim. "We're going for it. Worst-case scenario, we fail and get other jobs. But we're not going to fail."

"My parents think I'm wasting my time. They say there's enough caterers out there, we don't have any real experience—they are so negative." Kim turned around and started to move the cookies into a tin.

"Don't let them get into your head. Remember when you told them you preferred girls in high school, they lost their shit. But you were brave and followed your heart."

"They threatened to throw me out of the house, but I lived under their roof until I could move out and date who I wanted to date. I knew I always liked girls, but my family would never allow even a conversation around that topic. They said it would shame them and our family. That's why I rented a room outside the house right out of high school. I couldn't suppress my true feelings," Kim said.

"I remember; that took courage. Look, I have no idea what my love life is 'cause I never had one. Kissed a few boys in high school but didn't feel a thing. It could have been that I was a lousy kisser or he was or we both were. You know my family; they are always trying to fix me up with some Italian stallion, and I've told them, over and over, no thanks."

"We may not have time for any love life while we're getting our business going. Let's commit to making this business a success first and then we'll see what happens. Sound good?" Kim smiled at Gina.

"Deal. What are we making next? I want to have the full tasting menu ready before my aunt gets back." Gina's mind was spinning with ideas.

Kim laid out all the recipes from her family, the ones Angie had shared, and some from the *Scratch? My Ass!* cookbook. "We have fifteen appetizers to make. Let's get to it."

Gina played Chainsmokers on her phone, one of their favorite bands, and they rocked out while they laughed and cooked for the rest of the afternoon.

The music was interrupted several times by Gina's mom calling. She finally answered.

"Hey, Mom, Kim and I are busy cooking. Can I call you back tomorrow?"

"I'm so sorry, honey, just wanted you to know I am behind you both a hundred percent. I cashed in one of my IRAs and transferred ten thousand dollars into your account."

"Oh my God, Mom! Thank you so much! I'll pay you back with interest, I promise."

"You don't have to pay me back. I had that money set aside for if you went to a four-year college, so it was always there for you. You'll never guess who helped me at the bank."

"Who?" Gina was tapping her fingers on the kitchen counter. She needed to get back to cooking.

"Tim Cash, your prom date. He sure had eyes for you. He asked all about you and even gave me his cell number. I'll text it to you. He's excited to reconnect with you, he's single—"

"Mom, he was a terrible kisser, and you always told me, if they can't kiss, then forget about anything else. Gotta go. I can't thank you enough for the money. I'll call you tomorrow."

Gina glanced over at Kim, who was focused on the third boiling batch of pot stickers. She turned up the music and they both jammed in the kitchen. Gina was so focused that she didn't hear Thad enter.

"Yo, roomie, what smells so good?"

Gina turned and looked over at him and his girlfriend,

Daisy, who had dyed her hair bright green that week. "Hey, Dais, what's up?"

"Right now, I'm super high. Thad got a new batch of weed from his friend in California and it's intense, probably not for your aunt, but it's a great high. Got anything we can eat? The munchies are kicking in big-time."

Gina looked over at Kim. "Can we spare a few pot stickers for these stoners?"

"Absolutely, and then they have to try the almond cookies. That will definitely hit the spot. I love these when I'm high," Kim said.

Kim dished up pot stickers for them and placed them on the kitchen table with the dipping sauce. Thad and Daisy sat down and dove in.

"Whoa, these are freaking amazing, dude. I could eat like a dozen of these," Thad said.

"We have to save some for Gina's aunt. How about a few cookies instead?" Kim walked over and placed a small plate of cookies on the table, then stepped back and put her arm around Gina as Thad and Daisy devoured the cookies.

"Damn! I bet these are great even when you're not high." Thad licked the crumbs off his fingers.

"Family recipe, dude, glad you like them." Kim and Gina exchanged smiles.

Angie walked into the kitchen with a bag of groceries. She looked over and saw Thad. "Hey, Thad." A girl with green hair sat next to him at the table. "And you must be Thad's girlfriend. Love the hair, and it's not even St. Patrick's Day. Are we having a party?"

"This is my main squeeze, Daisy," Thad said. "We're chowing down on these flavor bombs—have you tried them?"

"Oh yeah, those pot stickers are beyond delicious." Angie pulled a half gallon of vodka out of the bag. "Cocktails, anyone?"

"None for me. Dais and I are heading downtown for a house party. Weed is my drug of choice, but feel free to party on."Thad and Daisy stood up, grabbed a couple more cookies, and headed out. "Later."

"How many martinis am I making?" Angie opened the cupboard and took out glasses.

"Make three—are we celebrating anything special?" Gina reached under the sink where she kept a martini shaker.

"Yes, we are, but I have to change into some comfortable clothes. You know how I like my 'tinis—be right back." Angie made her way to Gina's bedroom.

Gina made sure her aunt was out of earshot and whispered to Kim, "My aunt is in a bad way. She has no money and has to move out of her apartment and find a job. She really wants to be part of our business, and I hope you're okay with that—just until she gets on her feet."

"Of course I am down with that. She will be invaluable—who can say no to her? Plus, she happens to be a great cook."

Chapter 13

After Ralph sent Angie off in a cab, he went back in and sat at the bar. "I'll have a Four Roses, neat." He thought about his long conversation with Angie earlier. What a sweet, funny, salt-of-the-earth woman she was, a real straight shooter. *She's a smart lady, good heart too. But maybe a little naive about how the world works sometimes. She reminds me of my wife*, he realized. *How could Vinnie have left her with nothing?* There just had to be more to the story. He knew Vinnie to be a stand-up guy. *I'm going to make sure she lands on her feet. She deserves that much.*

The bartender put the drink in front of Ralph. He took a sip, then glanced at his phone; Rebecca had called several times. *This has got to end—now—it has to be in a public place—no more temptation.* He took another sip of his bourbon and sent her a text: *Meet me at Gibsons for a drink at seven.*

She responded immediately: *SURE, then your place*, with a heart emoji.

Ralph didn't respond to her text. He enjoyed his bourbon and recollected when he and Rebecca had discovered each other after a ribbon cutting at one of the buildings his firm had built for the city. The chemistry between them was maddening, pure lust. But now it had to end; his whole career was at stake. If her husband or anyone else caught them together, Ralph would have to pack up and leave town. The sex was amazing but not worth the cost of losing his business. He had an entire office staff who depended on him—and faithful clients who knew he could get their projects built navigating all the red tape from City Hall.

He checked his watch, finished his drink, and hopped into a cab to Gibsons. He rolled down the window. A cool breeze came off the lake, the sky was blue, and sailboats were sprinkled on Lake Michigan. *I love this city*, he thought. Heavy traffic afforded him a chance to relax and close his eyes for a few seconds. The cab pulled up to Gibsons and he walked inside.

"Hello, my love," Peaches greeted him.

"Just drinks tonight." He leaned over and kissed her soft, full cheek. "I need to make a reservation for next Monday night for two, corner table, please."

Peaches made a note. "You got it. I think your guest is waiting in the bar." She winked at him.

"You don't miss a trick—do you?"

Peaches batted her eyelashes and smiled back at Ralph.

As soon as Ralph entered the bar, he saw Rebecca sitting at a table window-side, sipping a martini. He made his way over.

"Lovely to see you." Ralph looked at Rebecca, then caught the eye of a waitress walking by. He pointed at Rebecca's martini and put his thumb up.

"You look dashing as always. I love it when you wear that blue suit, perfect fit in all the right places." Rebecca's eyes drifted from his chest down to his crotch.

"Thank you for meeting on such late notice, Rebecca," he said, as the waitress placed the drink down in front of him and slipped away. "Cheers to what has been a fabulous interlude that must now come to an end." He looked directly into her eyes and took a sip of his martini.

"We won't be cheering to that, love. I believe I was clear. I decide when we're done—not you. I thought we had sorted this out already."

"Unfortunately, recent events prevent me from continuing this relationship. It's entirely too risky and we need to end this amicably. Make no mistake, I will miss you terribly. Please understand." He placed his hand gently on hers, and she pulled away.

There was a moment of silence between them, then Rebecca threw her drink in his face, stood up, and stormed out. Her martini was dripping down his forehead, eyebrows, eyes, and cheeks. He winced, and his chest tightened. This was his neighborhood watering hole; he didn't want a scene. *You have to pull yourself together*, he commanded himself.

Ralph took his napkin and wiped his face. He could feel the eyes of the patrons upon him. He stepped off the high-back chair—stood tall and made his way to the reception desk where Peaches was standing. He handed her his credit card. She quickly processed the bill and printed out the receipt.

"Trouble in paradise, my love?" Peaches slid the receipt over to Ralph.

He forced a smile. "It's always something. See you on Monday."

"Looking forward to it—you take good care, sweetheart."

"Will do." He left Gibsons and walked home.

The doorman greeted him outside and opened the door. "Welcome home. Flying solo tonight?"

"You got it, and if anyone comes calling, I am out."

"Aye aye, sir."

Ralph proceeded inside and took the elevator up to his penthouse. He took a shower, set his suit aside to be taken to the cleaners, and changed into his robe and slippers. He went into the living room and poured himself a Pappy Van Winkle bourbon, a gift from a developer. He sat in his Eames lounge chair and put his feet up on the ottoman.

He let out a long sigh. "What a day." The best part, he realized, had been having drinks with Angie. Just as his mind was lingering over his visit with her, his cell phone buzzed with a text message from Angie: *Thanks for the beautiful flowers, what a kind gesture. I look forward to dinner on Monday.*

He texted back. *I'm glad you liked them—see you at Gibsons Monday at 7.*

Ralph's phone rang; it was the doorman. "You have a visitor—can I send her up?"

"No, I told you to tell anyone who came to visit tonight that I wasn't home. You've done this before. No company tonight—get it?" He hung up.

The phone rang again; he let it go and slowly sipped his bourbon—finally, the phone stopped. He turned on the late-night show with Jimmy Fallon and enjoyed a few laughs in the opening monologue. Ralph felt his head start to nod, so he got up, put his empty glass in the sink, and went to bed. Rebecca's scent still lingered on his sheets. He was too tired to change the bed linens so he inhaled deeply, recalled their fabulous sex from the night before, and fell sound asleep.

The next morning Ralph awoke at his usual time—five—donned his running outfit and took a long run along Lake Shore Drive to clear his mind. He turned left out of his place, took the underground pass, and enjoyed the cool breeze off Lake Michigan; the water was choppy. Other runners and bicyclists passed him going the other way; the fresh air felt good. He got to his turnaround point and headed home. As he approached his building, sweat dripping from his brow, he checked his watch. *Five miles—perfect.*

As he walked through the lobby, the doorman stopped him. "Mr. Conti, there's a note someone left for you last night."

"Thanks." He got in the elevator and opened the note. *You better watch your fucking back, no one breaks up with me! R.*

Ralph shook his head, went up to his place, showered, and took a car to his office. Eunice greeted him as she did every day—with his printed agenda, a hot cup of coffee, and a warm chocolate croissant.

"It's going to be a hectic day. The city building inspector called and insisted you be in his office by ten sharp, or they are going to stop construction on the Sinclair apartment building today. I moved around all your meetings. I'll need you back here no later than noon. Oh, and Cookie from City Hall called several times insisting to talk with you. Maybe you can swing by when you're done with the inspector."

"Never a dull moment, eh, Eunice?" Ralph sipped his coffee and sat at his desk, eating the croissant and checking his emails.

Eunice stood at his office door. "I'll make sure there's a car downstairs for you at nine thirty."

"I don't know what I'd do without you. You're the best."

"Thanks, boss."

The car dropped Ralph off at City Hall; he caught the elevator up to the building department. His least favorite inspector was sitting at his desk, a Cubs baseball hat on his head, a pencil hanging out of his mouth. "About time you got here, asshole. I have to leave in ten minutes. You got real big problems on the jobsite, buddy. They're not building to code—who the fuck gave this job the green light in the first place?"

"Nice to see you too, Barry. I'm sure we can straighten this out. Show me the drawings." Ralph walked over to Barry's round table where a thick stack of drawings was sprawled out.

Barry pointed at the areas of concern. "Here's the problem.

Your fucking fancy architects forgot to put in handicap bathrooms on the first floor; that's all I need is to have the ADA people up my ass about this. I'm stopping this job until you get this rectified!"

Barry had a pungent, unpleasant body odor that took Ralph aback. "Smells like you've been working around the clock, Barry—been home lately?"

"Fuck you, Ralph—it's the city—nobody gets a day off. Fix this and call me when it's done. I already sent Mario over to the site to stop the job. You'll need to call your contractor before he signs on to another job. I don't have time for this shit, Conti."

Barry left his office.

Ralph was studying the drawings. "I have no idea how these got by the planning department—they usually catch this shit." Ralph paused. *This is something Vinnie would have caught.* Ralph made a few calls to get things back on track and then headed down to Cookie's office, her assistant escorting him to her office.

Cookie was standing, her arms folded, looking out her window at the Chicago skyline. "We have a big problem, Ralph." She turned around and motioned for him to sit.

Ralph sat. "What's wrong? The day can't get much worse."

"Oh, you should never say that. Our friend Mario is on a rampage. I'll spare you the details, but he will be getting Vinnie's pension in a few weeks. He made me change the beneficiary to him, and now I have to tell Angie she's SOL and doesn't get a dime, and I can't even share who the beneficiary is. The deed is done, and I need you on cleanup. Don't ask me any questions."

Ralph studied Cookie's face. "What he's done is illegal."

"'Done' would be the operative word. There's no proof it was any other way. And don't try talking to Mario, please, or he will have me fired, or worse—he has friends."

"So, what do you expect me to do?"

"You're smart and rich, figure something out to help her. She can never know who is getting Vinnie's pension. I'm going to find her a job with the city, but she doesn't have any real skills, so it won't pay much, but at least she'll have benefits."

Ralph sighed. "This is so wrong. I hear you—it's your ass on the line. Do me a big favor. Can you sit on this pension thing for a couple days? Don't say anything to Angie. Please."

"The best I can do is wait until Monday, and then I must process the paperwork. Mario is in a big hurry to get the money—he's going to take a one-time payment rather than get monthly checks. Seems he needs cash fast." Cookie stood up. "I have a meeting upstairs. Call me no later than Friday at three p.m. with whatever miracle you have up your sleeve." Cookie walked out and Ralph followed her to the elevators. The doors opened and out walked Rebecca with her husband, Alderman O'Brien.

Ralph took a few slow, deep breaths and looked down.

"Hi, Cookie—how are you?" the alderman said.

"Great, Alderman O'Brien. Nice to see you too, Mrs. O'Brien." Cookie's elevator came and she quickly boarded.

"Nice to see you, Ralph. I'm hearing good things from my precinct about your new low-income housing project. I know it was tough to get through the system, but you did it—thank you."

"We need to get to our meeting, honey," Rebecca announced.

Ralph avoided direct eye contact and looked straight at the alderman. "I'm glad it's working out. I'll let you both know when the ribbon cutting is scheduled."

"Please do." The alderman and Rebecca walked away arm in arm down the hall.

Ralph cleared his throat and took the elevator down. He could feel his own stomach acid making its way up to his throat. All the way back to his office he was trying to figure out a way to fix this pension thing and not get anyone in trouble or killed. He placed a call to a friend who had connections everywhere.

Chapter 14

Angie sat at the table in Gina's kitchen, her chest tightening as she listened to what Cookie was telling her on the phone. "Okay . . . if that's the only way I can get a job at City Hall, then that's what I'll do," Angie said.

Gina walked in the front door from working the late shift at Panera and gave her aunt a thumbs-up; Angie returned Gina's gesture with a thumbs-down. She shrugged her shoulders and motioned for her niece to give her five minutes.

What Cookie was saying was that she wanted Angie to be a cleaning person for the city and to start early the next morning. Angie swallowed hard to keep from crying. *I'm forty-five, I'm too old for this kind of work. My legs and back ache even when I clean my own place. I'm not cut out for it.*

"I appreciate any job you can arrange for me until Vinnie's pension comes through. I won't let you down, Cookie. I'll see you tomorrow morning at seven sharp."

"It's temporary. I know you need money and benefits, and this will get you on your way until we get Vinnie's pension sorted out."

"I'll be the best cleaner you ever had, Cookie." *I don't know how long I can do this, but at least it'll get my foot in the door.* Angie hoped her trembling chin didn't find its way to her voice.

"I know you will. My assistant will get you all set up with a name badge. There's paperwork to sign and you'll need to bring your birth certificate."

"Got it. I can't thank you enough, Cookie." Angie's hands shook as she put down her cell phone, covered her face, and started to sob. "How could I have let myself get in this position? I'm such a loser."

She felt Gina's hands on her shoulders as she sat in the chair. "You're not a loser, Aunt Angie. This is all temporary. As soon as we get our catering business off the ground, you can stop that job and work for Kim and me."

Angie turned around and leaned into Gina, tears flowing, while Gina rubbed her back. "You're a strong woman with a family who loves you so much. We're here for you." Gina handed her a tissue.

Angie blew her nose. "Vinnie always said what doesn't kill you will make you stronger. I know he stole that from someone, but it applies here. I'm not going to let this keep me down. We got a business to start. Who knows? I may be able to get us some clients from the city; people are always dying there."

Gina laughed. "I have an early shift tomorrow. How about I drop you off for your first day?"

"That would be great. I better get my cleaning clothes out and go to bed. Morning will be here before you know it." Angie gave her niece a kiss and a hug goodnight and went to her bedroom.

Angie tossed and turned most of the night, finally got out of bed around five, showered and made coffee to go. She had on an old pair of loose-fitting black pants that would allow her to get up and down off the floor—as she cleaned under the desks—and a gray sweatshirt with pockets. Her tennis shoes would have to do until she got some better shoes to help support her legs.

On the way downtown, Gina and Angie sipped their coffee while listening to the morning news.

"I wonder what cleaning products they use? I bet they have some tips and tricks on cleaning such a huge building," Angie said.

"You're a talented housekeeper; I'm betting you can teach them a thing or two." Gina pulled up to the entrance on LaSalle. "Good luck, you'll be great. See you tonight."

"It's like the first day of school. I'm a little nervous and excited. It's an adventure." Angie kissed her niece on the cheek. "You have a good one too." She hopped out of the car, went inside and up to Cookie's office, where a young red-haired man wearing big black-rimmed glasses was waiting behind the desk.

"I'm Angie Sortino reporting for duty. You must be Irish with that beautiful head of hair."

He smiled. "Good morning, Angie. I'm Bud, and, yes, I'm Irish. I work with Cookie. I have all your paperwork ready. Please follow me to the conference room."

She followed him into a small room with a round table where a stack of paperwork was waiting for her.

"When you're done, we'll get your photo ID, and then I'll introduce you to Lorna, the supervisor over housekeeping. She'll orient you to our system, and then you'll be off and running. Would you like a cup of coffee?"

"No, thank you, I already had mine." She sat down and moved the stack of papers in front of her.

"I'll be out front when you're done." Bud left Angie to it.

Angie read every form carefully and completed each one until it came to next of kin. She gently touched her heart. *I'll use Gina's name and contact info.*

She brought all the completed forms out to Bud. An hour later, she was ready to start cleaning. Lorna's orientation was short and to the point. She handed Angie a sheet of paper.

"Here's a list of all the cleaning supplies. If it's not on the list, you don't need it. The utility closet with the refills is in the basement. Be careful down there; we have rats. We tried to get rid of them, but they're not leaving." Angie read the list. All the necessary items were there, not her preferred brands, but these would get the job done. "No time to dillydally around here," Lorna said. "We have to keep this place spick-and-span. You'll have the first two floors to start with. I'll be on the eleventh floor if you need me. You don't look like you'll need any cleaning tips; you're no spring chicken. Start with the bathrooms."

As Lorna was talking, Angie watched the penciled-in, large brown beauty mark on the left side of Lorna's lip moving up and down, likely a nod to Marilyn Monroe.

"One more thing, on the morning shift, we clock out at five sharp, no matter what. Don't try to be a hero; we don't go for that here. I've been cleaning here for over twenty years." Lorna left, her long, dyed blonde hair tied up in a bun on the top of her head bouncing.

Angie pushed her cart through the dimly lit first floor of the Chicago City Hall. She hummed as she went about her work, her eyes darting around, taking in the grandeur of the building. She had cleaned a toilet or two in her life, so this wasn't difficult work.

As she turned a corner, she saw a group of young men in suits huddled around a conference table in a heated debate, their voices rising. Angie paused for a moment, her curiosity piqued. She cleared her throat, making her presence known. The men turned to look at her, their expressions ranging from surprise to annoyance.

Angie smiled warmly at them. "Good morning, gentlemen. I'm just here to clean up."

One of the men nodded curtly and then returned to the

discussion. Angie watched them for a moment longer before continuing her route. She knew better than to get involved in the politics of the building, not that anyone was inviting her.

As she made her way to the next room, Angie noticed a pile of papers scattered on the floor. She bent down to pick them up and felt her eyes widen. They were official-looking documents, bearing the seal of the city. She knew that these papers could be important, and she couldn't just leave them lying around. She quickly gathered them up and put them in her cart. Lorna would tell her what to do with them. *Maybe I can do a little research on where Vinnie's pension is when I clean HR on the eleventh floor tomorrow. No telling what files I might find on Cookie's desk. I better watch myself—I don't want to get fired, or worse, arrested.*

As she moved on to the next room, Angie couldn't help but wonder what else she might find out about City Hall doing this job. She might be just a cleaning lady, but she knew from Vinnie that the building had its fair share of deep, dark secrets.

Angie kept moving forward, knowing that she had a job to do. She stopped briefly to eat the peanut butter and jelly sandwich and apple Gina had made her the night before and put in a brown paper bag with a note: *Good luck on your first day—go get 'em, Aunt Angie. Love you, Gina.* She smiled. After she finished lunch, she moved on to her next room. It felt good to be working, and come payday, it would feel even better.

Lorna found her at five sharp. "Quitting time. I'll show you where to stow your cleaning cart for tomorrow."

"I found these important papers on the first floor and wasn't sure what to do with them." Angie handed her the papers.

"You'll be finding a lot of these. We have a lost and found basket in HR; drop them there on your way out. Write the floor where you found them. See you tomorrow." Lorna cracked her gum and left.

Angie took the bus home, dozing off and on until it got to her stop on Diversey. Getting off, she walked two blocks to Dayton to Gina's apartment.

As she approached the door, smells of buttery garlic greeted her. Once in, she saw Kim cooking up a storm, all four burners going with pots of food simmering.

"Smells amazing! What's for dinner?" Angie glanced over at the stove.

"We're having some of my famous wonton soup, with garlic shrimp and chestnuts, homemade egg rolls, and egg foo yong—all my great grandmother's recipes. You're in for a real treat. Gina is on her way home. We have lots of great news. I can't wait to share. Why don't you go get changed and I'll pour you a glass of wine."

"Sounds wonderful, I'll be back in a bit." Angie showered and put on her Juicy sweatpants and sweatshirt that Gina gifted her and came back into the kitchen.

Over a delicious meal, Kim brought everyone up to speed on her productive day. "I called our friend Louie Rago, and he graciously offered to have us at the monthly funeral directors' meeting at his place next Monday. I told him we'd supply all the food and drink and to be sure he brings his appetite."

"This soup is amazing, Kim, and the shrimp and garlic, a flavor party in my mouth." Gina licked her lips.

Kim continued, "I drafted a list of finger foods for every type of ethnic service, and I got a great potato latke recipe from a Jewish friend. We can make small ones and serve them with applesauce and sour cream."

Angie smiled. "I have a good feeling about our company. I can make homemade applesauce this weekend. It's an old family recipe. I do have a full-time job now, so I'll have to do my prep at night and on the weekends."

"Let's look at the list after dinner. How was your first day at work, Aunt Angie?" Gina asked.

"It was so interesting. The cleaning part is easy. So much going on at City Hall, all kinds of people coming and going—it's fascinating. I met my supervisor, Lorna, who is a kick in the pants. She looks to be about fifty, but she's got a Marilyn Monroe thing going on, put a fake beauty mark over her lip. She has no time for idle conversation."

After dinner they cleared their plates and went into the small living room and focused on the draft menu. Angie could hardly keep her eyes open. "It's bedtime for me. Whatever you decide on the menu is fine with me. I gotta be up at the crack of dawn to catch the bus. And thank you for that sweet note in my lunch bag, Gina. Dinner was exceptional. Good night, my two young entrepreneurs."

Chapter 15

After Angie went to sleep, Kim and Gina decided to review the tasting menu for Louie at Rago Brothers. Everything had to be perfect, since his first experience with them at Uncle Vinnie's funeral had been such a disaster.

Kim sat next to Gina on the couch and pulled up the menu on her laptop. "You do remember we have our final presentation in our class tomorrow?" she asked. "I put together a slide deck; we already talked that through. We are so getting an A in this class."

"You're damn straight! We're getting an A-plus. I got in deep shit at work because I asked for the day off tomorrow. My boss said no more requests like that, or I'll be looking for another job. He's such an asshole."

"Sooner than later, you won't have to ask anyone for time off—we'll be our own boss." Kim pointed at the menu. "I thought we should focus on our menu for Italian wakes and funerals first, then we can arrange another meeting for our Chinese clientele. Here's what we thought we could pull off without too much expense and still look professional—I think we need to pare this down, but let's decide together."

They both stared at the screen:

—Caprese skewers with fresh mozzarella, cherry tomatoes, and basil

—Antipasto platter with sliced meats, cheeses, olives, and roasted peppers

—Garlic toasted crostini with pesto

—Seasonal roasted vegetables

—Biscotti

Beverages:

—Red and white wine

—Italian sodas

—Coffee and teas

"I think this is all doable. My aunt said she could make a simple olive oil, balsamic vinegar garlic dip for the bread, and she has an easy biscotti recipe we can knock out in no time." Gina couldn't contain herself—especially her shit-eating grin—and she put up her hand. "High five!"

They slapped hands.

"I went to Jewel and Trader Joe's, and we can absolutely get an assortment of premade items, and then it's just some assembly with a dash of Aunt Angie's magic. But reality check, Gina, do you really think your aunt can handle all this? I love her, but going from not working at all to having a full-time job *and* catering with us is a lot," Kim said.

Gina took a deep breath. "I don't know, but we have to give her a chance. She looked so tired tonight. I think we keep her in the loop, and on the weekends, she can cook and bake. She really needs to know she's a part of our operation; we're her ticket out of the land of poverty and toilet cleaning."

"I'll pull up the slide deck for tomorrow, and then we both need to get some sleep. I have to keep working at my parents' store in Chinatown until we start making money. Of course, they have me opening at six every morning."

They quickly reviewed the slides and then Gina walked Kim to the door. "I'm so excited we're partners, Kim. I have a really good feeling in my gut."

"Me too."

"I'll pick you up for class tomorrow. Good night," Gina said.

After Kim left, Gina made Angie another lunch, then wrote the Rago's menu on a piece of paper and included a note: *Good luck on day two*, with a heart. She got ready for bed, lay down in Thad's room, and snuggled under his comforter. She fell sound asleep and didn't even hear her aunt leave early the next morning.

Gina's alarm went off at six thirty; she wandered into the kitchen and saw her favorite coffee mug that Uncle Vinnie had given her, CUBS WIN, sitting by the coffeepot. Her aunt had put a Post-it note on the mug: *Good luck today at class—you & Kim will knock it out of the park. Proud of you.* Gina enjoyed her coffee, reviewed the slides, and got ready for the day. She texted Kim that she was on her way, got in her car, and called her mom.

"Hey, honey, last day of school, you ready for your presentation?"

"Kim and I got this. I'll show you the slides when we have dinner tonight—are we still on?"

"We'll get some Portillo's beef sandwiches and take them over to Angie's place; I promised her I'd help her start packing. It would be great if you and Kim could come too. It's going to be tough for her."

"Aunt Angie was exhausted last night. Today is her second day of work. Did you hear she got a job in housekeeping at City Hall?"

"Housekeeping? What the hell?"

"It's all they could give her with just a GED. She's keeping her spirits up, but it's hard labor. Sounds like there's some kind of problem with Uncle Vinnie's pension," Gina explained.

"What's going on with her pension? I sure hope they're not messing with that. Vinnie earned every penny he made," Connie said.

"I don't know any details, but Angie is pushing as hard as she can without pissing off Cookie. Maybe we should wait until this weekend to pack her up. I don't think she'll have the energy after a full day of work." Gina's car was inching toward Kim's apartment.

"We have to go soon. Beatrice has been up my ass about that damn storage unit key, and I told Ben I'd come by to get it from him. Apparently, he took it upon himself to search for it at the apartment. Knowing how close Ben and Vinnie were, he maybe knew all along. Anyway, he said he and Angie will need to go to the locker before Beatrice gets involved."

Gina tapped her fingers on the steering wheel. "I'll talk to her when she gets home around six."

"That Angie. She sure is a good sport, getting herself a job."

"She is determined to be independent as soon as she can. Kim and I are planning on going to the credit union at school after our presentation today and filling out some forms. We're not sure if we'd qualify for a business loan, but we want to try. I don't know if they'll give me a loan with my job at Panera, and I owe a lot on my credit cards too."

"That's a good idea; sometimes they have small loans for start-ups. I'm so proud of you for starting your business. I can certainly co-sign for the loan."

"That would help. I'll get the paperwork and we can go over it together. I'm almost at Kim's. We have our first tasting scheduled with Louie at Rago Brothers next week; we already have a draft menu. We're starting with Italian and then we'll do a separate one for Chinese, and maybe eventually do a combo." Gina felt a warm swell in her chest. Her mom's unwavering support was something she realized not everyone gets. Kim didn't have the same.

When Gina pulled up in front of Kim's apartment, Kim was waiting outside with her backpack on.

"My mom's on the phone," Gina said when Kim got into the car.

"Hey, Mrs. Paloni, what's up?"

"All good here. Good luck on your presentation. Gina, call or text me afterward and let me know how it went. I'll plan to come by your place tonight around six so I can talk with Angie—and I'll bring the sandwiches. Sound good?"

"Perfect. We can go over the loan papers together. Gotta go."

Gina shrugged her shoulders, glanced over at Kim, and started driving to school.

"Did your mom say anything about the loan?" Kim asked.

"She cashed out an IRA that was supposed to be for college if I went. She is totally with me using it for this. That'll give us ten thousand."

"My parents are a hard no unless I marry a nice Chinese guy, and that ain't gonna happen. I have my savings, so they can't say anything about that."

"I can't believe they still can't accept that you're gay." Gina thought again about her mom's support. Though they'd never talked about it, Gina knew her mom would love her unconditionally, gay or straight, though she'd have to adjust a few expectations.

"They think it's a fad that I'll outgrow. They're also still mad I'm not going to medical school like my brother. I don't care anymore what they think. I am who I am."

"I know it took a lot of courage for you to come out in high school. They'll have to come around eventually, or not, I guess," Gina said.

"Right now, we're still in the 'or not' phase, so I only see them for Sunday dinner and when I'm working at the store. Thanks for always being there for me, Gina. It means a lot."

"Always got your back. Ready to kick some ass on our presentation?"

"Absolutely. It will be so good to have this behind us; I know we're going to ace it. I also did an Excel spreadsheet showing the initial investment and when we can expect to make a profit. I'll show you when we get to school," Kim said.

Once they got to school, Gina and Kim reviewed their presentation one more time. Kim added all kinds of fun visuals and had even designed a simple logo for Last Bite. They were first up, and everyone, including their teacher, Mr. Spiro, clapped after they were done.

"Very creative approach, ladies," Mr. Spiro commented. "I have a good feeling about this. Please let me know if I can help you."

"Do you know if there are any places we can apply for a loan or maybe find investors?" Kim asked.

"Let's talk about it after class—I have some ideas."

The rest of the class presentations paled by comparison, and once all the students left Kim and Gina approached Mr. Spiro's desk.

He took out a folder labeled "Financial Backing" and spread out about ten forms in front of them. "There are several small companies that support entrepreneurs. You can send your prospectus to them, and I'm happy to give them a heads-up. Be reasonable and start small—I have no doubt you'll be successful."

"Thanks, Mr. Spiro," they responded in unison.

Gina looked over at Kim once they were back in the car, her eyes gleaming and her face sporting a huge grin. "Let's go celebrate. I know it's early, but we have to celebrate every little step."

"Why not? How about we park by your house, and we can walk to Durkin's, just in case we drink too much."

"Sounds good." They talked about their next steps as Gina drove home and got lucky finding a parking spot right in front of her place. "Let's dump our backpacks inside."

They walked up the stairs. Once they were inside, they heard moaning coming from the living room and smelled marijuana fumes permeating the air. "I think my roommate is having an afternoon delight with his gal. Let's leave our stuff in the kitchen."

They grabbed their wallets, left their backpacks, and headed out.

"At least someone's getting some," Kim chuckled.

"Got to give Thad credit. He hasn't said a word about Angie living with us, and I'm using his room, so he can have all the fun he wants during the day," Gina shared as they walked to Durkin's.

Kris, the bartender, greeted them and put two coasters in front of them on the long wooden counter. They entered through the large wooden door with windows into the dimly lit bar.

"Hey, Gina, good to see you. It's been a while. Sorry about your uncle. It was always fun when you both came in together. I'll need to check your IDs, you know it's the law." They pulled out their wallets and showed him their licenses.

"Thanks, Kris, it's been tough, so unexpected." Gina needed a break from thinking about her uncle right now. Since her aunt moved in a week ago, it seemed that was the only subject they discussed most of the time. It seems whatever they discussed led them both to thinking of Vinnie. They both missed him so much.

"May he rest in peace. Old Style on tap?"

"You got it. This is my best friend and business partner, Kim Yang. Meet my buddy Kris."

Kim put her hand out and they shook. "Nice to meet you, Kris. How about two shots of tequila?"

"Must be celebrating something—finally left Panera?" Kris started to draw their beers.

"Not yet, but hopefully soon. We're starting a catering company, just finished the entrepreneur class at Daley College, got an A," Gina shared with pride.

"What kind of tequila would you like?"

"Do you have Don Julio Blanco?" Kim asked.

"Sure do, nice choice." Kris placed their beers in front of them, then grabbed the tequila and two shot glasses, and poured them to the brim. "Here's some lime and salt if you like, but this is smooth, so you may not need them."

Gina glanced around the bar. It had a classic Irish pub interior with dark wood paneling, exposed brick walls that were decorated with a mix of vintage Irish advertisements, sports memorabilia, and local artwork. Plenty of screens to watch any sport that was on; the White Sox were playing now.

Gina and Kim sipped a little off the top and then lifted the shot glasses. "Here's to our new business and being our own bosses," Kim toasted.

They both downed the tequila. "That goes down smooth; we could get in trouble fast." Gina took a sip of her beer.

"I'll get in trouble with you anytime," Kim said, then ever so briefly closed one eye and smiled.

Wait, did she just coyly wink at me? Gina wondered, but then shook it off. *I must have been seeing things.*

"This is a big step for us." Kim sipped her beer. "I did some preliminary calculations, and I think we can start booking as soon as we get the call from the funeral director. We'll have to use your small kitchen until we have enough money to rent a better space. I think we should require a fifty percent down payment up front, and we'll use that money to purchase most of the ingredients. I asked my parents for more shifts at their store, and they were more than happy to oblige, mostly because they can watch my every move. I have about ten grand in my savings account."

"Another shot?" Kris asked.

"Yes, please." Gina shifted her attention back to Kim.

Kim raised her shot glass again. "Cheers."

They downed the second shot, and over the course of the afternoon, each had another beer as they discussed their pitch to Louie. But Gina found herself having a difficult time keeping her mind focused on business when Kim started applying gloss to her smooth, full lips. As Gina stared at Kim's mouth, a thought came to her: *I wonder what it would be like to kiss Kim?* But just as suddenly as the notion had entered her mind, she pushed it away. *Okay, this is ridiculous. Clearly, I've had too much booze.*

Gina glanced down at her watch. "Oh, shit, it's almost six. I forgot my mom's bringing us sandwiches, and we have to figure out when Angie wants to pack and move. I'm ordering us an Uber."

Kim pulled a couple of twenties out of her wallet and put them on the bar. "Here you go, Kris. Keep the change."

"Gee, thanks, Kim." Kris looked over at Gina. "And you take care, Gina. Don't be a stranger."

"With my schedule and starting this catering company, you may not be seeing me for a while, but if you know anyone who needs their wake or funeral catered, give me a call." She jotted down her cell phone number on a napkin and slid it over to him. "I'll drop off some business cards once we get them printed."

Kris laughed. "Hopefully I won't be calling you anytime soon. Take care."

"I'm feeling a nice buzz. How about you?" Gina glanced over at Kim.

"Oh, yeah, that's why I love my tequila. A nice, gentle high," Kim said.

Before she could stop herself, Gina put her hand on Kim's cheek. "That gentle high looks good on you."

"You're not so bad yourself." Kim smiled.

Gina looked away. *She is so beautiful. Yikes! Why am I looking at my business partner like this? Slow your roll, Gina! Enough with the tequila brain.*

Canceling the Uber, and needing to walk it off, they walked to Gina's apartment, finding Angie sitting in the kitchen, sipping a glass of wine, while Connie put out huge beef sandwiches, wrapped in white butcher paper. "Nothing like Portillo's beef, sweet peppers, giardiniera, and grilled onions—and lots and lots of broth."

"Thanks for doing this, Mom," Gina said.

"Of course, honey. How did your presentation go today?"

"Mr. Spiro said we nailed it. He was impressed that we're only twenty-two and we really seemed to have a grasp of what it would take to launch our business. He gave us some leads on where we could apply for loans and some start-up money," Gina said as she dove into her sandwich.

"What about you, Angie? Any news about Vinnie's pension?" Connie asked, as she refreshed her and Angie's wineglasses.

"No news is good news for now, but the wheels move slowly at City Hall."

Connie nodded. "Not to pile on, but I talked to Ben today.

He wants us to come over to his place so we can handle this storage unit situation. We should take care of this as soon as we can, Angie."

"Let's go first thing Saturday morning," Angie said.

"Hey, what did you think of the tasting menu I put in your lunch bag?" Gina asked.

"I have some fun ideas that will punch it up, but it's a good start," Angie said.

Connie stood up. "I have to work at the office tonight. See you bright and early Saturday."

"I hate to be a party pooper, but I'm tired. Good night, girls," Angie said.

"I have the early shift so I can drop you off if you want," Gina said.

"That would be wonderful," Angie said, and made her way to the bathroom.

"I need to head home too." Kim walked to the door.

"Let's talk tomorrow after work. Maybe we can bang out the loan papers together," Gina said.

"Sounds good, partner."

Chapter 16

Ralph was having dinner at home alone when his cell phone rang. The screen said *private number* and he picked up reluctantly, hoping it wasn't Rebecca using someone else's phone.

"This is Ralph."

A man's raspy voice answered. "Ralph, an attorney friend of yours called me and said you may need some help with someone at City Hall."

"Who am I talking to?" Ralph asked.

"I don't discuss anything on the phone. Meet me at the McDonald's on Rush Street in twenty minutes. I'm tall and dark-haired. I'll be wearing a black leather jacket."

"See you there." Ralph hadn't expected such a quick response to the call he put out to his friend.

McDonald's was a quick four-block walk from his house and was crowded as usual. He saw the guy sitting at a table in the back, facing the front entrance, eating french fries. He walked over and sat across from him.

"Before we get too far," the guy said, "I need to know who exactly at City Hall you're having issues with." The guy put a bunch of fries dripping with ketchup in his mouth.

"Mario Longetti," Ralph said.

The guy stood up and wiped his face with a napkin. "Can't help there, pal. Have you heard of his family? Half of them are in prison for murder, and the other half make it a point never to be made. You need to import someone from Vegas if you're going after Mario. My advice? Forget about it and figure something else out." He pushed his fries over to Ralph. "You can finish these."

After the man left, Ralph sat there shaking his head. *Now I get why Mario is such a blatant asshole. He's well protected.*

Ralph looked down at the cardboard box in front of him. *McDonald's does make the best fries*, he thought as he dipped some in ketchup.

It was a perfect fall evening—as Ralph strolled lost in thought—and the streets were packed with the convention party crowds that frequented Chicago.

The next morning, Ralph went for his usual run, hoping he could figure out a way to work around Mario and get Angie her pension—or maybe he couldn't help her. He usually wasn't one to give up, but risking his life seemed like pretty high stakes. Once he got to the office, Ralph spent the morning returning calls, answering emails, and attending meetings.

Eunice knocked on his office door. "You want lunch? I'm bringing in Chinese for the staff today."

"No, thanks, I'm heading down to a jobsite, then over to City Hall; I need to get a master list of all my projects from the building department. But thanks." Ralph took a car to the jobsite, and Barry from the building department was waiting for him out in front. "Your job is officially on hold. Your architects gave the contractor shit drawings, and we don't have time for that crap."

"Oh, Barry, what do I need to do to get this back on track? Just tell me and I'll do it."

"Too late for that, I have Mario up my ass. He's riding me like a racehorse, and if he says jump, I say how high. And he's definitely no fan of yours. If I were you, I'd steer clear of him. Work with his second-in-command, Dennis. If anyone knows how to handle that hothead, it would be him."

"Thanks for the heads-up; I'm heading over to City Hall now. I'll see if Dennis can meet with me, and we can get things back on track." Ralph shook Barry's hand and noticed he still hadn't showered.

City Hall was bustling as usual. There was a protest out front by some labor union. Ralph wanted to support unions, but if he honored every picket line at City Hall, he would have no jobs to give to his union tradesmen.

He took the elevator up to the building department and was greeted by a young, curly-haired woman at the reception desk. *Looks like another temp; just when I warm up one assistant, they leave.*

"May I help you?" she asked.

"Yes, is Dennis available? I'm Ralph Conti. I have several projects with the city."

"Just a minute, I'll see if he's in. Sometimes he sneaks out the back door." She picked up her phone and dialed his extension. "Hi, Dennis, you have a visitor here, a Mr. Ralph Conti."

Ralph studied her face as she listened to whatever he was saying. She kept saying, "Oh, okay, all right. I'll tell him."

She put the phone down. "He has meetings all afternoon. He can see you at four thirty for fifteen minutes."

Ralph checked his watch; it was three. "I'll be back here at four thirty sharp. Thanks."

He headed to the records department and received a warm welcome from Misty at the front desk. "Hello, Ralph, what a nice surprise. I didn't see your name on the meeting agenda today. What can I do for you?"

"I was hoping I could get a master list of all my projects under construction and their status. I think the planning commission is meeting tonight, and I want to make sure someone from my team is there and up to speed."

"Funny you should say that, because Mario just asked me for the same thing yesterday. I made copies for the commission and I have a few extras." She took out a file and handed him one. "He's taken Vinnie's place temporarily. He'll be at the meeting tonight." Misty leaned in toward Ralph and whispered, "If you ask me, I think he's counting on getting the job, but he's not Vinnie and he has a short fuse. He yells and swears at everyone. I've suffered his wrath more times than I care to count."

"He's probably under lots of pressure since Vinnie died. Any inside scoop on who will be making the final decision on who replaces Vinnie?"

"I'm not sure, but there is a hiring committee that Cookie Cunningham leads. You may want to ask her."

The desk phone started ringing; Misty picked it up and waved at Ralph as he left.

Ralph headed to HR and was greeted by Bud, the assistant. "Can I help you?"

"Yes, I need to see Cookie. Is she available? I'm Ralph Conti."

Bud called Cookie and told her she had a visitor. "She said to ask you to wait; she's finishing up a meeting in ten minutes. You're welcome to take a seat."

Ralph elected to stand, browsing the reading rack and glancing at the latest city newsletter. The door opened behind him and he turned to see Angie, wearing a cleaning uniform, walking in with a stack of papers. At the sight of her, he forced a smile, which she did not return, as the corners of her mouth turned down and she looked at the floor. Ralph cleared his throat. "Fancy meeting you here. I didn't know you were working at City Hall. No grass grows under your feet, huh?" When she didn't answer at first, he thought, *God, I'm so embarrassed for her. I can only imagine how much she wishes she hadn't just run into me.*

Finally, she spoke. "A gal has to do what a gal has to do. I need a job until Vinnie's pension check starts coming in and likely after that. Good to see you, Ralph—can't talk, I'm on the clock."

"Hi, Bud, good to see you." She handed the stack of papers she'd found during her second day on the job over to him. "Here you go, I wrote down the floor and office I found them in. Not sure if there's anything important but Lorna told me to drop these here."

Bud took the papers and placed them in a bin on his desk. "I'll make sure Cookie sees these. If there's any confidential information, I feel sorry for the person who left them. Cookie gets upset about such things. Will you be cleaning our offices today?"

"You're next after I finish the bathrooms. Please let Cookie know I didn't read them. I'm just doing my job," Angie said, and turned to leave.

"See you Monday?" Ralph asked.

"Yes, but we'll need to make it an early evening. I have to be up by six for work."

"No problem. Take care, Angie."

As she left, Ralph watched her pushing the heavy cleaning cart down the hall. She so reminded him of Alice the other night when they had cocktails. Now she was mopping floors. *I respect her for doing what she needs to do, but there must be a way for me to help her out.*

Cookie came out into the reception area. "Hey, Ralph, let's go for a walk."

As they were leaving the office, he glanced down the hall to see Angie briskly pushing her cart, her shoulders hunched and head down, and his heart sank.

Chapter 17

Angie's heart raced as she pushed her cart down the hall as fast as she could, holding back tears. *I am so humiliated that Ralph saw me.* She parked the cart outside the women's restroom, then took the yellow plastic CLOSED TEMPORARILY FOR CLEANING sign and put it in the doorway. She checked to make sure no one was in there and closed the door. Sobs trapped in her throat, she found the closest stall, locked the door, sat down, and started to cry.

"I'm exactly the kind of loser my father and my first husband said I was. *I was just fooling myself when I was with Vinnie.*" She allowed herself to let it all out, and then a switch clicked in her head.

"No, no. I am not that old Angie! I am *not*!" she said, fighting the sobs that persisted.

She blew her nose, wiped her tears, splashed cold water on her face, and cleaned the bathroom with newfound energy. *I'll show them.*

Angie was determined to get what was due to her, one way or another. She checked her watch; it was close to quitting time, but she needed to finish her last office. She wheeled Hazel—as she now endearingly called her cart—to the HR department;

Bud was gone and the door was locked. She unlocked the door with her master key and started cleaning the reception area, then moved to the offices behind closed doors.

Angie headed straight to Cookie's office, dusted off the plants, then the perimeter of the desk, and came to a halt when she saw a thick file with Vinnie's name on it. Her eyes darting around, her heart racing, she frantically took it to the copy area and made copies of everything. She put them under the paper towels lying atop Hazel and returned the original to Cookie's desk. Her palms were sweating as she quickly finished cleaning the rest of the areas in HR and took Hazel down to the basement. On the way out, she decided she would hail a cab. It wasn't in her budget, but she had to get that file home and read what was inside as soon as possible.

Fortunately, Thad and Gina weren't home when Angie locked herself in her bedroom and started to read Vinnie's file. It was thick, but she found a section labeled "Retirement," and she quickly flipped to that section.

And there it was, in black and white; the beneficiary of Vinnie's pension was Mario.

"What?" she yelled out. "What the hell?" *This can't be right*, she thought, as she quickly flipped each page and read the highlights. But no, it was crystal clear. Mario would be getting Vinnie's entire pension. *How could this be?*

Her fingers suddenly weak, the papers fell to the floor and Angie lay down on Gina's bed trying to make sense of everything. She picked up the remote control for Gina's TV and hit the on button. *The Wizard of Oz*, one of her favorite movies in the world, was playing. It was one of the last scenes where the characters were sending Dorothy off, and Glinda, the good witch, looked at Dorothy and said, "You've always had the power, my dear. You just had to learn it for yourself."

Angie stood up, all the muscles in her body tightened, and she screamed, "I'm not letting anyone take that pension away from me!" She slammed her hand on Gina's dresser. Her cell phone rang. She took a deep breath so she wouldn't sound like a maniac answering the phone. "Hello."

"Well, it's about damn time you answered your phone. I've been leaving you messages for days. Didn't anyone tell you it's rude not to return calls?"

"I'm done taking your shit, Beatrice. Do you ever think about anything else besides yourself and your money? Vinnie always said you were the most selfish person he knew, and he was spot-on. When I have something to tell you about whatever is in that storage unit, I will call you. If you call me one more time, you won't ever hear from me again. Do I make myself clear?" Angie was stunned by the power in her voice. She'd always buckled under intimidation. And Beatrice was nothing if not intimidating. Angie felt herself puff up with her newfound forcefulness.

"I want what's rightfully mine, and you don't intimidate me for a minute. You were nothing before you married Vinnie, and you're nothing now. You better get your ass over to that storage unit sooner than later or I'll—"

Angie cut her off, "Or what? You'll come after me in your electric scooter with that rat dog of yours? Please, save your bad breath threats for someone else, you waste of space. No wonder you've been single all your life. Who could stand to be around you? I will call you when and if I'm good and ready. If you bother me one more time, I'll sue you for harassment. I work at City Hall now; I have friends there. And stop calling Connie because that's not going to get you anywhere either. Too bad you weren't really dead like Vinnie told us." Angie ended the call, let out a huge breath and smiled. *Man, that felt good.* She went into the bathroom and washed her face and neck with cool water. *Wait until Ralph hears about these pension papers.*

Angie called Ralph next, her heart still racing. When he answered, she said, "Ralph, are you sitting down? You're not going to believe this."

"Yes, I'm sitting down. You sound upset. What's going on?"

"Is this a secure line?" For all she knew, someone could be bugging his phone.

He laughed. "I think so, but I'm not a hundred percent sure. Do you want me to go find a pay phone?"

"That's not necessary. I just got off a call with Beatrice so my engines are running hot right now," Angie said.

"You okay? What's going on, Angie?"

She could hear his concern.

"I am just fine. After I saw you, I cleaned the HR offices and found Vinnie's file on Cookie's desk." Angie laid out what she had discovered and her rush to photocopy the file. "Mario is the beneficiary. He's going to get all Vinnie's money. I need your help, Ralph. I know we're just getting to know each other, but I didn't know who else to call. I don't want to bring Ben into this; it could jeopardize his pension at City Hall."

"Wow, no wonder you're all riled up. I would be too. Do you have any evidence that can prove that Mario did this?" Ralph asked.

"No, I just found this all today. It appears like it was always Mario if you look at the paperwork. I know for sure that Vinnie would not have done this. Who else would have but Mario?" Angie walked into the kitchen and poured herself a glass of wine.

"Well, I'm no attorney, but if we can't prove that your name was on there first, then changed, I'm not sure if we can do anything. Did Cookie ever tell you that your name was on the pension papers?"

"She led me to believe that it was when I met with her. She said things take time at City Hall. Maybe I can wear a wire and go into her office and ask her point-blank. Or I could corner Mario and get him to confess," Angie said.

Ralph laughed. "I think you're watching too many detective movies. It's an idea, but we'll have to figure out another way to get to the bottom of this. When I saw Cookie on Friday and asked her about how your pension paperwork was going, she all but bit off my head and told me to mind my own business. She also demanded I stop asking questions about Vinnie's replacement. I'm walking a tightrope at City Hall right now. They're shutting down all my jobs, so I need to stay in Cookie's good graces."

"I'm so sorry to hear about that. Will your company be okay?" Angie finished her wine in a gulp.

"Honestly, I don't know. The majority of my jobs are with City Hall. I have several others outside, but things with those could go south too if word gets out. Don't you worry about me, Angie. I'll land on my feet. I do think you should destroy the copies you made from Cookie's file. That's a criminal offense that could get you into serious trouble if someone finds them."

"Right now, the only people who know about them are you and me. Thanks for the heads-up on that. I'll hide them in a place where no one would think to look." *My underwear drawer*, she thought, grinning to herself. "I'll see you for dinner on Monday night. I'm looking forward to it."

"Me too, Angie. Have a good weekend."

Chapter 18

Gina yanked off her dirty apron, threw it in the Panera staff laundry basket, and headed out to her car, shoulders slumped, thinking, *I've never hated a job so much. I get paid like shit and they work us hard.* She had even texted Kim on her break that she didn't think she could wait much longer to quit.

As she reached into her purse for her keys, she heard someone call her name. "Hello! Earth to Gina!" Kim yelled.

Gina looked up; she had walked right past Kim, who was leaning against the trunk of Gina's run-down sedan holding a bouquet of sunflowers.

"I didn't even see you. I'm so sorry; it's been another shitty day," Gina said.

"I got your text. I brought you some flowers." Kim handed her the bunch of bright yellow blooms, Gina's favorites. When they were both in high school and Gina's parents were fighting all the time, Gina would always buy her mom some sunflowers because she knew it would make her smile.

"You are so sweet." Gina studied Kim's face. *No one has ever been this kind and thoughtful to me.* She set the flowers down, wrapped both her arms around Kim, and gave her a long embrace. As Kim leaned into her, Gina thought, *This feels so good, I could stay here forever.* She finally stepped away and picked up the flowers again, her heart beating rapidly.

"You're a great hugger," Kim said, and Gina felt herself flush. "I have another surprise for you. Follow me to my car." Kim walked a few parking spaces from Gina's car. "I want to take you for a fun getaway right here in town. You game?"

"Are you kidding? Yes, please." Gina let out a sigh.

Kim drove to Montrose Beach on Lake Michigan, parked, and took a small cooler out of her trunk. "Follow me."

They found a bench by the lake and Kim took out a couple chilled beers, removed the caps, and handed one to Gina. "Here's to us jumping in with both feet and making our catering company a success, no matter what it takes." They clinked bottles and each took a drink.

Gina glanced over at Kim. "Thanks for making the end of my day so much better and for the flowers. That was very kind of you."

"That's what friends and business partners do for each other," Kim said.

Gina sighed. "I could get used to this after-work thing. It's very civilized. I'm starting to get why there's been a five o'clock happy hour for decades."

"We all need time to decompress after working, so we'll have to build this into our busy schedules."

They drank their beers and enjoyed watching all the bikers and runners along the lakefront under the blue sky. "I love Chicago so much," Gina said. "I love the whole vibe."

"Same here," Kim said. "Coming to the lake always helps me shift gears."

"We should get home and start prepping for our tasting dress rehearsal with Ben tomorrow. He said he'd be there at noon," Gina said.

As they walked toward the parking lot, Gina noticed a food truck with the name *Sethna* painted on it, along with a line of people waiting. "I've heard about this; it's Filipino street food and supposed to be amazing. I forgot to eat today." Gina noticed several people eating and licking their fingers.

"Perfect, I'm starving too. One of my friends who knows that cuisine says it's the real deal," Kim said.

As they stood in line, an attractive, short woman with black hair, wearing a name tag with *Christine* written on it, approached them and handed them a small laminated menu.

"Welcome. We only have a few items. *Sum*, which is popular traditional street food. There's savory and sweet," Christine said.

"I've never heard of it. I love *pancit*," Kim said as she browsed the menu.

"Me too, it's one of my favorites. I just made a fresh batch so you're in luck. I would recommend you each try one sweet and one savory in addition to pancit," Christine said.

"What's in the sum?" Gina asked.

"Sweet sum is made with rice cakes wrapped in banana leaves, steamed with coconut milk; it has a rich and creamy texture. The savory"—she pointed to it on the menu—"is made with rice, coconut milk, and a mixture of taro and sweet potato, also served in banana leaves."

Gina was listening but was staring at her, sure she had seen her somewhere else. "You look so familiar, but I can't place where I've seen you. Do you by chance go to that karaoke bar on Rush Street?" she asked.

"I actually won the contest there a couple months ago. I can't believe you remembered me."

"Yes, now I remember. You were amazing! I was clapping for you the whole time," Gina said.

"Thanks. I need to put in your order. You can stay in line to pay. I hope you enjoy it and tell your friends." Christine walked to the truck and yelled out the order in Tagalog to the cooks inside the truck.

Gina and Kim devoured every yummy morsel, even licking the banana leaf. They gave Christine a thumbs-up as she walked by to help another customer in line.

"If we get a Filipino funeral, we'll have to hit her up for sure," Kim said.

Gina looked at her watch. "Time to prep for our official tasting."

"I'll drive you back to pick up your car." They got in Kim's car and blasted "24K Magic" by Bruno Mars.

When they walked into Gina's place, Angie was pacing in the kitchen with her hands on her hips, wearing a scowl.

"Before we start prepping for tomorrow, I have bad news to share," Angie said.

"What's wrong?" Gina asked with concern.

Angie slammed her fist on the countertop. "I've had it! I'm done with all this bullshit, once and for all. What do I look like? A stupid, spineless idiot? No one is going to fuck with me anymore, those motherfuckers."

Gina's eyes widened and she looked over at Kim, whose mouth was agape.

"What happened?" Gina had never seen her aunt this angry, ever, and she rarely used the f-word.

"Mario is trying to take my pension, and that is just not going to happen. I am not a victim. I won't be treated like a helpless damsel in distress. I am forty-five years old, and Lorna gave me some good advice, told me to pull my head out of my ass, put on my big girl panties, and stop depending on anyone, especially a man."

Kim and Gina stared at Angie, until finally Kim said, "You go, Towanda. You know, from the movie *Fried Green Tomatoes*, when the Kathy Bates character finds her inner bitch?"

"I know who Towanda is. I've watched that movie a million times," Angie snapped, then added, "Sorry, I shouldn't be taking this out on you two."

Gina got out a bottle of bourbon, poured three glasses, and handed one to Angie and one to Kim. "To Towanda."

They clinked glasses, and Angie said, "You're goddamn right. Nobody—but nobody—fucks with Angie Sortino. I'm going to get Vinnie's pension money. It's mine and that asshole Mario has no right to it. If I find out Cookie is helping him, her ass is grass."

All three women stood in the kitchen sipping their drinks until Angie calmed down and broke the silence. "Sorry about the outburst. I'm so done with all this game playing at City Hall. If I have to march into Mayor Borden's office and demand my money, then that's what I'll do."

Gina studied her aunt's face. "I'm behind you, and you're right, it's all bullshit. Kim and I can do the prep for the tasting if you want to go and relax."

"No. I want to help you. I'm too upset to relax. Cooking always takes my mind off my troubles and I love cooking with you both." Angie put on her apron. "Let's get started. Thank goodness tomorrow is Saturday, no work. After Ben comes for the tasting, we're going to this mysterious storage unit. Wait till he hears the news about Vinnie's pension. I'm sure he'll have some sage counsel. I called Ralph earlier and shared this news with him, but I'm not sure how much help he's going to be. He's in hot water with the city now."

Gina and Kim put on their aprons and started to take ingredients out of the fridge. Angie washed her hands. "Let's make some magic in this kitchen," Angie said.

Gina selected "Do You Wanna Funk?" by Sylvester, one of her favorite songs from the playlist on her phone. All three women started to dance, the energy in the kitchen ramping up.

Chapter 19

Early Monday morning, Ralph had already finished his morning run, showered, and had a cup of coffee. As it was, three out of ten of his jobs were on hold thanks to Mario. His morning would be filled with calls and meetings with the investors wanting an update on their projects. The only good news was that Rebecca had finally gotten the message and he hadn't heard from her, although he guessed she had something to do with his projects getting shut down. As he reflected on his dealings with City Hall over the last twenty years, most things got done or undone behind the scenes. No calls, no emails, just in-person meetings where nothing could be traced. He had usually been on the winning end of those meetings.

His cell rang; it was one of his contractors. "Hey, Joe, what's up?"

"What the fuck, Ralph. They closed two of the jobs I was working on, and now I'm scrambling to send my crews to other jobsites. These guys need to make a living, and we can't sit around waiting for you or the city to get your shit together. You promised me this was a sure thing, and I promised I could get it done three to four months early, bonus money all around. I'm letting you know that deal is off. Call me when you get the green light."

The call ended abruptly, and Ralph was sure there would be more just like that coming. He grabbed his briefcase and headed to his stakeholders meeting downtown. Eunice met him outside the conference room on the seventh floor of the Four Seasons, notebook in hand.

"Hey, boss, we've got some angry elves in there. Word is out that the jobsites were shut down. I made sure everyone had their coffee and pastries; if I had some Valium, I would have slipped them some." Eunice grinned.

"Too bad this wasn't an evening meeting—at least we could have plied them with good scotch. I'm a big boy, I can take the heat. Thanks for being here, Eunice. You're my anchor."

"Of course. We'll get through this, just another rather large speed bump." She handed him the printed agenda and opened the door for him.

The room was filled with women and men donned in suits, with several small groups clustered together talking, stopping as soon as he entered the room.

Ralph immediately took command. "Welcome, everyone, I hope you helped yourself to some refreshments." He sat down and called the meeting to order. Eunice was seated next to him, ready to type the meeting notes on her laptop. Ralph saw Eunice look down at her phone and slide the phone over to him to read the text message she had just received from Mario: *Tell Conti we just shut down two more of his projects.*

Ralph cleared his throat, then took a sip of water and began. "As you are aware, we are having some issues with our projects down at City Hall. My contact there, Vinnie Sortino, died a few weeks ago, and no one knows what's going on. I'm working with the building department, but there will be delays, no question."

There were groans around the table and one of the men

finally spoke. "How much is this going to cost us and will there still be a profit?"

"Great question. Please look at page five of your packet. I did a quick financial assessment on each of the jobs and made a conservative estimate and anticipated a longer delay." Ralph watched as they reviewed the numbers. He had worked with these investors for over twenty years and had made them a lot of money; now he could only hope that counted for something, but experience had taught him that the response was usually more like *What have you done for me lately?*

Hank, wearing his signature handlebar mustache, spoke. "Not good, Ralph. I have to say I am very concerned. You know we trust you, but these are big losses, and I for one don't know if my stakeholders are willing to shoulder this financial burden." Hank was Ralph's biggest investor, usually patient when they ran into delays.

"I hear your concern, Hank. I wish I had better news, but I am working with several folks at the city on a daily basis. I am not in a position to make any promises, and you know me well enough to know when I have bad news, I let you know immediately. I'm going to need some time to course correct."

"How much time are we talking about?" Hank closed his packet.

"I'm asking for a month. I spoke with HR at the city, and they are working on a replacement plan right now for Vinnie's position. Once I know who has the job, it will be easier for me to establish a relationship and move forward. Right now, it's a moving target."

The sound of cell phone dings interrupted the meeting, and everyone, including Ralph, picked up their phone. When he read the message from the *Tribune* on Twitter, his stomach clenched. When he looked up, all eyes were glaring at him. Clearly, they all had the same alert notice turned on. Ralph read the message aloud:

"Chicago City Hall just announced they are halting all construction projects run by the billion-dollar firm Conti Development Company. The CEO, Ralph Conti, was unavailable for comment. Alderman O'Brien stated that he was saddened by this news as several of the projects were in his precinct and were slated for low-income families."

Ralph stood up. "Excuse me, I'll be right back." He walked quickly to the private men's restroom, heat flooding his body and beads of sweat rolling down his face. "That fucking bitch," he mumbled. "She told her alderman husband to do this." As he locked the bathroom door, he dialed Rebecca's cell.

"Long time, Ralphie," she chuckled.

"What the fuck did you tell your husband? Are you trying to destroy me just because I won't sleep with you anymore? You vindictive bitch!"

"I'm sure I don't have any idea what you're talking about. I have to go. Please don't call me again. I'm blocking your number."

Ralph wanted to punch something, but knew he would break his hand if he did. He threw cold water on his face and neck, dried off, and went back into the conference room. It was empty except for Eunice.

"They left and said they wanted an update of the financials on all ten of their projects by end of business today. I called Molly, our attorney in charge, and she's going to meet us here in thirty minutes."

Sweat was still dripping from Ralph's face. "We need to lawyer up big-time, have our finance team run the numbers if none of these jobs go forward."

"Already notified the team and they will have a first draft to you in an hour," Eunice replied as she finished collecting all the confidential packets.

Ralph's cell phone was blowing up with calls and texts, which he ignored. He knew all too well never to fuck with Chicago contractors and unions, and he needed to have a plan before he responded.

Eunice and Ralph sat at the conference table. "How about I call Mary O'Sullivan, head of the Department of Housing, and have her place a call to O'Brien, put the pressure on restarting these projects? He's running for reelection. He needs all the votes he can get. The media is all over this, especially the low-income housing in his precinct. It would be positive PR for him."

Ralph looked over at Eunice. "That's why I love you and could never live without you, Eunice. Go for it."

Ralph started to review his texts. "I'll start responding to all these the-sky-is-falling messages," he said, as Eunice left the room to make the calls.

Ralph responded to each text with the same answer. *I'm actively working with the city. Give me a couple days. I have insurance; send my office your payroll details, and we'll be sure your crew gets paid during the shutdowns.* He copied and pasted this to each of his contractors. He received several thumbs-up. He scrolled down the voicemails and was about to start listening when Eunice returned.

"Mary is on it. O'Brien is on his way to her city office now. She said she'll call us after she meets with him. This could open the city to a huge financial lability. She was more than happy to handle this. She said she didn't know what the actual cause for the shutdowns was about, but some heads will roll at City Hall for sure."

"Hopefully one of them will be Mario's." Ralph paced back and forth in the conference room.

"Our lawyers are on their way over here now. I spoke with Molly, and she said we should be able to file for an injunction on these work shutdowns this afternoon." Eunice poured herself a cup of coffee. "We may want to wait until we hear from Mary before we file."

"I agree. In your own creative way, let City Hall know we're doing our best to downplay this and keep everyone out of the press's eye. I'll call the *Tribune* reporter as soon as Mary gives us the update."

Three lawyers, along with two other women and another man, walked into the conference room at the Four Seasons. Molly, the tall brunette, spoke. "Hi, Ralph and Eunice. I had my team draw up several legal options; we can pull the pin on any or all of these today. My team didn't find any just cause for these shutdowns—the city could be in for a very expensive lesson."

Eunice handed each of the attorneys sitting across the table from her and Ralph a packet containing the legal course of action spelled out on the cover memo. After they had some time to read all the legalese, Ralph checked his watch. "Why don't we all go downstairs for some lunch while I'm waiting to hear back from City Hall."

Over lunch, they continued to discuss all the legal options, and then his attorneys excused themselves.

"I'll wait to hear from you. If there is any way you can make some decision before four, that will give me time to meet with a judge, if we decide to go that direction," Molly offered.

"Hopefully we won't have to go there. Thanks as always for your prompt attention." Ralph glanced down at his phone, no new texts or calls.

Ralph and Eunice stayed and checked their emails, nervously waiting to hear something that would determine their next steps.

When Ralph next glanced at his watch, two hours had passed since Eunice had checked in with Mary.

"Do you want me to call her again?" Eunice asked.

Just as Ralph was about to answer Eunice, he saw Mario out of the corner of his eye flying toward him like a cannonball. Mario punched the side of his face, knocking him off his chair and onto the floor. He was breathless as he sat up, his entire cheek throbbing, blood oozing out of his nose.

Ralph blinked and tried to get up, but Mario pushed him back down and put his shoe on Ralph's neck. "What the fuck did you do, Conti? Who the fuck do you think you are calling my boss!"

Ralph shoved Mario's foot off his neck and caught his breath. Mario's comb-over was extra greasy and his clothes had dirt stains all over, likely from a jobsite. All eyes in the restaurant were on them; some patrons were taking pictures with their phones.

Mario pulled Ralph up by his suit coat. "Outside, motherfucker, you're going down. They put me on unpaid leave starting immediately—and it's all your fault."

Ralph pushed Mario's hands off him, looking up to see two security guards quickly approaching behind Mario. "Fuck you, Mario! I tried to play nice with you. You brought this on yourself. Maybe you can use some of Vinnie's pension money to tide you over."

Just as Mario raised his fists to punch Ralph again, the security guards grabbed Mario from behind.

"Sir, you need to leave now," one of the burly guards said.

As he started to escort Mario away, the other guard quietly spoke to Ralph. "If you want to file a police report, we can give them a call."

"I think that's a good idea," Ralph said.

Mario shouted one more threat over his shoulder. "You have *no idea* who you're fucking with. Watch your back, Conti!"

Eunice rushed over to Ralph and handed him a wet napkin to wipe the blood off his face. The restaurant manager was at his side. "I'm so sorry for this, Mr. Conti. Would you please follow me to my office? I've got our on-call doctor meeting us there to give you a once-over."

Ralph's eye and cheek still burning, he put his hand up to his nose, where he was holding the napkin. He glanced at the bright red blood that had stained the entire thing.

"Eunice, why don't you head back to the office. I'll be there after I see their doctor and file a formal complaint."

"You got it, boss. You're going to have a shiner for sure, and your nose isn't in the right place either. I'll keep you posted."

"Never a dull moment, huh, Eunice? I better get back to the boxing gym."

The manager of the Four Seasons escorted Ralph to his office. "I apologize that our team didn't spot that guy coming after you. Be assured everyone from the doorman to the restaurant hostess has been notified, and he won't be setting foot on our property again."

"I appreciate that," Ralph said, pressing the cloth to his still-bleeding nose.

Once they were in the manager's office, a thin redheaded man wearing khaki pants and a polo shirt entered carrying a small black bag. "I'm Dr. Jensik; you can call me Steve. Let me take a look at your nose. Looks like it may be broken."

Ralph removed the napkin and Steve gently moved Ralph's nose one direction, then the other. "Any pain?"

More blood oozed from his nose; Ralph soaked it up with a warm washcloth that the hotel manager handed him. "It hurts for sure. Can you tell if it's broken?"

"If I had to guess, I would say yes. We should get you over to Northwestern. I can arrange X-rays, and they can pack it for you. If it needs to be fixed, they can handle it right away." Steve looked over at the hotel manager. "Would you please get him an ice pack for the back of his neck; that should slow down some of this bleeding. And also an ice pack for right above his nose."

"On it, and Mr. Conti, we have a car ready to take you over to Northwestern."

"I'll call my friend who's a plastic surgeon," Steve said. "I'm sure she'll be able to get him in quickly. She's on the fifth floor of the professional building; her name is Dr. Mary Hoffman."

"Thanks. I appreciate you taking care of me."

The hotel manager returned and handed Ralph the ice packs. "If you give me the information on the man who assaulted you, I'll file with Chicago PD."

"His name is Mario Longetti. My office manager, Eunice, can give you the rest of the details." Ralph jotted down her phone number and followed Steve down to the lobby of the Four Seasons.

"Let me know if you need anything else, Ralph. You're in good hands," Steve assured him.

"Thanks, Doc." He got in the black limo, leaned his head back to hold the ice pack in place over his nose, and checked his phone. No updates.

Dr. Hoffman met him in her office, quickly assessed his injury, and asked him about his medical history. "I think you have a deviated septum; that punch must have been forceful. I'm going to have to get an X-ray. There's a machine right here, down the hall from my office."

"What's that mean?" Ralph gently touched his nose and winced.

"It's a thin wall of cartilage and bone that separates your nostrils, essentially a broken nose. I see a lot of this in football players, boxers, anybody who plays contact sports. Once I confirm this, I can straighten it out and pack it for you. You look like a healthy guy so it should heal just fine."

"Okay, then, let's get to it." Ralph pushed his hand through his hair.

Sure enough, his nose was broken, and after a few injections around his nose that burnt like hell, and some calming medication, she straightened it, packed it, put a nose guard on, and secured it with white tape.

"Here's a prescription for Tylenol with codeine; you should take some tonight and maybe tomorrow. I had my staff make an appointment for you in two weeks. I'll remove the packing, and you should be feeling much better by then. Looks like you'll have a black eye too."

Ralph stood up and checked himself in the mirror. "I've got a lot of meetings with my clients, and if I don't make up a good story then I know they will."

"Take it easy tonight and, if possible, tomorrow. You'll feel relaxed from the medication I gave you, so no drinking or heavy lifting."

"How about a glass of wine? I have a dinner date tonight at Gibsons."

"As long as you have a driver and don't overdo it, you should be fine. I love Gibsons—best steak house in Chicago."

"Can't thank you enough, Dr. Hoffman, for taking me in so quickly and handling everything so professionally."

"You can call me Mary, and it's what I do. By the way, the hotel is paying for all your expenses, and the hotel manager has a car waiting for you downstairs. You must be a VIP."

"I do a lot of business with the Four Seasons. They always take good care of me and my clients."

"Well, enjoy your dinner tonight. Here's my cell phone if you need anything else. Nice to meet you, Mr. Conti."

He checked his watch; it was already seven. He called Angie.

"Hi, Ralph, I'm looking forward to our dinner."

Ralph glanced down at the blood on his shirt. "I'll be a little late; I need to stop by my place and change. I'll be by your place around seven thirty."

"No problem. See you soon."

Ralph cleaned up at his place and checked out his face in the mirror. He touched his right eye, which was swollen half shut, and winced. "Ouch!" *I'm gonna need an ice pack for the road.* He grabbed an ice pack on his way out and took the limo that the Four Seasons had offered him for the entire evening. When the car pulled up in front of Gina's apartment, Angie wasn't waiting outside, so he walked up the stairs and knocked on the door.

A young man opened it. "Dude, who are you and what happened to your face, man? It looks gnarly."

The smell of pot wafted out into the hallway. "I'm Ralph, and you are? I'm here for Angie."

"I'm Thad, Gina's roommate. Angie's at her apartment; she's cool."

Ralph saw a young woman with green hair walk behind Thad toward the kitchen. "She didn't mention that on the phone. I'll give her a call and let her know I'm on my way."

"Awesome. Do you want a toke before you head out? I got some really good shit."

Ralph laughed. He hadn't smoked a joint since college. "I'll pass, but thanks."

Chapter 20

It was Saturday morning, two days before her big date with Ralph on Monday. Angie awoke to the sound of laughter and loud music playing. She glanced at the time on her phone: 10:03 a.m. She threw on her robe and hustled into the living room. Gina and Kim were dancing, wearing the aprons Angie had made for them, *Last Bite* printed on the front. They had moved the kitchen table into the living room, set with a tablecloth and two place settings, linen napkins, and silverware.

Gina looked over. "Good morning, sunshine. We've been going since seven this morning and we are ready for our official tasters."

Kim handed Angie a cup of coffee. "Ben will be here in a little bit. You take your time getting ready. We're so excited."

Angie smiled and said, "You two are so cute and full of energy. Thanks for the coffee, Kim, it's perfect. I'll shower. Can't wait to taste everything."

"We need you to be brutally honest about everything. Don't hold back, you won't hurt our feelings. We really want to get this right, and we'll do anything to make it happen," Gina said.

Angie gave them a thumbs-up and headed to the bathroom. She finished getting ready and checked her phone before heading into the official tasting room, still hoping to see a text from Vinnie with his usual daily greeting: *Good morning, my love. I hope you have a wonderful day. See you for dinner.*

The lack of a message from him was just another reminder that she would never get one again. Angie had kept Vinnie's old texts and a few voicemails so that she could hear his voice and attempted to conjure up his presence. But no matter how hard she tried, she knew the reality: *You think everything is perfect one minute, then things turn on a dime, and someone you thought would be here forever is just gone.*

When she walked into the living room, Ben was sitting at the table, smiling. "Aren't we the lucky ones, a private tasting." He stood up and pulled Angie's chair out for her. "Please, allow me."

As they sat across from each other, Angie gently touched Ben's hand. He was the one and only person Vinnie had trusted unconditionally. "So good to see you. How have you been?"

Before he could answer, Kim was standing in front of them. "Thank you both for bringing your taste buds and brutal honesty. We will be sampling the menu for an Italian funeral. We're serving this at the funeral directors' meeting on Monday. I've placed a pad of paper with each item listed on a scale of one to five. After you have tasted each item, we kindly request that you don't speak to or make eye contact with each other. One means the food is horrible; five means you ask the caterer for the recipe. We are setting a two-minute timer after you taste each item so you can quickly write down your answer and notes. What's important is that we get your immediate response; that's when folks register their likes and dislikes more accurately."

Angie glanced at Kim and winked. "This is some serious business."

"This is our future. We want to make any course corrections after we get your thoughts," Kim said.

"You will both go a long way with that can-do attitude," Ben said.

Ben and Angie quietly tasted each item as it was served. She tried hard not to look at Ben, but on a couple occasions, she heard him moaning and looked over when he was eating the roasted peppers and sautéed mushrooms. "Oh, yeah," he said. Angie chuckled.

After he tasted the pesto crostini, he couldn't help himself. "Can I get a few more of these, please? This is bank; you should serve this at every event. It's going to take you all the way to the top." He handed his evaluation paper over to Kim, then wiped his face and put the folded napkin on the table. "Would you two start-up chefs please sit down."

They pulled up two chairs to the table.

"After tasting this amazing food and seeing how dedicated you are, I've decided to invest some of my retirement money in your enterprise. How much do you need?"

Angie watched Kim and Gina stare at each other, their mouths agape. Gina finally spoke. "Like, for real, Uncle Ben?" Gina had called him that since she was young and hanging out at Uncle Vinnie's place.

"How much do you need?"

After a long silence, Gina looked at Uncle Ben. "We need about five thousand more. My mom is giving us some money, and Kim has savings she's going to use."

Without hesitation, Ben reached into his pocket. "I always have my checkbook. Some people call me old-fashioned. I'm going to write you a check right here. We'll figure out the rest later." Ben handed it to Gina, stood up, and looked over at Angie. "About time we go to that storage unit, don't you think?"

Angie clasped her hands over her chest. "You're the best."

"I never expected this, Uncle Ben. You won't be sorry, I promise." Gina hugged him.

"I believe in what you're both doing, and I know your uncle Vinnie would be so damn proud of you."

Angie had a lump in her throat as she stood up. "This is all delicious, girls. But I'm feeling a little itchy to get down to that storage unit, if you don't mind. I'll get my purse."

En route to the storage unit, Ben glanced over at Angie and asked, "Vinnie never told you he had a storage unit?"

"First I heard of it was at his funeral. Beatrice has been insane about getting her hands on whatever is in there. I gave it to her yesterday, so she won't be calling me a million times now." *Why does he keep looking in the rearview mirror?* she wondered. She glanced in her side mirror and didn't see anything suspicious, so she figured maybe Ben was just a little jumpy.

"Good for you," Ben said as he parked at the location. Angie followed him to the storage unit, where he pulled out a small piece of paper with a code written in Vinnie's hand and entered the numbers. A musty smell greeted them as Ben pulled up the heavy door. He looked to see if anyone was standing on either side of them, then motioned Angie inside.

"Why do you keep looking around? Is someone following us?" Angie asked.

"Not that I can tell, but from what little Vinnie did share with me, there are sensitive documents inside, and I don't want to take any chances with your safety."

The storage unit had boxes neatly lined up on each side all the way to the ceiling. Toward the back were piles of large black trash bags stacked high, stuffed with who knew what.

"What is all this about?" Angie asked.

Ben wrapped his long arm around her shoulders. "Vinnie was always thinking ahead; you know how he was. Over the years, he learned a lot about city politics and shenanigans."

"Uh-oh, the last thing I need to do is get arrested. I got bills to pay, a job at City Hall, and a business to launch. Maybe I shouldn't be here, Ben. Sometimes it's better not to know things. Don't forget I worked in enough Italian restaurants, watching the comings and goings, and sometimes some folks were never seen again." Angie stayed at the entrance.

"It's okay, Ang, I won't let anything happen to you. You'll be fine, better than fine." He pulled out two black folding chairs from behind the boxes and set them up in the back near the black bags. "Sit down and let me explain what this is all about."

Angie swallowed and gingerly walked to the back and sat down, clutching her purse. "Why do I have a feeling this is going to be a doozy?"

Ben grinned. "You're right, it is, but you of all people will understand. Let's start with all these bags. Want to take a wild guess at what's inside?"

Angie walked over to the bags and pushed down. Her hand sank in fairly deep. "Feels like clothes or blankets . . . am I close?"

"Yes, there's lots of clothes—and hats too."

Angie searched her memory. When had Vinnie ever bought lots of clothes? Never. He hated shopping. She bought all his clothes—from underwear to shirts. The only thing he would buy was shoes and always bought two to three pairs so he wouldn't have to go back. "I have no idea."

"Remember when the Cubs almost won the National Division? Or the time they almost went on to the World Series?" Ben started to open one of the bags.

"I remember it well. There were some sad days and nights

after we lost. I tried everything to cheer him up. He didn't even want to go to Vegas. My poor guy."

"Well, Vinnie was a loyal fan to a fault. He was so sure they were going to win that he ordered hundreds of T-shirts and hats. He was going to sell some and bring them to all his buddies as gifts."

Angie's eyes scanned all the stuffed bags—there had to be at least twenty. "So you're telling me he bought all of these each time? We didn't have that kind of money." Angie looked over at Ben who was gazing down.

"That's where Beatrice comes in; she lent him money each time. He promised she would double her money if they won. And if they didn't, he would still pay her double."

"Sounds like a dumb bet; I'm surprised she lent him anything. She can make the buffalo on a nickel squeal. He never said a thing to me, but then I wasn't the breadwinner. It was his money."

"You really understood him, and he loved you for that. His backup plan was to sell the sports T-shirts and caps to a third-world country vendor, so at least they would find a home. No one in Haiti knows who won the World Series or National Division, but they can always use new T-shirts and caps. Unfortunately, our boy pissed off the guy who was shipping the stuff overseas. Vinnie jacked up the price and they told him where he could shove his sports clothes."

"So that's why Beatrice never got her money back?"

"That's only a part of it. Vinnie borrowed money from her when he went to Vegas. Most of the time, he paid her back with interest, but then the last couple times he stiffed her. And that's when the shit hit the fan."

"I could always tell when he owed someone money; he got real fidgety and crabby. When Connie would call with a cheap Vegas deal, if money was tight, he'd say, 'It's not a good time,

Connie.' But then time would pass, and he would go back to being his sweet Vinnie self, so I always assumed he had taken care of things. And since he was the breadwinner, I didn't think it was my place to pry."

"So you knew about that?" Ben winced.

Angie put her hand on Ben's arm. "I'm not just another pretty face. I didn't know the details, but I could tell when he was nervous about money, even if I didn't have the checkbook."

Ben walked to the back and took one of the boxes down from the top. "Vinnie told me that you should look at the three boxes marked *For Angie's eyes only*. I have no idea what's in there, and he made it crystal clear that there was something important and potentially dangerous if these boxes got in the wrong hands." He placed the box in front of her. "I'm going for a short walk. Take your time. I'm going to speak with the manager here; I want to be sure the storage facility has my credit card so we can leave things here until you decide what you want to do with everything." Ben headed out as Angie was opening the first box.

There were manila folders neatly organized by year. She pulled out the first folder marked 2007, the year they were married, thinking how their eleventh anniversary was just around the corner. She flipped through the paperwork, which looked like a bunch of work orders from the city, "Confidential" stamped on every one. Now Angie was the one glancing up to be sure no one was peeking inside the storage unit. *I have no idea what this is all about, but I'll figure it out—hopefully.* She read the first two pages and saw a dollar amount jotted down in Vinnie's hand. After sorting through a few more files, she took a pen from her purse and started to record the amount from each. There was $10,000 for one job, $25,000 for another, and three more $10,000 line items from three more files. She totaled the amount: $65,000 so far. She recalled Vinnie always grumbling about competitive bids from contractors coming in for city jobs; there were always late-night calls after the bids were open, but she had never paid attention to what Vinnie was saying. Vinnie had explained to her that the city always had to go for the lowest bid to show the taxpayers the city was being careful with their money. Angie paused. *Hmm, then where did this extra money come from? I can't pretend to understand how the wheels turn at City Hall, but my hunch is that some of these contractors told Vinnie they would give him a kickback if he guaranteed them he would present them to the city as the lowest bidder for the job they wanted.*

Vinnie had written where the money had gone: half to an alderman of project X and the other half to Vinnie himself. On several payoffs, Mario's name and the amounts he had received were written. Angie finished thumbing through the rest of the boxes, and as she took out the last file, she found a savings account booklet at the bottom of the box. On the inside was a folded piece of paper with her name on it. She opened it and saw a note from Vinnie.

> *Angie, my love, if you're reading this, I am gone. All of this is for you; tell no one. If this gets in the wrong hands, you will be in grave danger, which is why I deliberately left out who was paying us under the table—so if you were asked, you could honestly say you didn't know.*

She flipped to the last page of the bankbook and let out a loud gasp. "One hundred and eight thousand dollars!" The last time Vinnie had put money in the account was the day before he died. She placed the booklet in her purse and quickly jotted down Mario's name as well as the names of the various aldermen. If someone did come after her, at least she had this information, even though she didn't know who the mystery payoff person was. Angie's hands were shaking, and when she tried to stand up, her legs were too wobbly.

Startled by a knock, she looked up and saw Ben standing outside the locker. "Okay to come in?"

"Not yet, just a minute." She mustered up all her strength, stood, and put the lid on the last box. "Come on in, I'm done for now." *I have to think about when and how I'm going to destroy all this paperwork.*

"You look white as a sheet. You okay, Angie?" Ben made his way to her and placed his hand on her shoulder.

"Not really, I need to go. Would you put this box on top of the others and take me to my apartment?" Angie kept thinking about all that money Vinnie had squirreled away. Her annual salary with the city was about $24,000 and included health care. Her rent was $1,500 a month, and then she had other expenses, of course. *At least this money can help me get on my feet until we get this catering company off the ground. That Vinnie, he could have gotten arrested or killed if the wrong people had found these files. No amount of money is worth that.*

Ben did as she asked. They locked up the storage unit and drove to their building without any conversation. He parked and opened the car door for Angie. "You sure you're up for packing?"

"I won't be packing today. I need to think about what I just saw. Thanks for your concern." She patted his arm.

As they walked toward the entry, a loud honking noise distracted them. As they turned around, they saw Beatrice's town car pull up. She lowered the window. "You don't scare me, Angie." Her shrill voice sent shivers down Angie's spine. She gathered all the energy she could find and walked right up to Beatrice.

"How much did Vinnie owe you, you miserable bitch?"

Angie watched Beatrice's face, her mouth wide open and her eyes wide.

"Well, how much?" Angie demanded. "What will it take so I never have to see you or hear from you again?"

"He owes me thirty thousand dollars."

"You'll get your money, unless you call or talk to anyone in our family, in which case you won't see a dime. Are we clear?" Angie didn't wait for a response before she turned around and walked into the building with Ben. *She'll be lucky if I give her twenty thousand.*

Chapter 21

Once Gina and Kim had finished cleaning up after the tasting, they both sat down for a break.

Gina looked over at Kim with one eyebrow raised and asked, "Ready for some fun news?"

"Of course."

"I've done some sleuthing and I identified the top five catering companies in Chicago. I checked their Yelp ratings and made a list of the owners. If we're going to be the best, then we should learn from the best. Success leaves breadcrumbs, and we are going to follow them."

Kim smiled. "You're a genius, always thinking."

"I'm fine to make new mistakes, but let's not make the same ones our competition has already made. The best way to learn what the competition does is to go work for them, so last week I put in our applications to become servers for one of them. I just heard back today, and we have a quick job interview this afternoon. You down?" Gina asked.

"I've never catered before. I wouldn't know what to do, can't even balance a tray with drinks, and I don't know the names of all those fancy appetizers, but what the hell."

Gina laughed. "Don't worry. You're a quick study. The guests usually have the same questions, they want to know if it's gluten-free, dairy-free, and then they rarely eat anyway. Everyone is always watching their weight; if they do take an appetizer, they usually take a small bite and wrap the rest in their napkin. Sometimes there's a few that chow down. You just need to smile and nod. The owner just wants to take a look at us and see if we're presentable enough to serve. We got this."

They both went downstairs and got into Kim's car. Gina gave her the address and started giving her directions. She opened the car window to let in the cool breeze.

"Bring it on. I love having this adventure with you." Kim grinned and drove them to the Food for Thought office, which was in an industrial warehouse area. She parked and then went inside. A bell on the door announced their entrance.

An older redheaded woman with a pencil tucked into her messy hair was slumped over a pile of papers, a lit cigarette hanging out of the edge of her mouth. Without looking up, she barked, "What do you want? We're closing soon."

"I'm Gina Paloni. I set up an interview for us today."

Still engrossed in the paperwork, she yelled, "Joyce, your interview people are here!"

"Send 'em back," a raspy voice responded from somewhere in the depths of the office.

They waited for permission from the redhead to pass her desk.

"You heard her, go on back—and watch your step. We just finished a big gig last night, so there's stuff all over the place. If you trip or fall, it's on you."

Gina raised her eyebrows and nodded for Kim to follow her. As they walked, they saw pots and pans piled high in a stainless steel sink on the right side, a mountain of dirty white tablecloths and napkins on a table to the left. All the way in the back of the building, she saw a yellow light shining from a small office.

A woman, presumably Joyce, though she didn't introduce herself by name, looked up from her desk and said, "Come on in, we need to make this fast. I have a client meeting in an hour, and we just finished a huge event for City Hall last night. There's barely time to breathe around here."

Gina noted the dark circles under Joyce's eyes and her short black hair with streaks of gray sprinkled throughout as Joyce looked her and Kim up and down.

"You both look like youngsters. Tell me about your catering experience, and I'll need some references before you leave."

Gina cleared her throat. "My name is Gina Paloni, and this is Kim Yang. As I told you on the phone, we have both worked in food service but not catering. We're smart, quick learners with a solid work ethic."

Joyce looked over at Kim and asked, "Do you speak, or does your friend here do all the talking?"

"I can speak for myself, but I think Gina covered it. I am willing to work hard and hope you'll give me a chance. You won't be sorry."

"Do you know how many people I interview? They sell me a line of bullshit and don't show for the gig. I can't have that. I have too many high-profile clients, and they expect flawless service and exceptional food every time. And they get it, which is why we have established such a stellar reputation."

"I checked you out on Yelp," Gina said, "and that's why we're here. We want to work for the best."

Kim chimed in, "Tell you what, you give us a chance to work one of your events, and if you don't like our work, you don't have to pay us. How does that sound, Joyce?"

Joyce glared at Kim. "Well, aren't you the little negotiator? Fair enough. I need two more servers for a brunch tomorrow afternoon. It's at a private home in the Gold Coast, starts at eleven and goes to three. Wear black slacks, black button-down shirts, black nonslip shoes, and black neckties, and be sure to tie your hair back neatly."

"Looking forward to it. Thanks for the opportunity," Kim responded.

"You both need to fill out these forms. Bring them with you tomorrow." Joyce put them in an envelope, wrote the address of the brunch down on top, and handed it to Kim. "See you tomorrow. And don't wear perfume! Customers don't like it."

They quickly walked out, passing the redhead, whose cigarette ash was getting longer by the minute.

"We need to stop at Ross on the way to dinner and pick up our uniforms," Gina said.

Kim steered the car to the closest store. "What a brilliant idea, Gina. This is going to be a blast." After they bought the required outfits, they stopped for a bite at a cheap sandwich shop near Gina's apartment.

"Why don't you come over and we can run through the Rago tasting menu one more time, maybe watch a fun movie," Gina said.

"Sounds like a plan."

Sunday morning, Gina and Kim took the bus that dropped them off right near Astor Street, close to the address Joyce had given them. Gina knew this area was known for its beautiful mansions, ranging from elegant Victorians to Georgian homes.

"When these people die, they will have a fancy funeral, don't you think?" Kim said as she looked at the three-story mansion.

"Oh, yeah, they will. I wonder which funeral parlor handles this crowd. I bet Louie will know." Gina rang the bell and the doorman admitted them and directed them upstairs.

Joyce was standing by the kitchen door barking orders to her staff and gave Kim and Gina a once-over.

"Look at you two, dressed perfectly and early. Impressive. Put on one of our aprons." She pointed to a stack on the counter. "I need you to start lining the silver platters with lace doilies. Put the smoked salmon on a cucumber slice and top each with beluga and a dollop of sour cream. Be ready to serve as soon as the first guests arrive."

They both nodded and walked into the kitchen, where things were bustling. Servers were shining the champagne flutes, plating various appetizers, and organizing the countertop, which was filled with champagne, wine, and water glasses.

"Can anyone show us where the smoked salmon and beluga are?" Kim asked.

The chatter in the kitchen halted and a tall, thin balding male server wearing large black glasses glared at Kim and Gina. "Surely you jest. Joyce usually asks one of her more seasoned staff to execute that rather expensive dish. And just who are you?" He raised his thick eyebrows.

Before Kim or Gina could respond, Joyce interrupted, "Jared, please don't be a jerk. These are our new servers, Kim and Gina. Show them where everything is and don't get in their way."

Jared let out a loud sigh. "Oh, I see, new teacher's pets. You'll be lucky if you last one day with her." He walked to the Sub-Zero refrigerator, pulled out the ingredients, and slammed them on the counter. "Here you go, bitches. Good luck."

Gina swallowed, glanced over at Kim and then back at Jared. "Thanks and fuck you."

Thanks, Uncle Vinnie, Gina thought. She remembered how her uncle had always told her not to let anybody intimidate her. He'd always told her that if anybody gets in your face, you hit right back.

Gina shut out the kitchen noise and got to work with Kim. As they walked out with their platters, Gina noticed several kind nods and smiles from some of the other servers, which confirmed that she had made the right decision handling Jared. They likely thought he was a jerk too.

As Gina offered each guest a napkin and an appetizer, she couldn't help but notice the sparkling jewels adorning the women's fingers, wrists, and necks. They wore elegant, tailored silk dresses with stylish jackets paired with four-inch Jimmy Choo heels. *How can these ladies stand in these shoes? How can they even see with all that bling shining right in their eyes?* Gina did recognize several of the guests, high rollers who made their way to the *Tribune* social pages weekly. The men wore dark blazers with white pocket squares, crisp dress shirts, beige slacks, and designer loafers. Gina thought it was funny that they had big bucks but still looked like they were wearing school uniforms, but pricier.

Gina went about the rest of the event with a pleasant smile, eyeing each person as a future customer. She gave them a score from one to three, three being one foot in the grave, one likely around for a while. *There could be at least several new customers who will need a caterer at their funerals in this crowd.*

Joyce walked up to Gina and Kim once all the cleanup was done. "You gals available this week? I have four events and could really use your help."

Gina glanced over at Kim, who smiled. "Yes, we are. Would you send me the dates and places? By the way, I was wondering, do you also cater funerals?"

"Nope, not interested, and I have more business than I can handle with customers above ground."

Yes! One less competitor, Gina thought, resisting the urge to do a fist pump.

Kim piped in, "So, Joyce, it seems like you're satisfied—when can we expect a check?" Kim handed Joyce the envelope with the completed forms Joyce had given them the day before.

"Yes, you were both great. You'll get paid in two weeks; your hourly rate is ten dollars." Joyce handed them each forty dollars in cash. "And here's a tip. I like to reward good work." Joyce folded the paperwork and put it in her pocket. "My next event is this Tuesday at noon in the Pritzker Auditorium in the renovated Chicago Library. I'll need you both there by nine sharp. It's a sit-down lunch and there's a lot of setup."

"We're there—love that space," Kim said. "Who's the client?"

"It's a big fundraising event put on by the city. Anyone who's anyone in city politics, even our dear Mayor Borden, will be there."

"Thanks for the opportunity, Joyce. We'll see you Tuesday," Gina said.

On the bus ride home, Kim and Gina reviewed every detail about the day's event and how they would recreate some of the appetizers with less pricey ingredients.

"I got a look at the guest list and took a photo with my phone. We should check the obituaries every day and see if any of their relatives have died and where their funerals are held, maybe even crash a funeral or two," Kim said.

Gina smiled. "That makes me think of my uncle. He always checked the obituaries every day. Said if his name was in it, no need to get dressed. We will be tracking this crowd for sure; we'll be funeral crashers instead of wedding crashers."

They hopped off the bus near Gina's, and she drove Kim to her place. "I'll pick you up around ten tomorrow morning, and then we can drive over to Rago's. We're scheduled to have all the food out and ready by noon."

"Sounds like a plan, see you tomorrow, girl. What a fun day. Thanks for setting up the gig. I'm up for more of those, and I get paid more than my parents pay me." Kim got out and ran up the stairs to her apartment.

On Monday morning, Gina drove to Kim's and found her waiting outside. Her straight, long black hair was pulled back in a ponytail, and she wore a crisply ironed, white collared shirt, black slacks, and black tennis shoes.

"Looking very professional," Gina said, glancing over at Kim as she got into the car. Gina took in Kim's dimples, her beautiful smile, and her perfectly proportioned figure and had to tap her fingers on the steering wheel to distract herself. *Why am I feeling like this?* She redirected her gaze forward and steered her car back onto the street.

"You ready to go blow Rago's mind?" Gina asked.

"Let's go get 'em, partner," Kim said, and gently put her hand on Gina's arm.

Gina felt a little tingle down her spine. "I talked to Aunt Angie before I left. She was in good spirits and she can't wait to hear how it all goes. Once they taste her pesto sauce, we will have them in the palm of our hands."

Louie Rago greeted them both at the door. "Uh-oh, the poison twins are back."

"Thanks for giving us a second chance, Louie. You won't be sorry; we promise." Kim shook his hand.

"Before you make any more fun of us, taste this." Gina handed him a small white bag.

Louie raised his eyebrows. "What have we here?"

"Old family recipe, almond cookies—try one," Kim prodded.

"It's not that I don't trust you, but why don't you both take the first bite." He handed them a cookie. Kim broke it in half and handed one half to Gina.

Gina savored the buttery almond flavor and crispness of the cookie. "I'll eat yours if you don't want to risk it, Louie."

Louie took a bite of his as they intently watched his face and waited. "Hmmm, these are delicious. No one would have spit these out at your uncle Vinnie's funeral."

"Now, Louie, you know we didn't have any notice, and Aunt Angie didn't have any money to hire a caterer. We are so ready to feed you and all your colleagues."

"I let all the funeral directors know there's free apps and to bring their appetite. Believe me, these folks can pound down food. Last count, there'll be about thirty attending."

Gina handed Louie the typed menu. "Here's what we'll be offering."

Louie held the menu and read it out loud. "Caprese skewers with fresh mozzarella balls, cherry tomatoes with fresh basil, antipasto platter with sliced meats, cheeses, olives, and seasonal roasted vegetables, and garlic toasted crostini with pesto." He glanced over the menu at them. "I hope you're serving breath mints after this."

"We'll have several bowls of breath mints available. Of course, we'll set those out with the coffee and tea along with the almond cookies," Kim said.

"Wow, sounds like you gals covered all the bases. Everything sounds delicious. I'm guessing your aunt helped you with some of this."

"The pesto is her recipe," Gina said. "We won't let you down, Louie. We even did a test run on one of our harshest critics, and he was almost licking the plates."

"Louie, you wanted everything set up in the kitchen, right?" Kim had one foot out the front door.

"No, I think you should set everything up here in the lobby." He pointed over toward the side near the ladies' lounge. "I put some tables out there for you. I assume you'll handle the rest."

"You can go back and relax in your office—we've got this." Gina propped open the door so they could unload quickly. Louie's cell rang as he was walking back toward his office; Gina overheard his side of the conversation.

"Another musician who wants to be buried with his baritone sax. No problem—we've done lots of those funerals. I'm glad he doesn't play the piano," Louie said.

Gina laughed and then helped Kim set up with linen tablecloths, a few small flower arrangements, durable white paper plates, and napkins. They put everything out on colorful platters and stood back to admire their first official display.

"Looks pretty darn professional to me." Kim took her phone out to take a "before" picture.

Louie greeted the directors—men and women wearing black suits, some with ties—as they arrived. Gina and Kim waited in the small kitchen to the right of the lobby where they could see when the platters needed replenishing. They could hear some of the shop talk interspersed with audible sighs indicating that they were enjoying the food; the pesto bites were flying off the platter.

Gina kept rubbing her hands on her pant legs, carefully watching their faces as they ate. There wasn't one smirk, and more importantly, no one spat out a single bite.

Louie started the meeting in the main room, and Gina and Kim kept replenishing the food. Several of the attendees preferred to stand up in the back next to the buffet table and listen, which afforded them easy access to more food. Topics such as cremation, green funerals, a less toxic approach for the environment, and celebration-of-life-themed events were heavily discussed. There were the older directors, who shook their heads reflecting on the good old days, and younger ones, who embraced the new age approaches.

Cell phones went off sporadically, as death waits for no one, and the person receiving the call would step outside. At the end of the formal meeting, Louie invited Gina and Kim up to the front of the room.

"These are the young ladies who provided the free appetizers today. The name of their catering company specializing in funerals is Last Bite." Everyone laughed. "I'd like to thank them, and if you are so inclined to hire them to provide food at your events, they have cards on"—Louie glanced to the back of the room—"the empty table behind me. I believe we ate everything you brought." The room filled with applause and many comments.

"I'd like to hire them to teach my wife to cook!" one shouted out.

"Nothing like a delicious morsel or two to calm a saddened heart. Well done!" another director said.

Gina could not contain her smile, and when she glanced over at Kim, she saw her glowing. They practically pranced to the back, and as each person walked out, they handed them a mesh bag containing four almond cookies and their business card; not one person turned it down.

As they were cleaning up, Louie approached. "You both have my business. I will need to know that you can provide this level of service when I call you on a minute's notice. We can talk later; I have a funeral to arrange. Are you available on Wednesday?"

"Absolutely," Gina said.

"Great, I'll let you know what time to be here. It's a musician. You can let yourselves out. And, please, give my best to your aunt. She is a wonderful lady."

Kim handed Louie a small white box containing ten almond cookies, a sticker with their Last Bite logo sealing the top. "These are for you. Sometimes you just need a sweet treat."

"Thank you. I will enjoy these." He walked back inside.

After he left, they both jumped up and down. "We did it! We did it!"

They loaded all the empty containers, platters, and leftover paper products, and got in the car.

A knock came from the passenger's side window. Gina looked over and Kim put down her window. It was Louie with a small bag.

"Would you please give this to your aunt? It's Vinnie's World Series ring." Kim took the bag.

"We'll make sure she gets it," Gina said.

There was silence in the car as they drove away. Kim looked over at Gina and repeated, "We did it!"

Gina nodded. "Amen. And we're not working for anyone else but ourselves once this gets going. I can't wait to tell Aunt Angie."

Chapter 22

Angie awoke early Monday morning, city hall was closed so she got to stay home and had to orient herself. When she realized, *I'm home and in my own bed; I don't have to move*, she snuggled under her soft down comforter and glanced at her bedside clock. It was 6:28, right when she usually got up with Vinnie to make his breakfast and lunch and see him off to work. She reached over to the other side of the bed, searching for Vinnie's hairy arm, which she always gently patted to wake him up. Not finding it there, she sighed. "I miss you." She fondly recalled that after she sent him off to work with a smile, she'd straighten up the house, then get ready and go volunteer at her local church, making sure she got home early enough to have his dinner ready when he got home.

She took a shower, wrapped a towel around her body, and glanced in the mirror. Her face was thinner, and under her brown eyes, it was puffy, probably because she had cried herself to sleep the night before. *I'll need some cucumbers over these before my date tonight.* She removed the towel and glanced at her naked body in the full-length mirror on the back of the bathroom door. Angie sized herself up from the front and side. *I've definitely lost weight.*

At five foot two, she had always been slim, never one to sit still, and loved walking. She stepped on the bathroom scale: 115. Ten pounds down. She laughed out loud remembering what Vinnie would tell Ben: "I have to shake the sheets in the morning to find her; she's got the body of an eighteen-year-old." It always made her blush and Ben chuckle. Angie threw on her robe, went into the kitchen, and started the coffee, half the amount she'd always made when Vinnie was alive. She noticed all the subtle things now that she was home; being back in her own apartment brought back constant reminders of the life she had.

Angie relished all the creature comforts she had become so accustomed to: their comfy chairs with her handmade crocheted blankets, familiar paintings and photographs on the living room walls. The wooden sign mounted on the kitchen wall that Vinnie had bought her, engraved with "Home Is Where My Honey Is." Her own pots and pans were a welcome sight, given what she had used at Gina's, as was her treasured collection of fresh spices. She had missed cooking in her own kitchen.

After her coffee and some yogurt, she got dressed and started to deep-clean the place. It would take her the better part of the day, but she put on the morning TV game shows followed by her favorite soap operas as background and occasionally sat down to watch who was sleeping with whom. She could feel Vinnie's presence as she dusted and vacuumed and especially when she cleaned out the refrigerator. Cans of Old Style beer, a few jars of sauerkraut, which she would never touch, and various hot sauces he collected over the years. All those could stay for now. He would pour copious amounts of hot sauce on his morning eggs and then wonder every time why he had heartburn. Angie always made sure he had bottles of antacids by his TV chair, next to his bed, and in his glove compartment.

After she washed and put away all the clothes that she had at Gina's, she started to scan her wardrobe for just the perfect dress to wear to Gibsons.

As Angie pushed Vinnie's clothes to the far end of the closet, she leaned into one of his shirts and inhaled. When the spicy scent of his aftershave filled her senses, her chin started to tremble. It was near a month since his funeral and her life had changed in ways she could have never imagined.

She left the closet, sat on the edge of their bed, and patted her tender heart. *It will be a long time before this new normal sinks in. Be gentle with yourself in the meantime.* She let her tears flow, then blew her nose and went into the bathroom to rinse her face with cold water. She looked in the mirror. "Best foot forward, Angie. You get to go have dinner with Ralph. Vinnie would want you to." Angie remembered Vinnie's words: "If I buy the farm, I don't want you wearing black like those old Italian widow crows always do. You live on. Go for the gusto and have fun; I'll be smiling down from heaven." *Why did it have to be so soon, Vinnie?*

As she ran her hands through her hair, her thoughts returned to the contents of the storage unit. She hadn't decided yet if she would share what was in the storage unit with anyone, and she reminded herself she didn't have to do anything with that information right away. In the meantime, Vinnie had noted to move the journals that detailed all the payoffs into a safety deposit box at their bank, which she had done. There was enough evidence in there to put Mario away if he didn't give Angie the pension money.

She glanced at the kitchen clock; it was close to five. "Yikes, I haven't eaten lunch." She assembled a plate of cheese, crackers, and olives, poured herself a glass of wine, and put on some Tony Bennett. Angie nibbled on the treats and sipped her wine as she surveyed her dresses. Several made her feel like a million bucks.

Her most glamorous girlfriend, Wanda, had taught her to dress up even when she was low, and it had always worked. She took out a black fitted dress and a floral-colored silk one that flared out from the waist, deciding to wear the floral one. She chose her red pumps. She had bought the outfit in Vegas after Vinnie had gotten a big win. She showered, dressed, did her makeup, and even sprayed on her finest perfume, Black Opium. Humming to Tony Bennett, she was ready for her date.

Angie kept peeking out the window and checking her watch. Her cell rang. "Hello, Ralph, is everything all right?"

"I went to your niece's place and met Thad. I'm on my way over now. I have a driver for the evening so look for a black limo."

"Goodness, I forgot to tell you I moved back home. Sorry about that. Long story, I can share over dinner."

"Yeah, I should tell you I got in a bit of an altercation this afternoon. I have a black eye and broken nose, but it's fixed. There's a huge white bandage on my face so don't be alarmed, I'm fine. I'll see you in about ten minutes."

Angie gasped and touched her throat. "You poor man, we should cancel. You need to go home and take care of yourself, for goodness' sake."

"Seeing you will make me feel better, and I want to take you to Gibsons as long as you don't mind people staring at your date. I'll come up with a good story. I'll see you soon." He ended the call.

Angie poured herself a little more red wine. *I wonder who Ralph got in a fight with? I didn't take him for that kind of guy.* She stood by the window. It was a warm fall evening, and the leaves were just starting to turn shades of red, orange, and yellow. *And he met Thad.* She couldn't help but laugh a little thinking of a very stoned Thad greeting Ralph at the door.

The limo pulled up. Angie went downstairs and was greeted by the limo driver, who opened the door for her. "Good evening."

"Good evening to you and thank you." She slid in and then glanced over at Ralph. "Oh my God! Are you sure you want to go out? Your poor handsome face." She kissed her hand, then put it gently on his bandage.

"Gibsons is holding our reservation, and we're going to go directly to the table. I was hoping to have a cocktail in the bar, but we can have an after-dinner drink there if you'd like."

"Let's see how you feel; you've been through a lot. So, what happened?" Angie asked.

Ralph recounted the entire event, how gracious the hotel manager was, and how quickly he received medical attention.

"Who would walk into the Four Seasons, of all places, and punch you?" Angie asked.

"If I tell you, do you promise not to do anything about it?" Ralph said.

"Hmm, that's not fair, but okay," Angie said.

"It was Mario."

Angie crossed her arms. "That son of a bitch."

"Now, Angie, there's nothing you need to do. I'm handling this. Let's change the subject. How about your friend Thad?"

She laughed. "I'm sure he and his green-haired girlfriend were stoned."

"And then some. He offered me a joint, but I declined. He's a character."

"He's harmless and very kind," she said.

The limo pulled up in front of Gibsons and the driver opened the door. Angie and Ralph walked inside. Peaches looked up at Ralph and walked around the reception desk. "Oh my Lord, man. What the hell happened to your beautiful face?" She placed her hand on his shoulder, leaning in a bit to get a close look at the damage.

"I'm fine, Peaches, thanks for your concern. Could you get

us a corner table in the back so I don't have to explain to anyone else I might run into?" Ralph asked.

"You got it, baby." She handed the young, buxom hostess two menus with a table number in the back. They were seated without incident and perused the menus until their waiter arrived.

"Good evening, Mr. Conti, your usual?"

"Yes, please. Angie, would you like a cocktail?"

Angie sized up the handsome waiter who was sporting a waist-length, white linen jacket, crisply ironed shirt, and a tie secured with a Gibsons' tie bar.

"What a fancy work outfit," she said. "What would you suggest? I'm not a big drinker, maybe something a little sweet."

"How about a lemon drop? It's vodka with fresh-squeezed lemon juice and sugar around the rim."

"Sounds yummy."

Ralph leaned in toward Angie. "The steaks are the best in the city and the portions are very large. May I suggest we split a steak, baked potato, and some creamed spinach? We can enjoy their crab cakes as a starter."

"That sounds wonderful." Angie scanned the prices and consciously tried to keep her eyes from widening and her jaw from dropping, then looked up at Ralph and frowned. "Are you in a lot of pain?"

"Nothing a stiff martini won't fix. I decided to skip my pain pill; I don't like drugs."

When the waiter brought over their drinks, Ralph ordered their meal. He lifted his martini and said, "Here's to you, Angie. You're a strong, kind woman. I'm glad we met, and by the way, you look very lovely tonight."

They clinked glasses and Angie took a sip. "This is a delicious drink; you can hardly taste the vodka. I bet these can get you into some serious trouble." Fueled by her wine at home and now this, she let out a deep, gratifying sigh and added, "Thank you for the compliment. It has been quite an adventure helping Gina and Kim start a new catering company, and starting a new job—I've hardly had time to think."

Over the course of dinner, Angie explained Last Bite to Ralph and he chuckled at the creative name and the target audience.

"I know several businessmen who have funeral parlors throughout the Chicago area, and I'd be happy to introduce them to Gina and Kim when they're ready. I can't recall ever having any delicious food at any wake or funeral I've been to over the years, so they may really have something here."

"I think it's a brilliant idea. I'll be part of their team. I'm planning to help them with all the culinary aspects, having worked in several restaurants over the years. I know a thing or two about what folks like when it comes to comfort food." Angie enjoyed the last of her baked potato just as the busboy approached to clear their plates.

"I did go over to Vinnie's storage unit with Ben on Saturday, and while I can't share all the details, it seems I will be able to stay in my apartment and pay my bills. I ran across Mario's name many times in Vinnie's files, and if this information leaked, Mario's job with the city would be over and he could be behind bars. So if he's still messing with you, let me know."

"Thank you, I may need to take you up on that offer. Be careful out there. He's very connected to some dangerous people who wouldn't think twice about killing anyone," Ralph said.

"Don't worry about me; those documents are tucked away in a very safe place now. I made a visit to the bank."

"You know, Angie, I don't know much about you, just that Vinnie bragged about your cooking and, of course, he was a devoted husband."

"I must excuse myself to go use the ladies' room, then we can talk about me. I'll be right back." Angie stood up to leave.

"Do you like chocolate?" Ralph asked. "Their desserts are amazing."

"Yes, please, and a cup of coffee too."

Angie found the ladies' room upstairs. As she finished washing her hands, she saw Rebecca, the alderman's wife, enter. She glanced down at Rebecca's heels and thought, *That's Ralph's bathroom date from the funeral, all right.* She dried her hands, sure that Rebecca wouldn't remember their brief encounter outside City Hall, and Rebecca looked right through Angie as if she wasn't there.

Back at the table she was greeted with the biggest piece of chocolate cake she had ever seen. "This could feed an army! I hope you're planning to share some with me."

"I'm not much of a dessert person; I prefer a good glass of grappa after my steak. You can take home whatever you don't finish."

"If I was still living at Gina's, I'm sure Thad would make fast work of this. I'll do my best."

Angie watched Ralph sipping a clear liquid in a brandy snifter. "I know what grappa is; we always had it on hand at the Italian restaurant where I worked. It smelled and tasted like lighter fluid to me, but enjoy."

"This is much smoother; believe me, I've had the kind you're talking about. So, Angie, tell me a little about yourself before you met Vinnie."

Angie savored the sweetness of the creamy frosting and cake. After the drinks and the delicious meal, she was satisfied and a bit tipsy. She decided not to share about her first—before Vinnie—"loser" husband or her abusive father.

"I was born and raised on the South Side of Chicago near the steel mills. My father was a welder, and my mother was a homemaker. She was a very lovely woman and a great cook. I had two brothers who also worked at the mill after they graduated from high school. My parents were part of the community and were on a church bowling league. We'd spend a lot of time at the bowling alley. I'd do my homework and play some of the pinball games after I was done."

Just as Ralph was about to ask her a question, Rebecca appeared at their table and glared down at Ralph. "Another street fight, Ralphie?"

Ralph stood up and glared right back. "I have nothing to say to you, Rebecca. Have a good evening."

Angie held her breath as she watched them stare each other down for a few seconds.

"How's business, Ralph? I heard you ran into quite a bit of trouble today. Such a shame. To think you were on top, and now—well, it's not looking good for you, if I can believe the news."

Ralph didn't respond. He sat down and looked directly at Angie. "Anyway, tell me more."

Rebecca glanced over at Angie. "Honey, you look like a nice enough lady. You're not in this man's league and if I were you, I'd stay away from him. He's a big-time loser."

Angie stood up and leaned into Rebecca. "I don't recall asking you for any advice."

Rebecca's face turned red, and she backed away from Angie.

Ralph quickly stood up and got between them. "This is not the place for this. Rebecca, I think you should leave. Angie, please don't pay any attention to her—why don't you sit down and finish your dessert."

Angie clenched her fists and stood her ground; she was done being treated like a second-class citizen by anyone, including Rebecca—or Ralph. She'd had enough of that from her ex-husband and her father. "Ralph, I'm not sitting down and finishing anything. I am done with men telling me what to do. That is over. I know you both had sex in the bathroom at Rago's. Seriously, you two deserve each other. I'm too angry right now to be good company; I need to excuse myself."

Angie grabbed her purse. "Thank you for dinner, Ralph. I can see myself home."

She ignored him calling after her, stomped out of the restaurant and into a cab. Part of her was glad Ralph stood up to Rebecca for her, but she needed to stand up for herself. Her heart was pounding out of her chest, and she had to take a deep breath before she could tell the driver her address. Her cell phone kept ringing. She glanced down and saw Ralph's name and turned off the phone. *I'll speak to him after I cool down.* Thankfully she had a quiet driver, so she stared out the window. *Calm down and breathe, Angie.*

Once inside, she quickly undressed, threw her clothes on the bedroom chair, and poured herself a bourbon. She sipped it as she paced back and forth in the living room. "I am done with people treating me like a second-class person! Fuck them!" she yelled to no one.

After Angie was able to calm herself down, she turned her phone back on and saw ten missed calls and voicemails from Ralph and one from Gina. She listened to Gina's. "Hi, Aunt Angie, we did it! It was awesome and everyone loved your pesto bites. Louie is going to use us, and many of the other directors took our cards. We couldn't have done it without you. Call me. I'm home."

Angie decided to call Gina back but knew she couldn't handle a long discussion.

"Hey, Auntie, it was beyond our wildest dreams. Kim and I have lots of ideas for other menu items and were hoping we could meet you tomorrow morning before you go to work."

Angie took a long, deep breath and said, "I am so proud of you both. I knew it was going to be a success. I want to hear every detail, but I am exhausted. How about I call you tomorrow?"

"Are you okay?" Gina asked. "You sound stressed."

"Actually, I'm not okay. I had a terrible run-in with Ralph at Gibsons and I don't want to relive it now. I'll tell you everything after I get a good night's rest."

"I can come over now if you need me to."

"No, honey, I'm swearing off men. Who needs them anyway?" There was a silence on the other end. "Gina, are you there?"

"I am. I hear you. Did you happen to open that little housewarming present I left on your kitchen counter?"

Angie walked over and saw a large-sized box covered with colorful wrapping paper. "Should I open it when you're on the phone?"

"Yes, I want you to open it now."

Angie carefully unwrapped it so she could reuse the paper and opened the box. There was a book and an oblong box with a label that read "Good Vibrations."

"*Our Bodies, Ourselves*?" Angie read the cover of the thick paperback.

"Yes. This is the best book for a newly single woman like you. I read it when I was in high school. Open the smaller box."

"I never heard of this book, but I'll give it a try." She opened the smaller box and let out a gasp. "Is this what I think it is?"

"Yup, I got you your very own vibrator—might be a while before you have a boyfriend."

Angie took the phallic-shaped vibrator out of the box. *A little bigger than Vinnie*, she thought, and chuckled. "Well, I guess there's always a first time. I'll be doing some reading tonight and let you know how things go."

"Don't forget to put the batteries in it. I'll call you tomorrow. You take care and sleep well. I love you."

"Love you too, sweetheart."

Angie looked at the book and vibrator. "Should I watch a rerun of *Mike & Molly* or give this a go?" She turned off the living room lights, took her new presents into the bedroom, and closed the door.

Chapter 23

Ralph sat at the table in Gibsons after Rebecca laughed in his face and Angie stormed out. As he sipped his grappa—which he really needed now because he was having heartburn from all the drama—he kept calling Angie, but every attempt went straight to voicemail. He left one message after another, hoping that she would listen to them and give him another chance. Had he had sex with Rebecca at her husband's funeral? Yes. The only way she would have known is if she was in the bathroom. She must have been in one of the stalls when they were going at it. Embarrassing to say the least. Rebecca was a great lay, but not the kind of woman he wanted to be in a real relationship with. He was more attracted to Angie as a person; she was as solid as they came. She wasn't the looker that Rebecca was, but her beauty came from within, just like his late wife's.

"Would you like another grappa?" The waiter had been standing at his table for who knew how long.

"I'm sorry, I was in another world. I'll take the bill. I have fires to put out on the home front," Ralph said.

The waiter put the leather-bound folder on his table, bill inserted inside. "Whenever you're ready." Ralph immediately handed him his credit card without looking at the bill. As he left, Peaches came back around and gave him a hug. "You take care of that handsome face, sweetie."

Ralph walked home, changed, and kept calling Angie. No luck. *Leave her alone for a while; she'll cool down. I can't blame her for being mad. I'm as much to blame for the bathroom sex as Rebecca. Not my proudest moment.* He poured himself a bourbon. So far, the alcohol had kept his pain at bay, so he decided to continue holding off on taking the pain pills Dr. Hoffman had prescribed. He started to look at his emails on his laptop and stopped when he saw one from Eunice marked "URGENT." She rarely sent urgent messages, so he called her.

"Hey, Eunice, just saw your email. Sorry it's a bit late."

"No worries, boss. I didn't want to put anything in writing—best we don't leave any trace of discoverable evidence if we have to go to court."

Ralph's stomach clenched. "Court, for what?"

"Our friend Mario is stirring things up at City Hall. Even though he's on leave, he's not. He said to tell you the hotel didn't file a police report; manager thought better of it after Mario let him know about his connections. He threatened that if he doesn't get his job back by end of week, he's going to sue us, the city, and several of the contractors we work with."

"For what? We haven't done anything wrong."

"That's not his story. He said Vinnie told him everything about the deals you made with the city and the contractors. Said he's taking it to the press end of business Friday, unless he's back at work."

Ralph shuffled back and forth in his chair. "He has no hard evidence, only hearsay. I'll call him first thing in the morning to see what he thinks he's got and get back to you."

"Good idea. He is such a hothead. He's laid off, and I have a feeling he's going to make our lives miserable. How are you feeling?" Eunice asked.

"Not too much pain, I'll survive. The sooner I can get this bandage off my face, the better. I'll be in bright and early tomorrow. Hopefully we can get a few of those jobs back on track."

"Looks hopeful. I've been going back and forth with the city, and it does look like the projects for low-income housing will restart soon. Alderman O'Brien is pushing hard on this, in time for his reelection. Oh, and don't watch the news tonight. They're bad-mouthing us right now and the city is on top. I don't think it will last another news cycle."

"Sounds good, thanks for the heads-up. See you in the morning. Thanks for everything you do, Eunice. Would you please send a dozen roses to Angie Sortino with an apology note from me?"

"Will do. Got yourself in a little trouble, eh?"

Ralph sighed. "You could say that."

Ralph sipped his bourbon and went through his email. His head started to hurt so he decided to go to bed early.

Early the next morning, Ralph awoke with a pain on the side of his face and grimaced. "Oh shit," he said as he studied his reflection in his bathroom mirror: black eye, swollen cheek, the white bandage thankfully still intact. While he was making his morning coffee, he grabbed a bag of frozen peas and placed it gingerly on his face. *Ahh, relief.* The local morning news reported the usual traffic jams on all the major expressways leading into the city, and if he believed the weather report it was going to be a beautiful fall day. No mention of his company or the City Hall issue, at least in the first hour.

He checked his phone for any messages. None. Not even from Mario, so he called him.

"What the fuck you want?" Mario asked.

"Good morning, Mario, right back at you. You need to stop

threatening me and my staff. You have no idea what kind of information I have on you. You weren't the only one Vinnie confided in, so watch your back. I'm sure you'll get your job back, but there's nothing I can do about that."

"You have no idea what you're talking about. I better have my job back by end of the week, or else."

"Best of luck with that." Ralph ended the call and tried Angie again. It went straight to voicemail. He got ready for work and arrived early. Eunice greeted him at the elevator and let him know Alderman O'Brien was waiting for him in his office.

Ralph paused before he walked in. "Alderman O'Brien, what brings you here so early?"

Ralph watched O'Brien's reaction to his face. "Who did you piss off, Conti?"

"Not worth the time to talk about. What can I do for you?"

"It's come to my attention that you are the one responsible for stopping my projects, and I need them restarted today. Whatever you need to do, I don't want to know about, just get it done. Do you understand me?" O'Brien pointed his index finger close to Ralph's face. "You've been through a lot, Mr. Conti. You certainly wouldn't want anything more to happen to you. This can be a dangerous city, after all. Do we understand each other?"

"Loud and clear. To clarify things, City Hall shut down the jobs, not me. I plan to spend the day there, so hopefully you'll hear good news end of day."

"I'd better. It would be so sad to see your successful company be destroyed, a tragedy after all you've done to build it over the last twenty years." Just as he was walking out, he stopped and looked at Ralph. "I hear rumors you and my wife were having some fun. I don't give a fuck about her, never did. She's just arm candy and looks good in my campaign flyers. But since I'm running for reelection, you need to keep your dick in your pants and stay away from her."

"Not sure where you heard that from, but you have nothing to worry about from me. Have a good day, Alderman." *What was I thinking screwing his wife? Not a good idea on any level.*

Eunice entered the office and looked at Ralph. "Your poor face, boss. You have a meeting with the building department in an hour; it sounds promising. I've blocked out your day to deal with that. Our attorneys are available immediately should we need them."

"Just be sure the rest of our projects are going as planned, and work with our public relations rep to get something in the media about all the successes we've had, or something like that."

"Already done. It will be in the *Tribune* tomorrow morning. Good luck today; let me know if you need anything."

Ralph quickly reviewed the paperwork on his desk, signed the checks for the contractors, and headed downtown.

After the meeting at City Hall, three of the jobs were back on track and the other ones would likely restart by the end of the week. When Ralph asked the guy in the building department if Mario was going to be supervising them, the man asked him to kindly mind his own business. He made his way to Cookie's office, where Bud informed him that she was out most of the day and offered to make an appointment, which Ralph declined. "Would you please ask her to call me at her earliest convenience? It's important."

"Will do." Ralph watched as Bud jotted down his information and placed it on a tall pile of messages.

"I ran into someone on my way over here who was looking for a cleaning lady. Any idea where they can find one?" Ralph asked. He was going to find Angie one way or another.

"I'm not sure when the next shift starts, sometime after five I think, but their carts are down in the basement if you want to go down and check."

Ralph checked his watch; it was just about two. He decided he needed a leisurely walk down Michigan Avenue to clear his mind. Then he'd come back and try to find Angie. He glanced over his shoulder and noticed he was being followed by two guys, one short and thick, one tall and thin, both wearing black leather jackets. He picked up his pace, quickly went down the stairs near the Wrigley Building, bought a ticket on the Wendella, a tourist boat attraction, and was able to board before the black leather jacket guys could catch up to him.

He waved at them as he positioned himself at the back of the boat. A man's voice drew his attention.

"Hi, my name is Charlie, and I'll be your tour guide today. I work with our local architecture institute and have been trained to share all the details of the beautiful buildings that adorn each side of the Chicago River."

Ralph kept watching the pier as the men stood with their hands on their hips. *These thugs must be friends of Mario's—am I going to have to hire a bodyguard?* But as the boat kept moving down the river and he lost sight of them, he finally sat down.

Charlie did a great job of explaining the various buildings: Willis Tower, formerly the Sears Tower, Tribune Tower, and the Aqua Tower, built by a famous female architect, Jeanne Gang. So much breathtaking architectural history. Ralph regretted how he rarely made the time to discover just how amazing his own city was. He decided to find a seat, put his phone away, and enjoy the rest of the tour.

Charlie knew his stuff. When the tour ended after about two hours, Ralph gave him a twenty and continued to make his way down Michigan Avenue. It appeared no one was tailing him. He stopped at Shaw's Crab House, had some raw oysters, a salad, and a beer and checked his watch. Time to walk back to City Hall.

It was just before five when he entered the lobby and a security guard stopped him. "Sir, we're closed for the day. You need to leave."

"I'm here to meet my wife. She's a cleaning lady, and we have a family emergency."

"What's her name?"

"Angie Sortino."

Ralph watched as a fifty-something woman with dyed blonde hair and a penciled-in large brown beauty mark on the left side of her lip approached the guard.

"Hey, Lou, I know where Angie is. I can escort her husband."

"Thanks, Lorna, but he needs to talk to her and leave the building. You know the rules."

"I've been here for over twenty years, hon, I know." Lorna led Ralph into the elevator and pressed the button. "So, you're married to Angie?"

"Yup." Ralph kept his eyes on the elevator buttons.

"Glad to meet you, Vinnie Sortino. I thought you bit the dust a while ago. Maybe Angie has been lying all this time."

Ralph could see Lorna was staring him down. The elevator door opened to the basement and they both stepped out.

"Look, buster, I don't know who you are, but you're not Vinnie and I'm Angie's boss. What do you want with her? Don't you even think about fucking with my friend."

Ralph cleared his throat. "I'm not going to mess with her. I really need to see her. It's urgent and she won't return my calls."

"Hmm, sounds shady to me. You look like you've been roughed up pretty badly. We don't want you bringing your troubles here. Wait here and I'll see if she's clocked in and, more importantly, if she wants to talk to you. What's your real name?"

"Ralph Conti. She knows me."

"We'll see about that." Lorna left him standing at the elevators.

Ralph waited. He had to talk to Angie. After about ten minutes, Lorna came back alone.

"She wants nothing to do with you, Ralph. You are a—how did she describe you? Oh, right—you're a 'fucking asshole who only thinks about himself and sleeps around.' Does that sound about right?" Lorna cracked her gum and waited for his response.

"Part of that is true. I just need five minutes, and I promise I'll leave. Please, Lorna."

Lorna took her time, continuing to size him up. "You're the guy who was on the news. Your fancy company ain't doing so well right now."

"That's me, and our company is in trouble, for now. That's why I need to speak with Angie."

Ralph heard the squeaky wheels of a cart coming around the corner. "Angie, is that you?"

As she appeared, Angie pushed her trusty cart right into him. "Out of my way, Ralph. I have work to do, and I don't appreciate you coming to my place of business. Please leave now. I have nothing to say to you." Angie pushed the elevator button.

"Please, Angie, just give me a few minutes. Please."

"You have as much time as it takes me to get to the fifth floor." Angie looked over at Lorna. "If you don't hear from me in five minutes, call security."

"You got it, girl."

Angie pushed Hazel onto the elevator and Ralph followed her in. The elevator began to rise.

"Angie, I understand you're upset with me, and I don't blame you."

Angie stared at the elevator doors as they ascended.

Ralph tried another approach. "It's Mario; he's coming after you for Vinnie's pension. He will not stop until he gets your well-deserved money and takes down my company."

"I don't care about you or your company. I've got the goods on Mario. It was in Vinnie's storage unit. He won't stand a chance of getting anything once I show HR the evidence I have, thanks to my faithful—loyal—husband."

The elevator opened and Angie pushed Hazel out. Ralph followed. "Please, Angie, I'm begging you to please consider forgiving me. I need your help. Please." He got down on his knees.

"Please, Ralph, save it. I'm sure your lawyers will save your ass. I need to get to work."

Ralph stood up. "No, they won't. Mario is having me followed. He is very connected, and he will kill me and you without any remorse. You have to believe me."

Angie stopped and turned around. "You're probably right. And for what it's worth, I thought we were becoming friends. I can't help you. Please stay away from me. Stop calling me and please don't send me any more flowers; I threw them away."

"Angie, I need you to know that I have become fond of you since we've spent some time together. I have no interest in Rebecca, and I haven't seen her since I began to get to know you. I was hoping we could spend more time together," Ralph said.

"If you weren't such an idiot, Ralph, I could see giving you a chance. I'm sure there's a nice guy in there somewhere, otherwise Vinnie wouldn't have called you a friend. He was picky about who he called a friend. Now I need to get back to my job. Please leave." Angie glared at him as she pushed her cart away.

Ralph summoned the elevator and, as he was getting on, he gave it one last chance. "I'm not giving up, Angie. Take all the time you need." He arrived in the lobby and was escorted outside by a Chicago policeman.

The minute Ralph stepped outside, he heard gunshots. He quickly turned around to try to get back inside City Hall as more shots were fired by a slowly passing car. The officer was down, and Ralph felt a searing pain in his arm and back, then fell to the sidewalk. He could hear the officer yell into his hand radio. "Officer down at LaSalle entrance to City Hall. Officer down!"

The sounds of sirens filled the air. Ralph gazed up and saw red lights swirling in his peripheral vision and police cars arriving en masse. The last thing he remembered was a warm fluid running down his arm.

Chapter 24

While she worked, Angie sang along to the Frank Sinatra playlist that Gina had made for her. It was five hours long and always helped get her through her shifts. She was right in the middle of belting out "My Way" when she felt a tap on her shoulder that caused her to jump. Angie turned around. Seeing Lorna, she pulled out her earbuds and put her hand on her fast-beating heart. "My, you gave me a startle."

"Sorry to sneak up on you. You got some pipes there, girl." Angie watched Lorna's concerned expression.

"What's wrong? You look upset."

"I wanted you to know that the handsome fella you were talking to just got shot along with one of our cops, and they're taking him to Northwestern. I thought you could hear all the sirens. I didn't realize you were listening to your music."

"Oh my God! I have to go. I was so mean to him. I told him never to bother me again. I'm a terrible person." Angie took off her work apron, pushed Hazel to the nearest elevator, and pressed the button.

"Here, let me take your cleaning cart downstairs and clock you out. You go," Lorna said.

"Thanks, Lorna, I'll go down with you. I need to get my

purse and coat out of the locker. What have I done? He's a nice man. I don't wish him any harm." Angie's hands were shaking; she needed to collect herself.

Lorna and Angie got into the elevator to go down. It seemed like it was moving way too slow.

"Girl, you need to take a breath; you're white as a ghost. You don't want to end up in the hospital too."

Angie put her hand on her heart and took some slow, deep breaths. "Thanks."

"What were you two arguing about? The little I heard before I got on the elevator sounded intense," Lorna said.

Angie kept watching the numbers on the elevator panel move slow—too slow.

"Oh, I accused him of being a big jerk, banging the alderman's wife at Vinnie's funeral, then pretending like he was into me. Seriously."

"Why would he come all the way down here to find you and try to talk to you? You can't blame a man for wanting sex. That's all men think about," Lorna said.

"That's true, and it's not like we're dating, although he did take me to Gibsons, which was quite lovely until that bitch Rebecca O'Brien walked up to our table, turned up her nose at me, and told me I wasn't in his league." Angie felt her face heating up as she spoke.

"Honey, honey. Rebecca has a reputation of sleeping with all the pretty boys; her husband couldn't give a shit. He just wants the prestige and power of his position. I've been around here a long time, and this is basically standard practice for most of the aldermen."

The elevator opened to the basement and Angie hightailed it to her locker, grabbed her stuff, and whisked past Lorna. "Thanks so much, Lorna. I'll make up my hours tomorrow; I know there's no overtime pay."

"Don't worry about that. Just go see if you've got a live body to make amends to. I hope he's not badly hurt."

Angie hustled outside, hailed a cab to the emergency room, and walked through the crowded waiting area directly to the desk.

"I'm Mrs. Conti. They brought my husband in with a gunshot wound. Can you tell me where he is?"

"One minute, ma'am." The young ward clerk barely glanced up as she started to type things into her computer.

Please don't let him be dead. Please don't let him be dead.

Time was moving slowly; nurses and doctors were interrupting the clerk, and she was clearly trying to serve everyone.

"Mr. Conti is in the operating room. The waiting room for those patients is on the second floor. You'll need to sign in, and when the surgeons are done, they can find you there."

"Do you know anything?" Angie asked.

"I'm not at liberty to give you any information down here. You'll have to go to the surgical waiting room." The clerk started working on something else and didn't even look up.

Angie found her way to the surgical waiting area and rushed up to the desk. "I'm Mrs. Conti. My husband was rushed to the operating room. Can you tell me anything? Please."

The receptionist glanced up at her and then checked the computer. "All I can tell you is that he's in the OR now; I don't know anything else. You'll need to sit down and wait. There's coffee and tea over there." She pointed across the room.

Angie poured herself a cup of coffee and sat down. A short, thin woman sat down next to her; she was dressed in a chic business suit. "Excuse me. I couldn't help overhearing you. You're Mrs. Conti?"

Angie leaned in and whispered, "Not really, but I just had a huge argument with him and then he goes and gets shot. If he dies, I just don't know what I'll do."

"I'm Eunice, his office manager. Are you Angie Sortino?"

"Why, yes, however did you know?"

"He's spoken about you, and I knew Vinnie. He also spoke very fondly of you. I'm sorry for your loss."

"Let's hope this isn't another loss. This is all my fault. If Ralph hadn't come to see me at City Hall, he would never have been shot." Angie finally allowed herself to break down and cry.

Eunice gently patted her back. "You should know that he is fond of you, and of course, he loved your husband. It wasn't your fault. Ralph is a strong man; he'll make it through."

Angie wiped her eyes. "Do you know how bad the gunshot wound was?"

"All they told me was that there were multiple shots and that Ralph and the police officer were both rushed to the OR. I'm on record as his next of kin ever since his wife, Alice, died. You know, you favor her a little."

Angie's eyes widened. "Really? I thought for sure he was married to a real glamour girl. I remember Vinnie went to Alice's funeral; I had to get his black suit pressed. What did she die from, if I may ask?" Angie sipped her coffee. It was bitter even though she had put cream and four packs of sugar in it.

"She had ovarian cancer that spread throughout her body; it happened so fast there was not a lot they could do but keep her comfortable and put her in hospice. Ralph was very dedicated to her. They never had children and he lost his mother at an early age, so this was a big blow. I was really worried about him. All's he did was work day and night."

Angie closed her eyes. "I'm a terrible person; I had him pegged for a real playboy. He's so handsome and dapper, could probably get any lady he wanted." She shook her head. *I'm always judging people without knowing them.*

"Mrs. Conti, please come to the reception desk," said the clerk at the front desk.

Angie stood up and Eunice joined her at the reception desk.

"The surgeon said it's okay for you to go up to the recovery room waiting area and he'll give you an update on your husband's condition. Take the elevator up to the fourth floor and follow the signs."

Angie and Eunice briskly left and found their way. They were greeted by a nurse who escorted them into a small room with four chairs and a small round table. She closed the door behind her and joined them at the table.

"Please sit. I'm Patti Bumby and I work with Dr. Belman, who operated on your husband." She looked back and forth between Eunice and Angie.

Angie chimed in, "I'm his wife."

Patti looked over at Eunice. "And you are?"

"I'm his emergency contact," Eunice said.

"Okay, well, Mr. Conti did sustain a chest wound and a wound to his left arm. He lost a lot of blood. Thankfully, the bullet missed his heart, but the bone in his upper arm was shattered. Dr. Bailey, our orthopedic surgeon, is finishing that surgery up now. He'll be in the recovery room soon, and once he's alert, you can both come for a brief visit. Then he's going to be transferred to our surgical ICU."

A tall, thin man entered the small room. "Hi, I'm Dr. Belman."

"I'm Ralph's office manager, and this is his wife," Eunice offered before Angie could speak.

He sat down across from them. "Mr. Conti lost a great deal of blood at the scene. The EMTs were able to slow it down, but we'll need anyone in your family who's willing to donate to come into our blood bank. I repaired his chest wound and put a tube in his collapsed lung. A few more inches closer and the bullet would have hit his heart. The ortho team is finishing up; his left arm will be out of commission for some time."

"Is he going to be all right?" Angie asked. She pulled a used tissue from her pocket and did her best to dry her eyes, then blew her nose.

"He's in excellent shape. Once we were able to give him blood and fluids, he stabilized quickly. His vital signs are normal. He will be in quite a bit of pain, so after they make sure he's comfortable in the recovery room, you'll have a few minutes with him, but he's going to need a lot of rest."

Dr. Belman stood up. "If he's stable enough tomorrow, they can transfer him to the floor. I have another case, so I'll need to go; Patti can answer any other questions."

Both Angie and Eunice nodded. "Thank you, Dr. Belman," Angie said. Relief washed over her as Dr. Belman left the conference room.

"I think you should both go downstairs to the cafeteria and get something to eat. He'll likely be in the recovery room for about an hour. If you give me your cell number, I can call you when he's ready to see you," Patti said.

Eunice jotted her number down and gave it to Patti, and they made their way to the cafeteria in silence. After they selected their food—chocolate pudding for Angie and a bowl of soup for Eunice—they ate.

Eunice finally spoke. "So what happened when you saw Ralph at City Hall?"

Angie described their conversation; the more she told Eunice, the guiltier she felt. "I should have offered to help him with this Mario thing. I have solid evidence that could put Mario behind bars and I didn't even offer that. I was just an angry, old woman acting like a teenager."

"You need to be careful, Angie. These people are not playing around. Not only did they shoot Ralph, they shot a Chicago policeman. Nobody shoots a Chicago cop—even the mobsters know that. It tells me they're not afraid of anyone and likely have connections inside City Hall that make them feel deserving of immunity." Eunice paused. "I hope the policeman is okay. This whole thing is out of control."

Angie explained in vague terms about the storage unit and what Vinnie had stashed over the years. She admitted that she had put the documents in a safety deposit box at her bank and that no one else knew the exact contents or had a key. Angie rubbed her hands together as she studied Eunice. *My gut tells me I can trust her, and my gut is usually never wrong.*

"Now, I'm taking a risk with you, Eunice, in case they try to off me. I'm going to write down the name of my bank and give you the extra key the bank officer gave me. I don't know you at all, but you don't appear to be the kind of gal who would have dealings with these thugs. I don't want my family to get in harm's way, which would be where they would naturally go. They don't know we know each other, so they would never come to you."

"I think that's wise, Angie. I've been with Ralph for over twenty years. He's more than a boss to me; he trusts me with his life."

"Well, you may have to protect him once he leaves the hospital. Remember Marlon Brando in *The Godfather*? He almost didn't make it out alive. Thank goodness his son saved him."

They couldn't help but laugh at that.

"No wonder Ralph has a crush on you. You're a strong, capable woman with a good sense of humor, just like his Alice. She always had me laughing. She was a beautiful human being all around."

Angie reflected back at how mad she was at Ralph at Gibsons. She'd stormed out and ignored his calls. Then she was yelling at him to leave when he found her at work. *I'm not so sure he has a crush on me anymore, but it's a sweet thought.* She glanced at Eunice. "We've certainly locked horns in the short time we've known each other. I'm guessing Alice was a lot nicer than I am."

"I wouldn't say that. She never tolerated any nonsense. Sound like anyone you know?" Eunice grinned at Angie.

"Well, who knows what the future holds? One thing's for sure, I'm no Rebecca. What you see is what you get," Angie said.

"Right now, we need to get him home to recover and make sure his business stays afloat," Eunice said.

"I'm here to help in any way I can. I need to get my pension money, and my friend Lorna has worked at City Hall for a long time, so I know she'd help me navigate inside. And we both have keys to almost every office, conference room, and closet in the building."

Eunice's cell rang. "Hello . . . okay, we'll be right up."

Five minutes later, they were standing over Ralph, who was lying in the recovery room bed. Beeping sounds emanating from various machines filled the room. He had two IV lines, a chest tube, and an oxygen mask covering his poor bruised-up face, and the white bandage was still covering his nose.

Ralph slowly opened his eyes but didn't speak. Angie softly placed her hand on his cheek. "You poor man, I am so sorry I was a bitch to you. I am so sorry I got you into this mess."

Ralph slowly put his hand on top of hers and shook his head sideways. He winced as he lowered his arm and the nurse came to his bedside holding a syringe. "I'll need you both to leave. I'm going to give him something for the pain. We can call you when he gets transferred, but it'll be at least three hours. Do you have somewhere nearby you can stay?"

"Yes, thank you," Eunice offered.

"Will you remind him that we came by?" Angie asked. "Sometimes when they get pain meds, the memory is a bit foggy. I'm Angie and this is Eunice."

"I will. Not to worry. Before you go, we'll need you both to go into the conference room. There are several Chicago detectives here who want to ask you questions." She pointed down the hall.

Angie gulped. "Detectives?"

"I'm just the messenger," the nurse said, before turning to her patient.

Angie and Eunice sat across from the two detectives as they fired away questions. They directed the first set of questions toward Eunice, who summarized her twenty-year work history managing his office. The detectives turned to Angie.

"How do you know Ralph Conti?"

She swallowed deeply before answering. "He worked with my late husband, Vinnie Sortino, on building projects for the city."

"Why was he at City Hall this evening?" The detective glared at her.

"He had offered to help me with my husband's pension paperwork." She wasn't going to tell them about their fight.

The detective sat back in his chair and looked at Eunice and Angie. "Do either of you know why someone would want to kill him badly enough to shoot a cop too?"

Angie shuffled back and forth in her chair and looked over at Eunice. She didn't know if these were dirty detectives who had a Mario connection, so she left his name completely out of her answers.

Eunice answered, "Nothing like this has ever happened to him. I can't imagine anyone trying to kill him. He's a well-respected businessman in Chicago. Feel free to ask around."

Angie shook her head. Even though she was sure Mario was behind all this, she had no proof, so she kept her own counsel. "I have no idea, but I sure hope you find whoever did this to him and the policeman."

After a few more questions, the detectives asked them for their phone numbers and home addresses and instructed them to stay in town in case they needed to contact them.

Cool, crisp fall air greeted them as they stepped outside the hospital. Angie took in her first long, deep breath since this whole thing had started. She gazed down at her wristwatch. "Oh my gosh, it's almost midnight. My family will be worried about me." She always called either Gina or Connie to let them know she arrived home safely, as she usually took a city bus around eleven thirty each night when she was working on the night shift. Sure enough, when she glanced down at her phone, there were multiple missed calls and unanswered texts from both of them.

"Why don't we go to Ralph's?" Eunice said. "I have a key, and it's a ten-minute cab ride from here. You can return your calls and texts, and I can check my work emails. With all this bad press, no telling how they're going to spin this in the media."

They hopped in a cab and entered the lobby of Ralph's condo. Hank, the doorman, recognized Eunice right away. "Where's the big guy?"

"He's been in an accident and is at Northwestern. I can't give you the details, but we're going to wait here until they call us and let us know. He's in the surgical ICU."

"Whoa, what a day he's had, first his nose, now this. You ladies go upstairs and relax. I'm sure you've had one hell of a day and night. I'll need you both to sign in; it's protocol."

When the elevator doors opened into his penthouse, Angie felt her eyes widen as her jaw dropped. "Wow, this is just like those places on *Lifestyles of the Rich and Famous*. It's beautiful and homey at the same time."

Eunice walked into the living room and put down her briefcase. "Can I get you something to drink? He has every liquor known to man. I'm having some of his bourbon."

"Do you think we should drink since we're going back to the hospital?"

"Absolutely. Name your poison." Eunice took crystal glasses off the shelf and poured herself a couple fingers.

"That looks good. I'll give it a try, thanks." As Angie sipped her bourbon, she slowly made her way over to each bookshelf where photos of Ralph and local and national dignitaries were arranged.

Angie picked up a photo of a younger Ralph standing with Harry Caray, who was holding a microphone. Every loyal Cubs fan knew Harry Caray as the best announcer to ever call a game. "Did Ralph sing the seventh-inning stretch with Harry? It's always been a dream of mine to sing it with Bill Murray. Vinnie almost made it happen, but some celebrity showed up so we got canceled."

"Yes, Ralph sang right along. He loved Harry back in the day, even invested in his restaurant. Ralph isn't a good singer. Thank goodness Harry drowned him out." Eunice was sitting on the couch pecking away at her keyboard.

"I'll go in the dining room and call my family, so I don't disturb you," Angie said.

Eunice nodded.

Angie called Connie, who picked up immediately. "Where the hell are you? The news has been covering the shooting and Gina and I are going nuts. The media is not releasing any details or names except a cop was shot."

Angie let out a long sigh. "It's been a hell of a night, Connie.

I'm safe but I can't really tell you a whole lot more until Chicago PD gives me the okay. The less people know, the better. I guess they want to try to figure out who did this. It's scary, is all I can say, and I'm so glad I have you and Gina. I'll let you know when I get home. It's going to be late." She didn't want to tell Connie she was at Ralph's as that would open up another can of worms.

"You be careful now. We love you. Want some good news?" Connie asked.

"I'd love some," Angie said.

"Last Bite is ramping up. Gina needs you sooner than later; they're already getting calls from the funeral parlors, two events tomorrow. They're going to have to expand their menu."

"That's the best news I've heard all day. Would you call Gina and let her know I'm fine? I'm so happy for them."

"And you too. Once this thing starts picking up speed you can quit that cleaning job. Love you, Ang."

"Love you too." Angie slumped back into the dining room chair. *If I'm still alive I can help. What if they come after me? Who can I trust?* She glanced across the room at the wall in the finely appointed dining room and saw a beautiful oil painting of a woman who had to be Alice. She was beautiful in a simple way, with sparkling blue eyes, short black curly hair, and a sweet smile. Some of her features were indeed similar to Angie's, and she felt a tingle down her spine. *Maybe he does have a crush on me.*

Angie glanced around the dining room and kitchen and then went back into the living room. Eunice was still at it on the computer. Angie slowly went from photo to photo. "Wow, he knows President Obama?"

"He does. He worked closely with him on his Chicago campaign. What a gift to our country."

Angie noticed Steuben crystal pieces placed on several shelves between the photos. She could tell Eunice was deeply engaged in her work so decided to sit down and put her feet up.

"Angie, honey, wake up. The hospital called. We can go over and see Ralph. We can't stay long."

Angie blinked and rubbed her eyes. "Gee, I must have fallen asleep. What time is it?"

"It's almost two. I called down and the doorman is calling us a car. They're going to drive us to the hospital and then after take us both to our homes."

They arrived at the surgical ICU and were escorted to Ralph's bedside where he was sleeping sitting up, hooked up to all kinds of wires and machines.

"Hey, boss." Eunice approached first. "What am I going to do with you? First your nose and now this. I'm so glad you're going to be okay. We spoke with your surgeon; you're not going to be in an arm wrestling contest with your left arm for a while."

Angie noticed the genuine affection in Eunice's voice. If this good woman regarded Ralph with so much respect after more than twenty years of knowing him, maybe Angie had been rash in her judgment.

He grinned at Eunice and then looked at Angie.

"Oh, Ralph, I am so, so sorry. This is all my fault." Angie's chest tightened when she saw all the bandages, IV lines, and monitors he was hooked up to.

"I promise I'll make it up to you; I've got the goods on Mario. We are going to take him down," Angie said.

Ralph grinned and gently shook his head back and forth. "Wait . . . until . . . I'm . . . better—promise me." He uttered the words slowly. The beeping sounds on his monitor started to go faster and the nurse came to his bedside.

"I'm sorry, ladies, you'll need to leave now. Mr. Conti has been through a lot with the blood loss and two surgeries today. He needs to rest. Hopefully you can come by tomorrow, but please call first in case he has a rough night."

Angie glanced back at Ralph. He was already asleep. She and Eunice left. *I was so angry with him and now I hate to leave his side.*

The car was waiting for Eunice and Angie downstairs. They exchanged few words as the driver took them toward Eunice's home first. She lived off Diversey, not too far away from Gina.

Before Eunice got out of the car, she turned to Angie. "Don't blame yourself, Angie. There was no way you could have known what was going to happen. Mario has been after Ralph since Vinnie died." She handed Angie her card. "I wrote my personal cell number on the back. Call me tomorrow and we'll talk. I will not let that bastard take Ralph down or the business we've built together. You get some rest."

Angie touched Eunice's hand. "Thank you for everything. I'll call you in the morning. Good night."

It was almost three when Angie got home. As she walked into her bedroom she saw the book and vibrator on her bedside. *Not tonight. I'm too tired.* She showered and fell into bed. Before she turned out her light, she texted Ben; she felt safe with him living down the hall.

I need to see you first thing in the morning. I need your help.

Chapter 25

Constant beeping noises brought Ralph back from the bizarre dream he was having. A nurse was at his bedside tapping his shoulder.

"Mr. Conti, wake up. You're having a bad dream. Your heart rate is too fast. Mr. Conti, can you hear me?"

Ralph opened one eye, then the other. A woman was standing over him, a stethoscope around her neck, her long brown hair pulled back. "Where am I? What happened?" He moved around in the bed and winced. "Ouch, what the . . ." He glanced down at his arm and then at the nurse. He touched his chest and felt a tube protruding out. "What the hell!" His lips were dry, it felt like there was cotton in his mouth, and his throat was sore.

The nurse lightly touched his right arm. "You're in Northwestern Hospital. You were shot at City Hall yesterday. You have a badly damaged left arm and a chest tube. You lost a lot of blood, and you were in the operating room for a long time. The doctor said you are in such good shape that you'll likely bounce back quickly."

Ralph opened both eyes widely, looking all around and down at his body, which was covered by a white hospital blanket. He lifted his right arm slowly; there was an IV in it. He tried to move his left arm and let out a yell. "Holy shit! What day is it? What time is it?"

"It's noon on Wednesday. How bad is your pain, one being nothing, ten being unbearable?"

"It's a ten, but I have to be at the office before my business implodes. I was shot? Who the hell shot me?" Random thoughts pulsed through his mind in no particular order. Sharp pains shot from his left arm up into his chest and neck.

"I'm going to get you something for pain, then we'll sit you up in bed." The nurse left and was back quickly with a syringe. As she pushed the medication into his IV, she said, "You should feel some relief right away."

Ralph felt a lightness in his head and then his whole body relaxed. "Wow . . . that was fast."

The nurse brought the back of the bed up to a seated position and adjusted the pillows behind his head. "Sometimes life is better with the help of pharmaceuticals. After you sit up for a while, we'll get you out of bed and walking. I'll be back in about twenty minutes." She gave him a glass of water.

"Sounds good to me, I have to get out of this place sooner than later. I have a business to run. Do you happen to have my cell phone?"

Before she could answer, a voice from the doorway responded. "I have your phone, boss. I knew you'd be going through withdrawals. We were pretty worried about you. Glad to have you back." Eunice walked over to Ralph and handed him the phone.

"Eunice, good to see you." He took the phone.

As the nurse was leaving, she looked at Eunice. "I'd be careful about leaving that phone with him while he's getting pain medication. He may not remember who he talked to or what he said."

Ralph watched Eunice's facial expressions as she studied him from head to toe.

"You look like you've been to war, Ralph. Angie and I were so worried about you."

"Angie knows I'm in here?"

"She feels awful that you got shot. She says it's all her fault. She was a mess last night. We both waited up until you were transferred to a bed. We didn't get home until after three this morning."

Ralph let out a long sigh. "I don't think she should come anywhere near me until we get this Mario thing resolved. I'm concerned for her safety. I think Mario likely hired a hit man to do this. He may go after Angie."

There was a knock at the door. "Mr. Conti?"

Two men in overcoats walked in. The taller one spoke. "We're detectives with Chicago PD. We need to ask you a few questions."

Eunice turned. "He's on pain medication and he just got through some intense surgery. Do you think it's really a good time to talk to him?"

"That's okay, Eunice. I'm a little loopy but I can talk." Ralph sat up a little more.

"I'm Detective Mars. We need to hear what happened yesterday, to the best of your recollection. No detail is too small, including who you think did this to you."

Eunice took a seat by his bedside. "Do we need to call our attorney?"

Mars shook his head. "Nice to see you again, Eunice. I don't think that's necessary."

Ralph looked at Mars, then Eunice. "You two know each other?"

"Detective Mars and his buddy here interviewed Angie and me last night while you were in the recovery room."

Ralph swallowed. He took a long sip of water, then looked at Mars. "These women have nothing to do with what happened to me. Please leave them alone."

"We're the detectives on this case, Mr. Conti, and we will speak to whomever we need to. We have an injured Chicago policeman, and whoever is after you is not going to stop. Nobody gets shot in front of City Hall. These people mean business."

"I may not recall anything with much accuracy," Ralph said.

"Why don't you tell us what you remember? We can always come visit you again if we need to."

Ralph explained that he was at City Hall checking on the status of his projects and then walked outside and heard shots.

"Any reason why someone would want you dead, Mr. Conti? Whoever did this appears to have been targeting you. The policeman—who is recovering, thankfully—may have just been in the wrong place at the wrong time. But again, it appears that whoever did this was intent on killing you."

Ralph wasn't sure he should mention Mario, then went for it. "Mario Longetti, who works for the city. He accused me of having him put on leave, punched me in the face when I was at the Four Seasons. I'm not sure if it was him or he had anything to do with it, but let's say he's not my biggest fan." Ralph watched the detectives' faces to see if either of them reacted to Mario's last name. No telling who was on the take. They were both wearing poker faces.

After fifteen minutes of questions, they told Ralph he needed to stay local. Ralph raised his eyebrows and pointed to his arm and chest tubes. "Not going anywhere fast."

As the detectives left the room, with a glance back, Detective Mars said, "Take care of yourself, Eunice."

Eunice returned his smile, her fingers never leaving her laptop.

The nurse returned, helped Ralph out of bed, attached his IV and chest tube drainage bag to a pole on wheels, and helped him walk around his room first, then down the hall and back.

The pain medication did the trick and made his walk easier. He sat in the high-backed chair as the nurse's aide made his bed and tidied his room. Eunice worked on her laptop all the while.

After he was settled back in the bed, he turned to Eunice. "Give it to me straight. Do we still have a company? Are any of our jobs back up and running?"

"You know that two jobs went back online before this shooting happened, and there are three more that should start in a couple days. The investors all send their best, but you know all they really care about is their money. Our lawyers have drafted the necessary documents to assure them that if they do incur any losses, we have reinsurance that will take care of things."

Ralph let out a sigh. "Please, let Angie know I'm on the mend and I'll be in touch."

"Angie did say she was going to get some papers Vinnie left her out of her safety deposit box, and she and her friend Ben were going to meet with someone at City Hall about her pension and Mario."

"Please tell her to be extra careful, Eunice. Mario is connected inside and outside City Hall, as you well know. I would hate anything bad to happen to Angie or Ben." Ralph closed his eyes for a moment. He was so tired.

"I'll take care of things, boss. I've got a handle on this. Get some rest." Eunice collected her things and left him dozing off.

Ralph spent the rest of the morning and part of the afternoon resting, interspersed with several walks up and down the hallway. He spent some time getting an X-ray to check the status of his lungs, and his pulmonary team came in to inform him that his chest tube could come out in the evening. If he did well, he might well be discharged the next day as long as ortho signed off on it. His lungs were in excellent shape since he was an avid runner, so he was healing well.

Eunice came in around dinnertime and brought him a fresh chopped salad and garlic bread, which he enjoyed. "Thanks for dinner. Looks like I may get out tomorrow. Ready to sleep in my own bed without a million interruptions. There's no sleeping in a hospital, I learned that when I was with Alice."

"I called Angie and told her you wanted her to know it wasn't her fault and that you'd call her in the next couple days. She's making up time at her job and said she's planning on seeing you with her own eyes. Apparently she didn't quite believe me."

"Sounds like Angie." Ralph cleared his throat. "I hope she'll talk to me now. The last time I saw her she said never to speak to her again."

"Why don't you wait until you get home and get settled to call her," Eunice said.

"Good idea. These pain meds are doing funny things to my mind, and I sure don't want to make her mad again. She's got quite a temper," Ralph said.

"Sounds like a plan. I'll see you tomorrow."

As Eunice was leaving, one of the residents from the pulmonary team walked in.

"I'm here to remove your chest tube, Mr. Conti. Your lung looks clear."

The rest of the evening went without incident and Ralph only needed pain medication once during the night. He was discharged the next morning, and Eunice brought him home after all the paperwork was completed and follow-up appointments were made. He was back in his apartment, tucked in bed, by lunchtime. Eunice helped him get settled and then went back to the office. Several large flower arrangements adorned his living room, one from his attorneys, one from the investors, and bright yellow daisies from Angie. He read her note. *Some fresh flowers to brighten your day. Hope you're feeling better. Warmly, Angie Sortino.*

He called Angie. "Hi. Thanks for the flowers, that was very thoughtful but not necessary."

"This whole thing was my fault; the least I can do is send you flowers."

"Angie, I want to be clear with you, this is not your fault. Mario is after me, and I don't think he'll stop until I can figure out a way to handle this. It's my problem, not yours. I'm home now and recuperating. How about you come by tomorrow for lunch before you go to work."

"Mario is my problem too. He took my pension money and he's not getting away with it; we've got the goods on him. By the time I get done with him, he'll be working on a chain gang. How about we work together on this."

Ralph started to laugh and then stopped. It hurt too badly. "I don't think they have chain gangs in prison anymore, but I like where you're going with this. I'm happy to be your partner in crime on this, Angie."

"Good, we're in agreement then. I'll bring lunch and we can map out a plan. See you tomorrow around noon. I'll be with Gina in the morning. Her new catering business is booming. They can't keep up with all the funerals they're booking."

"Well, my aunt Marge always said, 'Every day above ground is a good one, but when it's your time, it's your time.'"

"Thankfully it's not your time. Take it easy. I'll see you tomorrow."

Ralph took a few naps during the day, walked around almost every hour, his arm in a sling, taking deep breaths as instructed and blowing in some contraption that had three balls in three plastic tubes. *This is fun. Let's see how high I can get them to go this time.* He checked his email with one hand and reviewed some new potential projects. Good thing he wasn't a lefty, or he wouldn't be able to do anything. He looked in the mirror and startled himself for a moment. He'd been so focused on his lungs and arm that he had temporarily forgotten about the big white bandage over his nose, and his blackening eyes. He looked like a battered raccoon. *What a train wreck.* He called Dr. Hoffman, the plastic surgeon who fixed his nose, and asked when he could remove the packing and bandage. She informed him that she would not be removing anything for now, instructing him to not do it himself. He could come in at the end of the week and she would assess his progress.

Eunice called Ralph at the end of the day. "I saw your emails; you are not supposed to be working. I've got things covered here. Four of the ten jobs are back on track. The unions were happy with the downtime pay for their teams. Seems that one of the *Tribune* reporters was covering another story at the hospital when you were brought in, so you made the papers again. No details, just that you were shot, gunman at large, but no mention at all of the cop. Detective Mars told Angie and me that they didn't want the media to print too much about a policeman being shot, didn't want to rile up the public."

"Great, just what we need. More stories in the paper," Ralph said.

"I've gotten some calls from your colleagues genuinely concerned about you and sending you their best wishes for a speedy recovery. They offered to help you in any way they can. Other than that, all is well in the construction world. Now get some rest."

Chapter 26

It had been nonstop action for several days while Gina and Kim had worked for the catering company and hosted the funeral directors' meeting. Now they were getting calls almost nonstop.

On Friday morning, Gina's cell phone rang at 6:20. She pulled her warm comforter over her shoulders and answered. "Mom, are you kidding me, calling this early?"

"I needed to talk to you before your crazy day got started. I just read in the morning paper that Ralph, Angie's Ralph, was shot at City Hall and was hospitalized. That's why she didn't call us back. She called me when she got home at about three this morning. She's fine but exhausted. She couldn't tell me anything when we spoke because this is being investigated, but the paper leaked the story."

"Holy shit, poor Aunt Angie. She sure doesn't need this kind of chaos after all she's been through. I'll call her after I get up and have some coffee. Thanks for letting me know, Mom. I'll call you tonight. Love you."

"Love you too, honey. Be safe."

Gina got ready for her day, had several cups of coffee, and

then called her aunt. She was energized and ready to get prepared for her two gigs that day.

"Good morning, Aunt Angie. First, how are you and how's Ralph? My mom said he got shot. It's in the morning paper."

"So much for not saying anything to anyone. The Chicago detectives said this case was under investigation."

"Are you okay?"

"I'm fine. I was working at City Hall on the fourth floor when this all went down; I had no idea. Ralph's on the mend. Don't know about the policeman, but it was really terrifying. It happened after I told him to go to hell. Feeling pretty guilty right now. Thank God he's okay. Bumpy night for me." Angie shared all the details.

"Thank goodness you weren't standing next to him, or they would have shot you too. Sorry to hear about the cop—the newspaper left that part out of the story. Do you have any idea who might have done it?"

"If I was a betting woman, I'd put my money on Mario or one of his thug friends, but honestly I don't have a clue. I just feel so guilty. If he hadn't come to try and talk to me, he wouldn't have gotten shot."

"It's not your fault. How could you possibly have known someone was going to shoot him? Don't beat yourself up. And maybe I can help cheer you up. Are you ready for some great news?" Gina asked.

"I'm more than ready for good news. Tell me, tell me."

"You have your first official customers who want jars of your pesto; those bites were a huge hit at the funeral directors' meeting. Ben is finding me a kitchen and some storage space through his sister. We have two gigs today and we could really use your help, if you're up to it. It sounds like you may need some downtime, though, so don't think twice about saying no."

"Thanks, honey, but I need to take my mind off things and what better way than to come over and work with you and Kim. After all, it's my business too. I'll get ready and I can be there in about an hour. You need anything?"

"No, just some more of your pesto and a few new appetizer ideas, so put on your thinking cap on your way over. Take it easy, okay?"

"I will. I have lots of ideas, honey, and if you can have Kim pick up some mason jars and lids, we can make a huge batch and get those delivered to our new customers, strike when the iron is hot."

"I'll text her now; she's out shopping. See you soon," Gina said.

Gina cleared all the counter space in her kitchen and took the food processor out so it would be ready when Kim and Angie arrived. She perused the *Scratch? My Ass!* cookbook and flagged a few more easy recipes that could be cheap finger foods. She chuckled at the names of the items: Triscuit appetizers that consisted of Triscuits, hamburger dill pickles, and American cheese, assembled and warmed in the oven until the cheese melted. *Even Thad could make these and I bet they taste good.* There was a simple quiche recipe with five ingredients and they could bake them in small muffin pans. When she got to the desserts, she found a recipe for dump cake, where you literally dumped the six ingredients into a baking pan, stirred, and baked. *We'll come up with a fancy name for this and cut it into finger-sized bites.*

Gina was tagging each recipe so she could review them with her pit crew when her cell phone rang. She looked at caller ID; it was her boss at Panera. She gulped and then answered. "Hello."

"Gina, you were supposed to be at work early this morning. What happened? I thought I could count on you, of all the employees, to show up on time," her boss said.

Acid started to make its way up to her throat. "I'm so sorry. I've been preoccupied."

"Well, you've never done this before, so why don't you come in now and work late?" he asked.

When Gina paused to think about going to work that day, her stomach dropped. *I shouldn't quit until our business is off the ground, but I just can't go back in there. Plus, we have all these gigs today, so even if I wanted to, I just can't.*

After a minute, she told her boss, "Thank you for the second chance, but I think it's best that I quit now. I'm starting a catering company, and it's taking off. I'll swing by later today and drop off my apron and keys."

"I just quit my job, so this business better succeed," Gina mumbled to herself as Kim was walking in the door.

Kim looked over at her. "You talking to yourself again? Help me with the groceries and tell me what's going on."

Gina and Kim finished unpacking all the groceries and Angie came in. "I'm here to help."

"Yeah, our mastermind partner is here," Gina said. "We really need to make this business work because I just quit my job. I completely spaced that I was supposed to work this morning. My boss was going to give me a second chance, but I said no."

"They don't deserve a smart entrepreneur working there anyway," Angie said.

Gina walked over to Angie and threw her arms around her. "How are you doing? You've been through a lot with the shooting."

"Gina told me all about it. Are you going to be okay? How scary," Kim said.

"I'm better than I was yesterday at this time, just grateful Ralph is okay. Thanks for asking. Let's get our aprons on and get this show on the road." Angie put on her apron and started making the pesto, and Kim made a batch of the almond cookies. Gina reviewed the menus for the wake that afternoon and the menu for Louie's friend's granddaughter's First Communion. The three women worked over the course of two hours, listening to the Tony Bennett and Lady Gaga duet album, packing each big bin with the food.

After Angie prepared ten jars of pesto sauce and three huge batches for the bites, she removed her apron and washed her hands. She looked over the new recipes that Gina had tagged from Mindy's *Scratch* cookbook, saying, "I think they're all winners. Why don't you test drive them and see if they're as easy and tasty as they sound. If they pass the test, then let's add them to the menu options, with new names, of course. You're both doing a great job, and keeping an eye on low-cost, delicious items is key to putting more money in your pocket."

"Good idea. Where you off to?" Gina asked. "I thought you didn't start working until three? It's only noon."

"I have one stop on my way to work; I'm bringing Ralph lunch at his apartment. I'll be back tomorrow bright and early."

"Ralph's apartment in the Gold Coast?" Gina asked.

"That's the one. It's quite fancy. I was there waiting with Eunice until Ralph got transferred out of the recovery room. How many events do you have tomorrow?" Angie asked.

"Just one, another funeral at Rago's," Kim chimed in.

Angie went to put the pesto sauce in the fridge, but there was no room. "What's with all this potato salad? It looks delicious."

"My mom went for it and we only needed a big bowl for today's Communion party. Can you take one to work? I bet the cleaning staff and guards would love it," Gina said.

"Sure, everyone loves free homemade food. I'll take the smaller one. Listen, the pesto sauce doesn't have to be refrigerated until it's open, so I'll leave the jars on the living room table."

Angie pulled out the potato salad from the fridge, put it in her shopping bag, and walked toward the door.

"I'll let you out, Aunt Angie." Gina walked her to the door and opened it. "The potato salad isn't completely homemade. My mom bought it from Jewel—it was on sale. I doctored it up, took a cue from the *Scratch* cookbook. I tasted it. Not bad for store-bought and it saved us a lot of time." Gina kissed her aunt on the cheek.

Angie left laughing. "I love your mom. I'll see you both tomorrow; good luck at your events today. Knock 'em dead."

Gina and Kim both laughed and continued prepping and packing for their events. Just as Kim was ready to leave for the Communion party, she turned to Gina. "Do you really think I should serve this potato salad? What if someone notices it's from Jewel?"

"Just smile and say, 'Thanks, that's a compliment.' Do not confirm or deny," Gina said.

"Got it. Can you help me put all this in my car?"

Gina sent Kim off to the event, and as she was walking back in, she saw Ben parking his car.

"Hey, Ben, thanks for coming by and helping me with this wake. The funeral home is near Rago's, but he couldn't help them 'cause he's booked."

"You got it. I spoke with my sister and she said there's a place that would appreciate you renting some of their space and we can see it this afternoon. Maybe we can go after the wake."

"Absolutely, we need space—like now."

Ben and Gina packed the car and headed over to the wake.

"Shit, I forgot to stop by my old job. I have to give them their stupid apron and the keys. I quit today," she said to Ben. "Can we swing by there real quick?"

Ben drove and stopped at Panera, where Gina ran in and came out in five minutes.

"How did it go?" Ben asked.

"I apologized for no notice and thanked him for the opportunity and wished him and the team well. Didn't burn any bridges. Ya never know if I'll need to buy some of their stuff for an event in a crunch."

"Good thinking," Ben said.

Ben and Gina set up the food table for the wake, made sure everything was just right, and Gina tapped the grieving wife and let her know she'd be back in about an hour to check in with her. The woman nodded as she wiped her tears.

They headed over to the industrial kitchen that was tucked away in a warehouse area with car repair shops and other businesses. Ben parked and they walked to the back, knocked on the door, and an old, bald man answered.

Ben extended his hand. "Hi, I'm Ben Prescott and this is Gina Sortino. I called earlier."

The man extended his hand. "I'm Mike Daken. Are you the Ben your sister Linda called me about? We love her, such a talent in the kitchen. Are you a cook too?"

"I'm afraid not. I worked at City Hall for forty years and retired. My friend Gina here is a caterer. Her business is booming, and she needs to find a space." They followed Mike inside as he asked about her business, but he stopped cold when she told him the name of their company.

"Last Bite, now that's clever. I don't think I ever heard of a catering company that just targeted funerals. Creative young woman ya got here, Ben."

"Thanks, Mike," Gina said. "We just did a big event for all the funeral directors over at Rago Brothers and our phone is ringing off the hook. I'm so excited to see what you have."

"Rago Brothers, like in Louie Rago?"

"That very one."

Mike started to guide them into the space. "If you're in with Louie, you're in. Never cross him and he'll be loyal to you forever."

"Good to know. I'm not planning on crossing him, ever," Gina said with a laugh.

"Follow me in the back and we can walk through what space is available. We have several caterers who use our space, and this is where they create the meals for the public schools in this area." He pointed over to one side of the room. "These fine ladies, parolees from our own Stateville Correctional Center, are hard at work preparing the lunches for tomorrow."

Gina looked over and saw muscle-bound women wearing hairnets, jumpsuits, and aprons with the name "Peggy's Kitchen" on the front. *I wouldn't mess with them. I wonder if they did in any of Rago's clients?*

As Mike toured them around, he pointed out the entire layout. Gina could see that the space was well organized, with dedicated areas for different food preparation. There were multiple stainless steel countertops, cutting boards, and sinks for washing and prepping ingredients. She couldn't help smiling.

"This is amazing. Everything is so clean and tidy. Do you have storage space we could rent?"

"Indeed we do. What caterer worth their own salt wouldn't want good storage?" He walked them over to the area. "Here are our walk-in refrigerators and freezers."

"Wow, this is beyond perfect. Do you have any space available now, like today?" Gina asked.

"Why don't you and Ben come into my office and let's discuss the logistics and costs?"

Gina and Ben followed him to a small room; it was super orderly and his desk was clear. Gina was trying to hold herself back from getting too excited.

Over the course of the next hour, Mike laid out the rules of the kitchen and the fact that they were visited frequently by inspectors since they prepared school lunches. "Cleanliness and food safety are our top priority. We have a commercial-grade ventilation system to remove smoke and odors, as well as ample cleaning stations for sanitizing utensils and equipment. Our kitchen also follows strict hygiene protocols."

It was important to hear all this, but all Gina could think was, *How much, how much?*

"So is there space available now and, if so, what kind of rent are we talking?" Ben asked, leaning in.

Mike took out a black leather binder and opened it to the contract page. "We have a small space that just opened up. The caterer moved into their own brick-and-mortar." He wrote down the square footage and fifteen hundred dollars a month on the paper and pushed it in front of Gina and Ben. Gina held her breath and looked over at Ben and then back at Mike.

"That's a bit high for our budget. Is there any wiggle room on the price?" Gina asked.

Mike took the paper back, flipped through a few other pages, made some notes, entered some numbers into his desk calculator, wrote down one thousand dollars a month, and moved the paper back. "Since you're Linda's brother, I'll give you a break. I could give you a weekly or monthly rate and we can see how things go. It's a little higher but that way we can decide if it's working for us, our other renters, and you."

"That's a great idea. Any chance we can hire the lunch ladies to help us cook on occasion, when we have multiple events on the same day?"

"You'd have to ask their employer, Peggy Miggs. They're her workers, and they'd have to ask their parole officer. It's possible—if everyone gives the green light. Peggy is a bit gruff, but don't let that intimidate you."

"I'd like to suggest we try the kitchen for three months, and if it works then we can sign a lease. How's that sound, Mike?" Gina asked.

"Sounds like a great start." He pulled out some paperwork, put it in a folder, and handed it to Gina. "Fill these forms out. We always do a credit check, and if everything checks out then you can move in in a couple days."

"Amazing. I'll need to confirm everything with my business partners, Kim Yang and Angie Sortino, and get back to you," Gina said.

Mike stood up, handed Gina his card, and walked them out. "Give your sister my best, Ben. Nice to meet you both."

As soon as they got to Ben's car, Gina let out a scream. "Yes! It's happening, Uncle Ben, thanks to you and Aunt Angie." She gave him a big, long hug, her heart still pounding from the encounter with Mike.

"You and Kim are doing all the heavy lifting. I'm proud of both of you, going after your dreams at a young age, creating life on your terms. Your uncle would be so proud."

Ben drove them back to the wake, and Gina talked the whole way about the space and Last Bite. After they replenished all the food and drinks at the wake, Ben suggested they go to a nearby diner for a treat.

Over a celebratory homemade chocolate milkshake, Gina looked over at Ben and smiled. "Thanks for being there for all of us. I know you're helping out Angie too."

"You are my family. Vinnie was like a brother I never had. I'll always be here for you. I have a surprise for you. Remember I told you I would invest in your company? Well I would like to pay for at least the first three months of your new space and then we can go from there."

Gina's mouth opened and a little milkshake dribbled out; she quickly wiped it off. "That is a miracle. I wasn't sure how we were going to come up with the money."

Ben nodded. "I know you're short on capital right now, but I know you're going to make this happen. I'm glad I'm in a place where I can help."

For the first time since she had the idea for her own catering company, a sense of calm and ease washed over Gina. They both chatted while they enjoyed their drinks. Gina avoided asking about the Mario situation. She didn't want to put Ben on the spot since she knew there were things that only he and Angie shared. If and when they wanted to tell her anything, she knew they would.

Ben helped her clean up after the wake was over and dropped her at her place. "Let me know when you and Kim decide to send your paperwork."

Gina gave Ben another kiss on the cheek. "Will do. I can't wait to tell Kim and Angie."

Gina carried up the bin of empty dishes from the wake and went into her apartment. Thad and Daisy were in the kitchen and Kim was sitting on the couch, her feet on the table, eyes closed.

Gina walked into the kitchen and saw Thad and Daisy. "I can see you're trying out the Triscuit recipe. How's it going?"

"These things are the bomb, perfect combo of flavors with the pickle, cheese, and Triscuit. A must for my funeral," Thad said, and popped one in his mouth and offered one to Gina, who tasted it.

"You know, it's good. Thanks for test-driving this," Gina said.

Gina put a few on a plate, went into the living room, and gently tapped Kim on the shoulder. "Ready for some awesome news, partner?"

Kim opened her eyes. "Yes, please, and no more First Communions, please. They are exhausting. But I have to tell you, the potato salad was a hit, not a drop left."

"Score two for *Scratch? My Ass!* Try this Triscuit treat, our very own. Thad made it."

Kim ate one and then another. "These are addicting. So what's the news?"

"I found us an amazing kitchen. Ben took me over to see it; it's super professional." Gina recounted everything she and Ben learned from Mike, the whole layout of the space.

"This sounds too good to be true. What's the damage?"

"That's the best part of this. It's one thousand a month for a three-month trial and . . . wait for it." Gina could see Kim's eyes widen at the price tag.

"Ben is going to pay our first three months. Then we'll revisit how things are going."

"Did you tell them absolutely yes?"

"No, I said I had to discuss it with my business partners and get back to him. It felt so legit to say business partners."

"Where's the paperwork? Let's get it filled out and we can drive it over so you can show me the space," Kim said.

They quickly filled the forms out, gave a quick call to Ben who wanted to be informed, and headed out to deliver the forms to Mike after they grabbed a few more Triscuit bites.

Mike was at his desk when they walked in. "That was fast."

"Mike, this is my business partner, Kim Yang, and we are ready to close this deal. We know our credit check will pass. I should tell you I just quit Panera yesterday but that shouldn't affect my credit; I pay all my bills on time and Kim does too."

Just as they were handing him the folder, a middle-aged woman with short hair tucked into a hairnet, bright red lipstick, and large black glasses barked behind them, "Mike, I need to talk to you. I need more space, just got a few more schools signed up."

"Ladies, meet Peggy Miggs. She runs her lunch program here. She's the one who hires the parolees."

"You girls looking for a job? I don't care what you were in for. You paid your debt to society. I pay minimum wage and you'll be here on time or I'll fire you, plain and simple." Her voice was gruff and she wore what appeared to be a permanent frown. Gina watched Peggy eyeballing her and Kim. "A little young for doing time," Peggy said.

"Peggy, they are renting the new space if their paperwork passes muster. They have their own catering company."

"Humph, are you out of middle school yet?"

"Actually, we're out of junior college and we've already got clients. We're looking forward to sharing space with you." Gina tried to keep it professional and light.

"Yeah, you won't last long. I've seen you youngsters come and go. Catering is hard work, and it takes tenacity to stay in the game. Stay away from my girls." Peggy turned around and left.

"Her bark is bigger than her bite," Mike assured them. "She's a softy once you get to know her. You may see her son come by on occasion. He's a Chicago cop, and the sun and moon sets on him, according to Peggy. He's a rather large fella—you can't miss him."

Mike scanned the paperwork from the folder and looked up. "There shouldn't be a problem. I'll call you later this afternoon and let you know if you have the green light. I'll need the first three months' rent up front and then I'll get you both keys."

"We'll be waiting for your call, Mike," Kim said.

"Cashier's check made out to me."

Kim and Gina high-fived each other and in unison said, "It's happening!"

"We have to celebrate. Where should we go?" Kim asked as they got in the car.

"How about we go to Murphy's for a celebratory drink?" Gina asked.

"Sounds perfect, I always love their brats," Kim said.

Chapter 27

Angie took a cab to Ralph's, carrying her work clothes, her own lunch, and Ralph's care package that she'd carefully prepared before helping Gina and Kim out earlier. She walked into his apartment lobby and the doorman greeted her. "Good to see you, Mrs. Sortino. Mr. Conti is expecting you." He pushed the elevator button, held the door, and sent her straight up to the penthouse where Ralph was waiting. As soon as the door opened, he was there to greet her.

"Hello. It's so good to see you. I'd help you carry something but I've only got one good arm." He sweetly kissed Angie on the cheek, which sent a tingle down her spine.

"It's good to see you up and about. I was a bit scared I'd find you a horrible mess and here you are already walking around. Modern medicine is a miracle indeed." She gave him a kiss on his cheek, and his aftershave smelled divine.

Angie walked past Ralph into his kitchen, unpacked the meal she had prepared for him, and put it in the microwave to warm it up.

"You sure know your way around my place. Seems like you've been here before," Ralph said.

"Why, yes, I have. Eunice and I came here while we were

waiting for you to be moved into your hospital room. You have a lovely home, not a lot of food in the fridge, but plenty of fine wine and spirits." Angie took out two plates, silverware, and cloth napkins. Setting two places at the dining room table, she glanced up at the portrait of Alice. "Hello, Alice, seems your man has gotten himself into some trouble, but we'll keep an eye on him and hope you can work your magic from heaven as well."

"So you've also met my beloved wife," Ralph said with a smile. "Glad to know you are both acquainted. I must say you remind me of her in so many ways." Angie felt Ralph's eyes following her every move as she served her fresh pesto pasta, salad, and garlic bread that she had warmed in his broiler.

"Please sit down. I believe you can eat everything with one hand."

Ralph followed her orders, took a taste of the pasta, and let out a groan. "Oh, my, this is so flavorful and fresh. This will heal me faster than any drugs they give me."

Angie ate hers and had to admit it was delicious. "How are you feeling? You have been through quite an ordeal. First your business problems, a broken nose, and then shot. Yet you're able to sit up and take nourishment. You're like the Tom Cruise character who gets beat up, shot at, and can still jump off a moving motorcycle and save the day."

"I'm honored you'd compare me to him. I'm grateful I've been diligent with my fitness."

Angie watched him navigate everything with his right hand, and she felt the urge to reach over and help him but decided he could handle it on his own. They ate in silence for a while with an occasional sound of delight coming from Ralph.

Angie put her fork down, reached down in her bag, and pulled out some paperwork. "Ben took me to my safety deposit box at the bank, and I have all the evidence we'll need to put

Mario and several of the higher city officials away for good, if we need to. This could go all the way up to the mayor's office if we want to take it that far. I really don't want to destroy anyone's reputation, except Mario's. I'm not afraid to take whatever action is needed to get what is rightfully mine."

She cleared Ralph's place and put the papers in front of him, took the dishes to the kitchen and cleaned everything up, moving about the space as if she were in her own kitchen. Though she'd never cooked in such a fancy kitchen, Angie found that everything was arranged in a way that made perfect sense to her. She found every item in the first drawer or cupboard she opened. It made her wonder if Alice had set it all in place. Angie felt an unexplainable affection for Alice, this woman she'd never met.

Angie returned to the dining room and found Ralph studying all the papers she had brought. She was happy she could trust him with this information, knowing if it fell into the wrong hands it could cost her life.

Ralph finished reading and looked over at her. "I had no idea all this was happening behind the scenes. Vinnie sure was meticulous about dates and details. This will all hold up in a court of law if we go that far. Who else has seen these?"

"Just me and now you. Ben asked not to be part of this except to protect me, should I need him. He was inside City Hall long enough to know about all the shady dealings. He kept his nose clean and retired with a nice pension, made no enemies. He was smart enough to stay under the radar."

"Would you have any objection to me showing these to Eunice? I trust her with my life, and if they do take another shot at me and hit the target, at least you two can finish this off."

"We can't let you get hurt again; that's why we need to act fast."

Angie thought about his request for a bit. "I did speak with her about this and gave her my spare key to the safety deposit box when we were in the hospital. We just have to remember that whoever knows this information is in harm's way and could end up dead if and when Mario and the City Hall thugs find out."

"I appreciate you being protective of her. I won't say anything to her about the details until you let me know if it's okay."

"Thanks, Ralph. These are copies and I have the originals. Why don't you give some thought on how and when we'll execute our plan. It needs to happen sooner than later and I already mapped out my ideas."

The house phone started ringing in the background. "Do you want me to get that?" Angie offered.

"No, it's probably a messenger from the office dropping something off at the front desk. I'll have them bring it up after you leave." The phone stopped ringing for a few minutes and then started again. They both ignored it.

Angie made Ralph a cup of coffee and put a few of her homemade chocolate-dipped biscotti on a plate, which she placed on the dining room table. "Here's a little dessert for you. I need to get into work early. I promised Lorna I'd make up the time I took off when I went to see you in the hospital. Just so you know, I did tell the hospital staff I was your wife so I could get in to see you quickly. A little white lie here and there never hurts." Angie gathered her belongings and headed to the elevator, the house phone again ringing in the background.

"You never know what the future will hold for us, Angie. I hope we can spend more time together. I really do enjoy your company."

"I hope we can too, but I can't have you bossing me around like you did at Gibsons. That was totally disrespectful the way you spoke to me. Not okay. While I care about you and all the troubles you've had recently, I need to trust you, and that will take time."

"You're right. I was just so angry at Rebecca for what she said to you that I lost my temper. I guess I was being protective of you. I'm so sorry about that. I won't let that happen again."

"I'm a grown woman and I can protect myself. I want a relationship built on trust and mutual respect, just so we understand each other. I've been through a lot this past month, to say the least, and I need things to calm down in my life. I want to concentrate on getting my pension and getting our catering company off the ground. That's plenty of excitement for me."

"Fair enough, Angie. I don't want to be the one causing you any more stress, believe me."

"I appreciate that; now I need to get to work. Please take care of yourself. You're not getting any younger."

Ralph grinned. "No, I am not, and believe me, I am feeling that now more than ever. May I please give you a kiss on the cheek?"

Angie looked up at him. "Yes, you may."

He leaned in, and as his soft, warm lips touched her face, she felt her cheeks flush and a tingling sensation travel all the way down to her toes.

They were both standing by the elevator doors when they opened. There was Rebecca, carrying a huge flower arrangement. "I'm here to take care of my man," she said from behind the bouquet, unable to see Angie standing there.

Angie dropped her bag, looked at Ralph and then back at Rebecca, who had put the flowers down from in front of her face and was staring at her. "What the fuck are you doing here? I thought you got the message; you're not in his league. Seriously, you don't actually think he's interested in you."

Adrenaline rushed through Angie's body, and she walked right up to Rebecca. "I think you should mind your own business and leave; you're not wanted or needed here. I need to go to work. We'll talk later, Ralph."

As the elevator doors closed, she could hear Ralph yell, "Stop, Angie, I didn't know she was coming. Please!"

She hurried out of the elevator downstairs, tears flowing, and hailed a cab. *I hate that woman, barging in all the time.* She hopped in the cab. "City Hall." Her phone was ringing. She turned it off and let herself cry until she got to work.

"You all right, ma'am?" the cabbie asked as he dropped her off in front of City Hall.

She handed him a twenty. "I'm fine. Keep the change."

Angie stood outside for a few minutes to collect herself, then went in, got dressed for work, and made sure Hazel had all the supplies needed for the evening's work. Just as she was about to go up to the elevator, Lorna came around the corner with her cart. "Hey, Ang, how the hell are you? How's Ralph?"

Angie burst out crying and Lorna came to her side. "Oh, honey, come here, sit down." She led Angie to a small row of old office chairs in the hall by the elevators.

Angie sat down next to Lorna and let herself sob, snot running down her nose. "That bitch Rebecca barged into Ralph's apartment while I was there, treating me like a lowlife." Lorna kept her arm around Angie the entire time, handing her as many tissues as she needed, while Angie kept throwing the used ones on the ground.

"Take a deep breath, Ang. Slow down and tell me everything."

She blew her nose, wiped her eyes, and shared what had just happened at Ralph's place, leaving out any mention of the papers. The last person she wanted to put in harm's way was Lorna, who had been so generous toward her.

Lorna said, "Honey, I know the inside of this entire building, and we can get your pension back without the help of any man. I got you. Let's go out after work and put together a plan to get you your pension and move past all this bullshit. You're a strong woman with an exciting future in front of you. Your niece is counting on you, as her partner, to help her launch her business, and we need you here to keep things spic-and-span."

Angie stood up and gave Lorna the biggest hug. "What a godsend you are. Let's get this place in order and I'll meet you downstairs after our shift."

"It's a date. Now turn on that Frank Sinatra music and find your groove, girl."

Angie put the "do not disturb" on her phone, put on the playlist that Gina had made for her, and sang and danced her way through all the dirty offices and bathrooms on the fifth and sixth floors. She had no appetite, so didn't stop to eat.

She rolled Hazel downstairs where Lorna was already dressed and waiting. "I've got just the place where we can go and not be disturbed," Lorna declared. "They have great food. We can get a booth in the back and have a few drinks."

"Sounds perfect. I'll let my niece know where I am. She always wants to know I'm safe. Where we going?"

"The Rosebud on Taylor Street. I know the owner and they're holding a table for us."

Lorna and Angie got in a cab, and on the way over Angie turned on her phone to call Gina and saw numerous voicemails and texts from Ralph. She quickly texted him. *I need time to cool off.* She deleted all the voicemails without listening, and texts without reading them. She called Gina to let her know her whereabouts.

Lorna patted Angie's leg. "I got you, girl. No one messes with my friend Angie—no one."

They walked into the Rosebud, one of the oldest Italian restaurants in Chicago. The dim lights, cozy atmosphere, paintings of Frank Sinatra and the Rat Pack set the mood for the place. The hostess recognized Lorna and Angie right away.

"What a sight for sore eyes. Angie, I haven't seen you in over ten years; you look great. How's Vinnie?" She hugged Angie.

"He passed recently; I'm just getting my feet back on the ground."

"I'm so sorry, if you need a job, you know you can always come back here. You were one of our best."

"Thanks. I think my waitress days are over."

Mary Ruth hugged Lorna. "Always good to see you." She took two menus and led them to a plush leather booth in the back.

"Good to see you, Mary Ruth. We'll probably be here for a while," Lorna said.

"Take all the time you need. Jimmy will be your waiter."

Jimmy was there in a second. "Hey, Lorna, nice to see you." He took their food and drink orders.

"They sure know you here. Is this one of your favorites?" Angie asked.

"My parents came here back in the day and then brought me and my brother. They were close friends with the owner. After my parents died, they kept an eye on us. It was a safe place to come, not to mention they have some of the best Italian food in the city."

Jimmy placed two Manhattans in front of them. "Your garlic bread and calamari will be out shortly."

"Thanks, Jimmy," Lorna said.

Lorna lifted her glass. "This will be a real caper. Let's toast to getting that pension. We have to come up with a code name just for fun."

Angie raised her glass. "How about 'Mario and Ralph can go to hell'?" They took a sip and settled back in the booth.

"We may need to shorten it, but let's start figuring out what we want to do and how to get it done. You've waited long enough to get your money from the city and we need to make this happen fast. I know you want to invest money in your niece's catering business and since it's taken off already she'll need that money right away."

Jimmy brought over the appetizers and they both started to nibble.

"Here's what I know," Angie began. "Cookie in HR is letting Mario get away with changing the name on Vinnie's paperwork and she's not going to do anything to change that, so she's no help. I have copies of both versions of the pension forms, one with my name and then one with Mario's."

"Believe me," Lorna said, "Cookie's nice, but she's not going to do anything to piss off Mario, and that's smart. He's connected to the mob, and I think he put a hit out on Ralph. Best to stay as far away from that man as we can. It's no use going to Cookie's boss; he doesn't give a shit about any of this. We may have to go straight to the top and make some threats."

"You mean Mayor Borden?" Angie cleared her throat, thinking about how big this was getting.

"Yup, he's a reasonable man, but he's kept in the dark on a lot of things, and if we were able to get a few minutes of his time and show him evidence, he may just help us."

"Do you know him?" Angie asked. "Isn't there anyone else below him that we could talk to? This seems like small potatoes given everything else that's on his plate." Angie took a bite of the buttery, crunchy garlic bread with toasty cheese on top. "This is the best I've ever tasted."

Lorna nodded. "Here's my idea. I clean the mayor's office. I'm the only cleaning lady they trust. I get in and, no matter who's in there, get it done, keep my head down. Sometimes he thanks me, which no prior mayor has ever done. Tuesday nights before the Wednesday city council meeting he reviews the agenda, sips some bourbon, and makes calls. The city council meets the second and fourth Wednesday of the month, so we should make this happen next Tuesday."

Angie winced. "That fast?"

"Angie, you don't have much time. Mario is on a rampage, and he is not a patient man. You need your money and you need to get on with your life. And it sounds like you have enough evidence from Vinnie to get your money from the city and get rid of Mario for good. We'll have to plan it carefully, tell no one what we're doing. I think if we can make our case quickly, list our demands, we may be able to pull this off."

"This is getting serious, but then who would suspect a few cleaning ladies cornering the mayor?" Angie said.

"I've never played a card like this either. You write up exactly what you want to say, back it up with facts in writing, and we practice a couple times to make sure it's smooth," Lorna said.

"Do you think I should show him Vinnie's journal, with all the names, dates, bribes?"

"I'd have them ready so he'll know we mean business if he tries to blow us off. The mayor will not want that out in the world. It would make him look bad. He doesn't want that."

"Okay, Lorna, we're going big-time here. Even Jessica on *Murder, She Wrote* never pushed around a mayor."

"There's always a first, and if we do this right, no one but the mayor will be the wiser," Lorna said.

Angie took a deep breath. "I am bushed. I was up early helping my catering partners, then I had the Ralph incident and a full night's work. Let's call it a night and we'll keep planning every detail every night on our breaks, sound good?"

"Let's get you a cab home." They finished their drinks and appetizers.

Jimmy approached the table. "Can I get you gals anything else?"

"Just the check," Lorna said.

"Boss said it's on the house, Lorna."

"Please thank him. This is for you, Jimmy." She pulled out forty dollars and slipped it in Jimmy's palm.

Angie could hardly walk up the stairs when she got home. She washed her face and fell into bed. Her thoughts were reeling about the plan, and then she was off in dreamland. Her last thought before falling asleep was, *Can two cleaning ladies really pull off something like this? Thelma and Louise did a good job, until the end. I guess Lorna and I could drive off the end of Navy Pier if we had to.*

Chapter 28

"Leave now!" Ralph pushed Rebecca toward the elevator with his good arm. "Take your flowers and get the fuck out of my home or I'll call the police. Stay out of my life or I will get a restraining order. Imagine the front pages of the *Tribune*: 'Alderman O'Brien's Wife Slapped with a Restraining Order.'"

Before she could respond, the elevator opened and Ralph shoved her in with her flowers and hit the button.

Ralph called down to the front desk. "Don't ever let that woman up again, do you understand me? Never, or you'll lose your job. Let all the other doormen know too." He slammed down the phone. A sharp pain on his side stopped him. He gasped for breath and sat down on the nearest chair. He glanced down at the dressing on the side of his chest and noticed some blood that hadn't been there before.

"Shit, I've got to slow down."

He called Eunice. "Sorry to bother you, but could you please come over now?"

"On my way. Are you all right? You sound out of breath."

"I'll talk to you when you get here, just please get here."

Ralph sat in the chair taking slow, deep breaths, trying to slow his pulse. He kept calling Angie knowing she wouldn't pick up, but at least she'd see he had been calling. *How am I going to get her to trust me now? And after everything was starting to go so well. Every time it looks good for us, Rebecca shows up.* The pain on his side was dull and starting to ease. His arm hurt, but he wasn't going to get up and take any pain pills. He needed to be clearheaded.

He tried to recollect what was on the papers Angie had shown him: the names, the numbers, the dates, but he hadn't studied it carefully, thinking he would be able to do that after Angie left.

Ralph threw the plastic breathing contraption across the room. "Shit!" He and Angie had had a real connection. He could feel it and he could tell she did too, and now that was all gone. He was in no shape to go anywhere; there had to be a way to get back in her good graces. Maybe Eunice would help him; she always found ways. Ralph sat back, took some slow breaths, and waited for Eunice, his mind spinning.

It felt like hours but Eunice finally arrived. "You're white as a ghost." She put her finger on his wrist. "Your heart is beating way too fast. If it doesn't slow down we'll need to call the doctor. What the hell happened? No, wait, don't tell me. I'll get you a sip of bourbon, if you haven't taken any pain meds."

"Perfect, bourbon works better than any of those drugs."

Eunice went over and poured them both a single finger of bourbon, handed him a glass, and sat next to him. He could tell she was studying him and could read the concern in her eyes. He took a sip, a breath, and then another sip. "You always know how to calm me down."

They both stared out the window with a view of Lake Michigan, sipping their bourbon in the middle of the afternoon.

Ralph's pain subsided and he was ready to recall the whole Rebecca incident without getting too upset.

Eunice sat next to him and listened. "You may have to ask your attorney to send her a cease and desist letter. That would send a clear message!"

He nodded and took another sip. They sat in the quiet together.

After a few more minutes, Ralph broke the silence. "Angie and I had a real connection. She brought over lunch and shared some private papers Vinnie had left her. They would have gotten our company out of hot water and put Mario behind bars."

Eunice listened, waiting for him to go on.

Ralph paused and then said, "I'm falling for Angie and now I think it's over. If you could have seen her face when Rebecca barged in and trashed her. I hope I never see that look again. I have to get her back and I need your help. I could see spending the rest of my life with Angie."

He stared out the window again, until Eunice finally spoke. "We can figure this out. There are a few things I need to tell you. When you were in the hospital, Angie and I came over here to wait and, after a series of long conversations, she gave me the key to the bank lockbox where she put the evidence that could put Mario and his cronies away for good. She's a smart one; she wants to protect her family. She knew if Mario got wind of anything, he would come after them."

Ralph glanced over at Eunice. "Angie showed me some of the paperwork and we were going to map out a plan, until the Rebecca blowup."

"There's no way she is going to trust you now, but she may trust me. Ralph, she's nobody's fool. And family is the most important thing to her. Did she tell you about her friend Ben?"

"I know him; he was like a brother to Vinnie. Good man."

"He's the only man she really trusts. You may want to call him. Let him know what's happened and he may have some words of wisdom. Not sure he'll be able to help, but it's worth a try." Eunice put her hand on Ralph's wrist. "Your pulse has slowed down. How are you feeling?"

"Honestly, I'm exhausted. Glad to have you here to talk this through with me." He took a deep breath and noticed that his pain had subsided. "Thank you. You're a gem."

"We'll get through this as we always do. Your heart is in the right place, Ralph." Eunice got up and brought Ralph a glass of water.

Eunice watched as Ralph took a sip of water and continued, "We need to focus on saving our company and fast. I got a call from our attorneys. The investors are pulling out. They don't want any more bad press and there's plenty of other places to put their money. It's all legal, and we'll likely have to file for Chapter Eleven. Our accountants agree that the sooner we do it, the better."

"That was fast. I thought more jobs were going back online. That should have sent them a positive signal. This sounds fishy; someone is pressuring them." Ralph shook his head in disbelief.

"I thought so too, so I did some digging and I think Mario's connections go far and wide. I called one of the investors and was able to get them to spill a little. Seems there's some banker friends who quietly suggested that they get as far away from your company as possible. There was no room to negotiate. They already met and voted unanimously to sever all ties."

"Hmmm . . ." Ralph slumped back in his chair. "This is a fucking nightmare. I'll need you to go ahead and lay off most of the staff immediately with a reasonable severance package. You know which ones to keep on. I agree with the accountants, though it nearly kills me. Best to file for Chapter Eleven. I'm not sure what we can salvage. If there is any way you can go to the bank and get into Angie's safety deposit box and take some photos of Vinnie's journals, that would help. I need to go see our friend the mayor. He owes me."

"You are in no shape to go anywhere, but you would definitely get a sympathy vote looking all banged up. I'll head over to the bank first and back to the office. You need to rest if you think you're walking into City Hall any time soon." Eunice made her way to the elevator. "I'll call you after I leave the bank. Promise me you'll lie down for a while. You're going to need your strength."

"Promise, I got nothing left in my tank and I can't handle any more bad news."

"I do have a little good news. I moved some of our assets offshore to our account in the Caymans before I came here."

"Always thinking."

Eunice left and Ralph went to bed and fell asleep.

He awoke several hours later in total darkness, sat up and turned on his bedside light. His stomach was gurgling. He headed into the kitchen to get something to eat, saw the left-overs that Angie had carefully put away and warmed them up. The pesto pasta was better than any he had eaten at any Italian restaurant. He reminded himself that she had made it with love. Oh, how a day could change things.

Ralph decided not to put on the TV; he couldn't take any more bad news. He checked his phone, no calls and one text from Eunice. *The papers are not in the safety deposit box.*

He called Ben, who picked up right away.

"Hey, Ben, it's Ralph. I need your help. Do you have time to talk?"

"Sure, it's what retired people do, talk and help out friends. What's up?"

Ralph explained what happened with Angie and Rebecca and how he needed to get back in her good graces.

"Not sure I can help you with that, buddy. I've only seen Angie mad a few times and when her temper hits red, things start flying. I'd suggest that you stay away until she cools off, if she ever does. When she says she's done with somebody, she's done."

Angie had told Ralph that Ben had helped her with the storage unit and getting the journals into a bank safety security box. "Have you heard anything about what she's going to do to get her pension issue resolved?"

After a long pause, Ben responded, "I'm not at liberty to tell you. She has sworn me to secrecy, and I won't cross that line. I was watching the evening news and it looks like things have gone from bad to worse for your company. I'm so sorry. I bet you're really missing your buddy Vinnie now."

"You know it. I've tried calling and texting Angie and no response. Any suggestions on how I might get in touch with her? Don't want to go to City Hall—that didn't turn out so well last time. I landed in the hospital with a gunshot wound to my chest and a busted-up arm."

"Damn, if you didn't have bad luck, you wouldn't have any luck. Why don't you give me a little time to feel her out. I've been helping Gina with all the catering gigs. I'll see Angie tomorrow morning and see if I can bring up your name when she's cooking. She's always calm when she cooks. Don't get your hopes up, though."

Ralph paced back and forth in his living room. "I'd sure appreciate anything you can do. I have to tell you, Ben, I've become quite fond of her and I'll do anything I have to to get her back. I just don't know what."

"Maybe hire a biplane from Meigs Field to fly around with a banner saying, 'Please forgive me, Angie. I love you.'"

They both chuckled. "Crazier things have been done. I sure

appreciate your help. I know you're the only man she trusts. I look forward to hearing from you."

Ralph sighed, then turned on the TV and watched the Cubs. Baseball always took him away to memories of his time with Vinnie, eating a Chicago dog and drinking beer at Wrigley. Nothing like baseball to slow down time and chill with his buddy. You could cover all of life's problems in nine innings.

Ralph looked up toward the ceiling and said, "Vinnie, I gotta believe you're up there. I need your help, pal. I got a soft spot for your Angie. I could use your help and so could the Cubs."

Eunice sent Ralph a couple more texts at the end of the evening saying layoffs were in play and the accountants were preparing the paperwork for him to sign in the morning. She'd bring them by.

He responded, *Coming into the office tomorrow. I can't stay home anymore and do nothing. See you in the morning.*

Ralph stood and stared out at the beautiful lake, shaking his head. *Things sure went south fast; a month ago everything was going splendidly. Business was booming. Now I'll be lucky if I can pay my bills.*

Chapter 29

Over the next two days, Gina and Kim secured their space, catered two more events, and started to move everything they had into their new professional kitchen. Ben not only paid for the space but gave them an additional $5,000 for materials and groceries. Angie came by every morning before work, made some pesto and then taught them how to make it. Orders were flying in for multiple jars, so they wanted to have the stock. Angie didn't say anything about Ralph or the pension issue and Gina didn't ask.

As Gina and Kim were making a large batch of pesto sauce in the huge mixer, Gina looked up and saw her mom walk past Peggy's girls and up to them. "You gals are playing in the big league, and look at you two, fast at work like you've been doing this for years. Is that Angie's pesto I smell?"

Gina hugged her mom. "Sure is, it's selling off the shelves. We can hardly keep up with it. This is going to be a huge revenue producer."

"Who would have guessed? Say, how did the potato salad turn out? I haven't seen you since then." Connie pulled up a stool and sat across from the gals.

"Big hit, Connie," Kim said. "They almost licked the bowl,

but we're not doing any more First Communions. All those kids running around, parents enjoying their afternoon cocktails and asking for recipes—*PASS*. Dead people and mourners are way more manageable. We'll leave that to another catering company, or we could have Thad and Daisy take those over. I bet those kids would get a kick out of those two and they could make the Triscuit bites and a few other items. They couldn't go stoned, though." Kim laughed as she added a huge container of pre-minced garlic into the mixing bowl.

"Glad the Jewel potato salad did the job," Connie said. "Say, I've been trying to get ahold of Angie, but no luck. Have you seen her?"

"She came over and taught us how to make the pesto in large batches, and now we're flying solo. She's real busy at work, said she and Lorna have some big meeting in a couple days. Said she needs to stay focused." Gina added mass quantities of blanched basil leaves and quarts of olive oil to the mixer.

"Travel business is going crazy."

"Can't help you, Mom, but I'm glad business has picked up. We have back-to-back events for the next two weeks at several funeral parlors, mostly Rago's. He's our VIP. We'll be closing in on our first month of business and looks like we may even make a small profit. Uncle Ben invested so we may even get a small salary."

"That's unheard of, but good for you."

All of a sudden a woman yelled from across the large kitchen. "Whatever the hell you're making over there smells amazing. What is it?"

Gina looked at her mom's face; her eyebrows were raised and she stared at Gina. "Who is that lady? She looks a little scary."

"That's Peggy Miggs. She rents most of the space here, lunch orders for the schools." Before Gina could finish explaining,

Peggy marched up to Connie and looked her square in the face. "You look familiar. Did you date my son, Mikey?"

"If it's Mikey Biggs from Mount Carmel, yes, I did. He took me to prom senior year. How is he?"

"I told him to stay out of your pants. We didn't need his career interrupted by some loose woman getting knocked up and making him marry her."

"Well, that explains why he never called me again. We only went to prom as friends, Mrs. Miggs. He was such a sweet guy. How is he?"

"He is a full-fledged cop and married to an okay girl." Peggy walked over and looked over Kim's shoulder. "Damn, that smells good." Kim was blending everything together.

Peggy took a spoon, dipped into the mixer, and took a taste. "Now that's good. I'll take a couple of bottles at cost and serve it to my workers with pasta after they're done working today."

"You got it, Peggy. I'll bring some over as soon as we're done with this batch," Kim said.

Peggy left without another word and Connie looked over at Gina. "She's still rough around the edges. I guess it gets worse with age."

"I heard that!" Peggy yelled from across the room.

Connie stood up. "I better leave before she gets one of those women to come over here and beat me up. Can you girls come over for dinner one of these nights? Be nice to catch up. How about Sunday dinner, maybe Angie can come too?"

Gina pulled out her phone and checked her calendar. "Yeah, Sunday will work. I think Angie's project should be done and she doesn't work on Sundays."

"I'll leave her a voicemail; it's a date. Love you both. See you Sunday." Connie left and Gina and Kim decided to take a break and review all the events and menus.

"Rago wants us to change things up, keep the pesto bites but add some new items," Gina said. "I thought maybe we could make mini-Jell-O molds, kinda like Jell-O shooters without the booze. Thad said he could get a great deal on those tiny cups at the dollar store."

"You know, I've watched people when a Jell-O mold comes to a party and they scarf it down. It's comfort food in a weird way. I love the idea," Kim said.

Gina opened *Scratch* to the pages she had tagged to show Kim. "We could do zucchini bread bites and dump cake bites in small muffin tins. They're super simple."

"Those are good sweet treats and probably cheaper than the almond cookies to make," Kim said.

Gina continued, "Since Thad and Daisy want in on the action and need to make some dough, I thought we could have them assemble small sandwiches on those Hawaiian buns, slice of cheese and turkey, condiments on the side. Oh, and I forgot to tell you, there's a new Italian bakery that makes fresh breadsticks daily. I talked to the baker and he's so excited and said he'll give us a big discount. We could get that beer cheddar cheese spread that folks love and they could dip the breadsticks in that, or even a chocolate dip would be good."

"I love where you're going with this, Gina. A friend of mine who is a no fuss, no muss cook sent me this list of other options we can review. They look easy and a little more on the expensive side if money is no object."

Kim and Gina worked side by side the rest of the afternoon, testing the small muffins, which turned out perfectly. Kim cut one of the zucchini bites in half and said, "Open your mouth." She placed the bite in Gina's mouth, and as she pulled her finger away, Gina felt her face flush hot, hoping it didn't show.

"These are so yummy, moist, and just sweet enough," Gina said, and looked into Kim's dark brown eyes. Gina had felt something more than friendship toward Kim for a while but dismissed it, thinking it was just because they were spending so much time together. But this was more than that, if she was being honest with herself. This was a revelation: *I think I have a crush on my best friend.*

As Gina held Kim's gaze, Kim asked, "Why do you have a shit-eating grin on your face? It's not every day I see you smile like that. What is it?"

Gina covered her face with her hands and peeked at Kim through a crack in her fingers. "Busted."

"Spill, girl. We're partners—you have to tell me," Kim said.

Gina motioned for Kim to follow her outside the building. She didn't want Peggy hearing anything.

Gina stood near the door, looking around to see if anyone was walking by. There was no one. "I don't know how to say this, but . . ." Gina felt her cheeks flush. "I think I have a crush on you, like, a girlfriend crush. I've had feelings like this before, but kinda thought it was just admiration for other girls. But I'm getting the feeling that something more is going on for me than just admiration. Is that weird? You know, just to be figuring this out?"

Kim broke out into a huge smile that accentuated her cute dimples. "Everybody comes to understand themselves and their attractions in a different way. I've been attracted to you for a long time, but I didn't want to make you feel uncomfortable and ruin our business relationship. I'm so happy right now."

"I am too. I just had to tell you. I'm nervous, but I can't stuff these feelings down any longer. They're real. So, where do we go from here?" Gina asked.

"I think we take it slow and for sure not be demonstrative here. Peggy would have a field day with that. Let's finish our work, and we can talk about it when we leave," Kim said, her eyes sparkling.

"Okay, then for now I'll just do this." Gina pulled Kim in for a hug and kissed her sweetly on the cheek, feeling her knees weaken. Kim kissed Gina's cheek in return, and they squeezed hands before pulling their entwined fingers apart and walking back inside.

Kim started cleaning up and Gina grabbed two bottles of Angie's pesto, walked across the room, and handed them to Peggy. "Here you go, Peggy, on the house. And if you have any good ideas for small easy to make and not too expensive finger foods, we're all ears."

"Let me think on it; I bet I could come up with a few ideas. Working in school cafeterias most of my life I knew a million ways to cut costs and feed those brats. You girls gonna be in tomorrow?"

"Bright and early," Gina said.

"Good, I'll see you then. Hey, thanks for the pesto."

Gina and Kim headed out around seven. As Gina started driving, she could feel Kim's gaze on her. "You're staring at me. What?"

"I'm really happy that you said something. I think we should grab sandwiches and go sit by the lake and talk about how we want things to move forward," Kim said.

"Sounds like a good idea. Wow, I need to talk about my feelings. Who knew?" Gina said.

They picked up sandwiches from Portillo's, along with a nice bottle of red wine, and headed for the lake. Gina pulled the wine opener out of her glove compartment and found a bench away from the other folks. Kim opened the wine and poured some into two paper cups.

Gina looked at Kim for a long time, smiling, and finally said, "I have a good feeling about us. I can't tell you how glad I am that I found the courage to say something." She held her cup up and they toasted. When Kim leaned in and gave Gina a kiss, Gina felt her heart begin to race.

When they finally pulled apart, Gina said, "I guess I always thought I'd have a boyfriend, but I was never attracted to one, and even when I kissed my prom date, I felt nauseous. I could kiss you forever."

"I've been waiting for this kiss for a long time. I could tell you felt something for a while, but I wanted to give you the space to decide if you wanted to act on it."

"Thanks for letting me take my time. It feels right. That I know."

"Let's finish our food and relax right here; nothing like the waves to calm you down. Then when we're ready we can head home. How does that sound?" Kim asked.

"Perfect. You want to spend the night with me?" Gina asked.

"I thought you'd never ask."

No one was home when they got to Gina's. They each showered and then slipped into bed. Both were exhausted. After a few long kisses, they fell asleep in each other's arms.

The next morning, they cuddled for a while. "I'm not ready quite yet for our next step, but I promise I will be," Gina said.

"I'm in no rush. I'll follow your lead," Kim said. "And right now I think we'd better get going. We have a busy day ahead of us."

They grabbed coffee, and once in the car, they were touching each other's hands as Gina drove to their office.

As Gina and Kim were walking into their kitchen to pack up the orders and head over to Rago's, Gina came to a complete stop. Across the room she spied Mario talking to Peggy, who was laughing at whatever he was telling her. Gina's stomach dropped. *What the hell is he doing here?*

"I'll meet you in the back, Kim. I see someone I know, talking to Peggy."

"Okay, don't be too long. We have to be over at Rago's in an hour to set up."

Gina walked over to Mario and Peggy. "Hi, Mario, fancy meeting you here." She knew everything he had done to Angie but didn't know if he knew she knew.

Mario leaned in and hugged her. She almost gagged. "How's my girl? I sure do miss your uncle. Peggy here tells me you started your own catering company. Good on you. I think your aunt may have mentioned something. Small world. Peggy and I were having dinner last night and she mentioned you had moved into her space."

Gina swallowed hard. "Actually, we're renting our own space here." She pointed over to where Kim was packing things up.

"Peggy gave me a tour earlier. I see you're pushing your aunt's pesto. There's no better. I wasn't aware you could cook, especially after what you served at Vinnie's funeral."

Gina wanted to spit in his face. "We know some things and Angie has joined our business; she's an excellent cook. But of course you'd know that after all the meals you ate at her house. It's so sad about what happened to her pension, don't you think, Mario?"

"I don't know anything about that, honey." He gave her a dismissive look. "I haven't been here since Peggy and her crew moved in years ago."

"Mario is the one who got us all the school lunch contracts through the city. I had no idea you both knew each other so well." Peggy patted Mario on the back. "He's an important man to know."

"My uncle worked with him for years, treated him like family, didn't he, Mario? Excuse me, I need to get going. We have a catering event in an hour," Gina said.

Gina walked away feeling sick to her stomach and wanting to stab Mario with a kitchen knife. She took some deep breaths and started to help Kim finish loading the bins.

"What is wrong? Your face is beet red and the veins in your neck are bulging."

"Let's get the fuck out of here and I'll tell you on the way to Rago's."

While they drove, Gina gave her the background about Mario in more detail than Angie had already shared. She told Kim that it was likely Mario was the one who had put a hit out on Ralph.

"He's a fucking pig and I hate him. Wait till I tell Angie," Gina said.

"Calm down. Time to put on your smiling catering face. We have mourners waiting on us."

Gina and Kim put out a huge spread for the Italian family who had money to burn. They even ordered flower arrangements to decorate the tables. Large women, clad in all black, wearing black lace chapel veils wandered around weeping. Gina watched as they sampled some of the food and could tell it met with their satisfaction. They nodded their heads between bites and went back for second tastes.

Louie was pleased that they had added new items to the menu and made sure to try them. "You gals are doing a great job. I need a last-minute favor."

"Sure, Louie, what do you need?" Gina asked.

"My sister's having a kids' party out in the suburbs later this afternoon, and the person who was supposed to cater it just got taken to the hospital. So there's no food and she's freaking out."

"Yikes, I'm so sorry." Gina thought for a minute. "Kim and I need to be here, with this big crowd to serve. I have a friend, Thad, who could handle a kids' party. Would you be open to that? We have plenty of food at our kitchen. I can send him and his girlfriend there to pick it up and bring it to the party. They won't have to play games with the kids or anything, just set up the food, right?"

"Just the food. Those kids are wild, so they'll be running around, no games."

"Okay, Louie, let me give him a quick call."

Gina stepped outside and Kim followed. "You really think it's a good idea sending Thad to one of Rago's relatives?" Kim asked.

"They're in a bind, and it's a bunch of kids. The more we help Louie, the more he'll help us," Gina said.

Kim raised her eyebrows. "Okay, just proceed with caution." She walked back in to check on the food and drinks.

Gina called Thad. "Hey, dude, how are you?"

"All good, just chilling here with Daisy. What's up?"

"I need a big favor, but you'll make some good money."

"I'm down. Hit me with it."

Gina explained the situation and that he'd need to meet Kim at their kitchen and she'd help him pack up some of the simple treats; he could even make the Triscuit treats he had perfected at her house. There were lots of Jell-O shots in the fridge.

"Sounds cool, Gina, what's the address of your kitchen? We'll meet Kim there. Good timing on the call; we were just about to smoke a joint, but we'll do that after the party."

"You're a lifesaver. Kim will meet you there in thirty. Thanks, buddy."

"Sure thing. We could pick up some pizzas if you want."

"I'll order some to the house. You'll just have to put them out." Gina went back inside the funeral parlor and gave Kim the update.

"Okay, call me if you need me to bring any more food back here after I pack up and send Thad and Daisy on their way."

"Thanks, Kim. I'll take care of things here."

Kim headed out and Gina went in the back to Louie's office where he was busy with paperwork. "I've got a crew heading out in about an hour. Just so you know, Thad's girlfriend Daisy has purple hair this week. I hope your sister won't care."

"You should see my sister's older daughter. Multiple-colored braids, tattoos, pierced eyebrow. Thad and Daisy will fit right in. Thanks, Gina."

Louie's phone rang. "I'm sending someone out to set up, put out the paper products; the rest is handled." He winked at Gina.

She gave him a thumbs-up and headed back out to check on the food. Mourners kept coming and coming. Gina could hardly keep the food and drinks replenished.

Kim returned within a half hour with a full report. "Thad and Daisy are on their way. They have enough food for a small army. Thad is going to make balloon animals for everyone. He demonstrated one for me; he's good. Who knew?"

They both started to laugh but got a side glare from one of the old lady mourners.

The rest of the Rago event went without a hitch. They cleaned up and headed back to the kitchen, where they unpacked and cleaned up. Peggy's gals were fast at work as usual. Several strolled over and asked if they could try those Jell-O shots they had seen Kim packing up earlier.

"Sure, but there's no booze in them."

"We can't drink on the job."

Gina pulled out the last tray and offered all of them one.

It was after five when Gina and Kim headed over to help the caterer they had worked for in the Gold Coast. She had called begging them to help for just a few hours; several of her team had come down with the flu. It was the last thing Gina and Kim wanted to do, but they agreed. They knew there would be some seriously expensive, delicious food there. They were tired of all the things they had been serving.

The event in the Gold Coast ended around nine and they stumbled back to Kim's car. When Kim pulled up in front of Gina's, she leaned in and gave Gina a long kiss. "I hope we can go on a proper date soon, but right now all I can think about is passing out."

"Get some sleep, and I'll do the same. Let's talk tomorrow." Gina got out of the car and barely made it upstairs. She kept playing the same Katy Perry song in her head—"I Kissed a Girl"—until she fell asleep.

Early the next morning, Gina's cell phone started ringing. She kept ignoring it until she heard loud banging on her apartment door. She got out of bed and opened the door. It was Kim.

"What are you doing here? It's eight in the morning. I thought we agreed we'd get to sleep in today, no gigs."

"We've got big trouble." Kim handed her a large coffee. "Rago called me. He said he's been trying to get ahold of you and no answer. He's pissed. I've never been yelled at in Italian. Chinese, but not Italian. I asked him to slow down."

Gina was wide awake now. "Uh-oh, what happened?"

"Seems the kids at the party are all home throwing up and have diarrhea. Rago's sister said it was from our food. The families are furious and they want Louie to fire us."

"What the fuck! Do you think Thad and Daisy did something?" Gina asked. Her heart was pounding away now.

"You better call Thad now. I have no idea. But Louie wants us over at his place, like ASAP."

Gina called Thad at Daisy's place. He picked up. "What happened at the party? All the kids are sick and they think it's from the food. Did you guys put anything in it?"

"Uh, no, why would we do that? We set everything up. They were downing the Jell-O shots, loved the Triscuit treats, and inhaled the pizza. The balloon animals were a big hit and we left."

"Well, something went way wrong, and Kim and I are heading over to see Rago now. I didn't mean to accuse you of anything. I just can't figure it out," Gina said.

"All cool here. Sorry about the kids. They were fun."

On the way over Kim and Gina were racking their brains about what would have caused the problem. They went over everything they made and sent over to the kids' party; it didn't make sense.

Rago was waiting for them at the front door. They walked inside and followed him to his office in the back.

"What the fuck! My sister has angry parents who had to take their kids to the doctor for dehydration. You both need to get to the bottom of what caused this. I don't care how you do it, but until you do, you're not catering any more events for me or anyone I referred. I have a reputation to uphold." He shook his head in disgust.

"Louie, you have to believe us. This isn't our fault," Gina pleaded. "No one from your service yesterday got sick, did they?"

"Not that I know of, but it only takes one bad experience. Call me when you have an answer, and if you don't figure this out, then I'll call the city and have your catering license revoked."

"Please don't call the city. Please," Gina begged.

"I'll give you one day and then you girls will need to find a new career because your name will be mud in this town." His phone was ringing and he motioned for them to leave.

Gina called Angie on the way back to their kitchen.

"Hi, honey, can't talk long. It's a big day for Lorna and me. We're meeting for lunch before work. We have a big night ahead of us."

"Whatever it is, I need your help." Gina recounted the kids' party and aftermath.

"Something sounds off. I know you're both so careful about your food preparation. Even Thad is a freak, washing his hands all the time. I've watched him. Is there anything you can think of that you did differently? Anyone besides you two working in the kitchen?"

Gina thought for a moment. "Fuck!" she screamed.

"What?" Angie asked.

"Yesterday when we got to work, Mario was at the kitchen. Seems he knows Peggy and she gave him a tour of our area before we got in. You don't think he could have, would have, put something in the Jell-O?"

Angie let out a gasp. "I got this weird text from him yesterday. He hasn't returned any of my calls since the pension thing went down."

"What was the text?"

Angie read the text. "'I wouldn't try anything or you and your family will pay.' I excused it because it didn't make any sense, but now it does. I bet he put something in your food."

"We have to prove he did this, but how? We pissed off Rago and no one does that." Gina slammed her hand on the dashboard.

"Leave this up to me. I'm so done with Mario's crap. You and Kim go back to your kitchen, clean everything out of the fridge. Check all your ingredients. Throw away anything that doesn't look or smell right. That pig has gone too far, going after you two."

As soon as Gina and Kim walked in the kitchen door, Peggy was waiting for them, hands on her hips. "What the fuck did you feed some of my girls yesterday? They called in sick." She shouted and threw aprons at them. "Put these on. You bitches are working for me all day, for free. I've got lunches to get out!"

Mike, the owner, was standing next to her. "When you're done there, I need you both to come see me. If Rago calls the food inspectors, they'll come turn this place upside down and you'll both be out of here."

Chapter 30

As Angie ended the call with Gina, adrenaline rushed through her body. She had never had such a strong urge for vengeance in her life. "It's war, Mario, and you're toast!" She got ready for work and texted Lorna that they needed to meet as soon as possible near City Hall; things had escalated with Mario.

Lorna sent back a brief text: *Go time—see you soon.*

Angie packed her work bag and threw in a few pairs of underwear in case she got arrested. As she was leaving her apartment, she saw Ben coming in. She noticed him check his watch before he said, "You look like a woman on a mission. Isn't it a little early to be going to work?"

Angie put her bag down and threw her arms around him. "Wish me luck. Don't ask. And keep your phone on. I may need you to come bail me out tonight."

"Slow down there. What's going on?"

"Could you go over to the kitchen? Gina needs you."

"Okay, what's going on with Gina?"

"It's a long story, but Rago fired them this morning. Apparently his sister's kids and their friends got food poisoning from a party that Gina and Kim had Thad and Daisy run. Now they have to clean out their entire food stock at their kitchen. I know you were good enough to arrange that space. Since your sister knows the landlord, you may be able to smooth things over until they get to the bottom of it. I have a strong hunch Mario has something to do with it."

"I'll head over there now. What's this about possibly bailing you out?" Ben asked.

"I can't explain all that now; I have to get going. Thanks, Ben."

Angie went downstairs and grabbed a cab to City Hall. Lorna was waiting for her at a nearby café in a back booth. She slid in with her bag, ordered a cup of coffee, and settled in. She told Lorna what had happened to Gina and watched Lorna's face turn bright red. "What a class-A asshole. God, I want to see that bastard go down. No one goes after family."

They both ordered a full breakfast, eggs, sausage, hash browns, and toast. "This could be our last meal on the outside if the mayor decides to throw us in the clink," Angie said.

"Unlikely, but just in case, chow down, girl."

While they ate, Angie looked around to make sure no one was watching her. Only one other couple sat near them and they were quarreling. She took copies of Vinnie's journals from the storage unit out and placed them in front of Lorna and watched as Lorna studied them.

"Holy shit, Ang. This is a gold mine. There's no way Mario can talk his way out of this one, or the mayor, for that matter. Let's rehearse one more time."

Lorna and Angie leaned in toward each other and went over every step of their plan, detail by detail. Lorna looked over at Angie. "We got this, girl. Let's go for a walk and window-shop on State Street before we go in. It'll calm our nerves."

"That's a great idea. I love to window-shop." They walked down to State and meandered up one side and down the other, crowds of people rushing past. Angie tried to enjoy all the pretty dresses she saw, but there was an empty feeling in the pit of her stomach gnawing at her. She kept silently repeating, *Please, God, help us. Please, God, help us.* Angie glanced up toward the sky. *Vinnie, you up there? I need you, baby.* She kept following Lorna but glanced over what was in the windows.

They clocked in just an hour early, as they wanted to get their regular work done before they headed to the mayor's office just after eight. That's when he'd be at his desk looking over all the council agenda items, and his bodyguards would be around. Lorna had assured Angie that they were used to seeing Lorna in and out of his office, so there would be no problem walking in. If they asked about Angie, Lorna would tell them she was training her.

"The guards, the cops, no one messes with me," Lorna said. "I'm usually quiet during my cleaning shift, but if someone pushes my buttons then I respond in a clear and firm way and they back off. They usually just think of me as a cleaning lady, after all, trying to make a living, minding my own business."

"Good to know. Sounds like you've trained them well," Angie said.

They changed into their work clothes, packed their street clothes, clocked in, and pushed their carts to the elevator.

Angie looked at Lorna, who smiled at her, then winked. "The adventure begins," Lorna said.

Angie forced a smile. "No turning back now." She pressed the elevator button and they both boarded. Lorna got off at three. "Keep your phone on you. I'll only call you if I need to; otherwise see you at the mayor's office at eight sharp."

"See you then, Thelma," Angie said.

"You got it, Louise." Lorna chuckled.

Angie pushed Hazel off on six and went to work in her assigned offices and bathrooms. She cleaned them better than she ever had, channeling all her nervous energy into scrubbing, vacuuming, and dusting. She locked up the office she had just finished and rounded the corner to find Cookie standing by the elevator. Angie froze, didn't make a sound, holding her breath hoping that Cookie hadn't heard her.

Cookie turned her head toward her. "Hey, Angie, haven't seen you in ages. How are you holding up, honey?"

"Just great. I love my job, can't thank you enough for helping out." Angie was biting the inside of her mouth. *Get lost, you bitch.* The elevator door opened and Cookie stepped in. She was saying something, but Angie couldn't hear it with the sound of blood rushing through the veins behind her ears. Angie finished all four of her floors, seven bathrooms, and six conference rooms a little before eight and slowly pushed her cart toward the mayor's office.

Lorna was waiting for her near the mayor's office. "Leave the cart here. Take your folder and follow me," Lorna said.

Angie followed Lorna's clear, decisive voice, grateful for her confidence and strength.

Lorna and Angie walked past one set of guards, who nodded at them. Then they entered the outer office where the mayor's assistant was busy on her computer. She glanced up and then back down. Angie took in the rich, dark carpet, leather chairs, and oak coffee table in the waiting area. Photos of past mayors lined the wall, interspersed with photos of the beautiful Chicago skyline, aerial shots of Wrigley Field, and the Magnificent Mile and Michigan Avenue at night.

Angie stopped looking when she heard Lorna tap on the mayor's door. Lorna waited a second, then opened it and walked in. "Good evening, Mayor, just cleaning up for the day."

Without lifting his head from his computer, he muttered, "Okay, Lorna. Busy time for me as usual, the night before our city council meeting tomorrow."

Angie admired his large oak desk set in the middle of the room. The office had such an elegant and professional feel. *So this is where it all happens.* She followed Lorna, taking in every detail she could without gawking.

As they cleaned the small work areas, Angie could see people coming and going, phones ringing, and heard some swearing. Just as they were finishing up everything but his desk area, Lorna motioned for Angie to come stand next to her. Angie watched Lorna scan the office to see if there was anyone else there at the moment. It was empty. This whole conversation had to go down in less than five minutes or the cops would literally knock down the door.

They had rehearsed this part over and over.

Lorna pushed her cleaning cart right in front of the door leading to the outer office and locked it. "Mr. Mayor, I need your help and I need it now," she said with a commanding voice.

He briefly glanced up. "Lorna, what's wrong?"

There was a knock on the door.

"I need you to tell them to come back in five minutes. It's all I'm asking," Lorna said, her voice calm yet bold.

"Come back in five?" Mayor Borden said. He looked at Angie and back at Lorna and raised an eyebrow. "Lorna, what's going on? I need to prep for the city council meeting."

Angie's heart galloped like a wild horse. Lorna hit Angie's arm. "Take a breath, for God's sake."

The mayor's phone was ringing and there was another knock at the door.

"I'm busy. Give me five minutes," the mayor called out.

"You okay, boss?" one of his bodyguards asked.

"All good," he replied, before turning back to Lorna. "Okay, Lorna, get on with it. I'm a busy man."

Lorna cleared her throat. "This is my good friend Angie. Her husband, Vinnie Sortino, worked here at City Hall for over twenty years. He died recently and your city staff have cheated her out of his pension."

The mayor's phone kept ringing.

"Mario Longetti replaced her name with his as the beneficiary and took her pension. He put a hit out on Ralph Conti—who you know—and Ralph was shot. And now Mario's after Angie." Lorna pointed over to Angie. "She's an innocent woman and I need you to put a stop to this."

"I'm sorry to hear all this. Lorna, can I deal with this after the city council meeting tomorrow? People are coming at me in all directions right now and I have to work through the night as it is."

"No, you can't. People's lives are in danger. We already have one Chicago cop shot; we don't want any more of that. Please, I promise I'll leave you alone if you give me this," Lorna said.

The mayor sat back in his chair. "I can't Lorna, not tonight. The press is up my ass with all the corruption going down with the city planning department. The *Tribune* has already sent a request for public information, which requires a quick turnaround by law. Who knows what they'll find?"

Angie swallowed and stepped up to his desk, trying to hide her trembling hands. "Mayor Borden, I am so pleased to meet you and thank you for your commitment to our fine city. I need you to listen to me for just a few minutes, and then if you want to send me down to Cook County Jail, I'll go freely."

He smiled. "I'm listening, Angie, but please, be brief."

His phone kept ringing, and there was another knock. "All good, need some more time," he called out. Angie figured that was code for *No murderers in here—the coast is clear*.

"Here's what I need. I need Mario Longetti behind bars tonight. I have enough evidence right here to put him away for life." She spread the papers in front of him on his desk; she had used a yellow highlighter showing Mario's name and the amounts of the bribes he had collected. She watched as the mayor skimmed them.

"Angie, this is incriminating evidence. These documents could hurt more people than just Mario, including me."

"Mayor, I only want what's mine—and Mario behind bars. That's all. I will destroy the original and this copy. I need to see him in handcuffs tonight before I leave this building. That's all I'm asking, sir."

Angie watched as he looked at her and over at Lorna. "Okay, then, I can tell I'm not going to get rid of the both of you until this is done. My city attorney is in the outer office. I'm going to bring him in and we'll get this matter over with. Lorna, move your cart."

Lorna pushed her cart aside and unlocked the door. The mayor's bodyguard immediately stuck his head in and looked at the mayor. "All good, boss?"

The mayor gave him a thumbs-up. "Send Richie in. Now!" The guard looked at Lorna and Angie and went back out.

A heavyset, bald middle-aged man in a tailored black suit walked in. "Mayor."

"Richie, I need you to look at these documents." The mayor handed him Angie's papers.

In less than ten seconds, Richie read them, looked at the mayor then over at Angie and Lorna and then back at the mayor.

He can read faster than our mayor, a lot faster, Angie thought.

"Okay, exactly what do you ladies want? It's not a good time to be bothering the mayor."

Angie walked over to Richie, stood tall in her five-foot-two frame, and looked up at him. "I am Angie Sortino and I have two demands. I need Mario Longetti in handcuffs tonight, and I need my husband's pension reassigned to me." She swallowed deeply and stood her ground.

Angie watched as the attorney sized her up. She had never felt so clear and strong in her whole life. She kept looking him directly in the eye. She wanted to throw her arms up in the air, the soundtrack of *Rocky* playing in her mind.

"Make it happen—and fast, Richie. Tonight. Now," the mayor demanded.

"Yes, Mayor."

"Lorna, I'm going to need you and Angie to wait in the outer office while Richie gets Mario here." He glanced up briefly from his computer.

"I've never asked for anything ever, and I will never again," Lorna said.

"I hear you, Lorna. You can trust me. Now if you kind ladies will let me get back to my business here, when Mario comes in, I'll invite you in to watch him get his due."

"Thank you, Mayor," Angie said. "And please forgive me for this intrusion." Angie walked out and Lorna followed.

They both made a beeline to the nearest bathroom. Inside her stall, Angie had to check her pants, worrying she might have generated a bit of a trickle when she stood up to Richie with her demands.

While she relieved herself, she called out to Lorna, "We did it! We really did it!"

"We can't declare victory yet, Ang. When I see that motherfucker in handcuffs, then we celebrate," Lorna announced from the adjoining stall.

Angie washed her hands and looked over at Lorna, who was doing the same. "You know, that was the most fun I've ever had. It scared me to death, but I feel so liberated. I've never stood up for myself like that."

"You had Richie on his toes, and that's saying something. I've watched him eat high-powered politicians alive in seconds in this building. You are a badass, Ang. I'm so proud of you."

"Couldn't have done it without you, Thelma." Angie threw her arms around Lorna.

They walked into the outer office and the mayor's assistant stood up and said, "May I offer you two something to drink? The mayor sent out his favorite bourbon if you'd care to calm your nerves."

"How lucky are we to have such a gentleman running our fine city," Angie said.

"I think we'll both take a little of that; it's been a stressful evening." Lorna walked over to the assistant's desk and brought the crystal filled glasses back to their seats. Angie watched as several visitors walked in and out of the mayor's office, even though it was late in the evening.

Almost an hour had passed since the mayor had sent Richie off to fetch Mario. *Is this whole thing going to go south?* Angie wondered. Lorna was sipping her bourbon and watching all the different people coming and going. "You think he's going to have us arrested and they're just waiting for the bourbon to calm us down?" Angie whispered.

"No, he's a man of his word. I'd stake my life on it." Lorna sipped.

Angie's cell phone rang. She quickly walked into the hallway to answer it without checking who was calling.

"Hello."

"Angie, don't hang up. It's Ralph, I'm worried about you. Ben called me and told me what was happening with Gina. He's worried you're going to do something dangerous at City Hall."

"Ralph, it's none of your business what I'm doing. I can't talk now."

"Please be careful. I would hate for anything to happen to you."

"I appreciate your concern, but I need to go. Please don't call me again. If and when I want to speak with you, I'll give you a call. But don't hold your breath."

Angie ended the call and went back into the mayor's outer office. She started to tell Lorna that Ralph had called when two of Chicago's finest, bookending Mario Longetti, walked straight into the mayor's office. Lorna motioned for Angie to follow her into the mayor's office.

The bodyguards closed the doors behind them.

The mayor stood up. "Mario, seems we have a serious problem that has to be resolved tonight. I don't have time for this bullshit."

"Mayor, I have no idea what's going on here." He looked over at Angie. "This woman is an alarmist. Disregard anything she has to say. She is mentally unstable."

Angie marched up to Mario and punched him in the face with all her might. "You are pure evil. How dare you mess with me and my family!"

One of the policemen moved Angie away; Mario wiped the blood off his mouth. "Who knew you had a good right punch. Vinnie would be proud." Mario snickered.

Angie went at him to hit him one more time and the officer intervened.

"Settle down now," the officer said as he stood between Angie and Mario.

"Don't you ever speak my husband's name again, you scum of the earth," Angie practically spat. "You're not half the man he was. And one more thing, Mario. I know you tampered with my niece's food and got all those people sick."

Mario's creepy smile made her want to hit him again, and she was not a violent woman; she'd never punched anyone before.

"If she's dumb enough to leave the fridge door unlocked, don't blame me. It was just a little syrup of ipecac, soaked right into the Jell-O," Mario said.

"You fucking pig! Her catering business has been shut down because of you. But you didn't just mess with her, you messed with Louie Rago. And when he hears it was you, good luck finding friends in prison."

Richie shook his head. "You messed with Rago? He's been here longer than any mayor. You've really dug yourself into a deep hole you're never getting out of. You're on your way to Cook County Jail now." Richie read Mario his rights. "We have sufficient evidence to arrest you for multiple crimes. You have put the City of Chicago and the Mayor's Office in grave danger." Richie motioned toward the officers, who handcuffed Mario and started to escort him out.

"You'll regret this, Mayor," Mario bellowed. "My people got you where you are. Good luck getting reelected—or with whatever political move you're seeking next."

Mario glared at Angie. "I may be in jail for now, but I have a lot of friends." The officers pulled Mario out.

The mayor looked over at Lorna and Angie. "Now can I get back to work?"

"One more thing, Mayor, if I may." Angie stepped toward him. "My pension. I need Cookie to change the paperwork tonight so I can leave with the papers in my hand."

The mayor yelled for his assistant. "Get Cookie here immediately."

"Yes, sir," she responded from the outer office.

The mayor sat back down and continued working on his desktop computer, his phone ringing.

He answered the call and started speaking, motioning for Angie and Lorna to leave the room. They took the hint, walked out of his office, and closed the door.

His assistant finished her call and looked up at them. "May I offer you anything else?"

"We'll just have another sip of that delicious bourbon and wait for Cookie. Any idea how long it will take?" Angie asked.

"She's still in the building. I've sent security over to escort her here. It won't take long. I instructed her to bring your husband's file. We'll get this all closed out in no time at all." She continued working at her desk, fielding calls to the mayor's desk and clicking away on her computer.

Lorna looked over at Angie. "One more thing to check off and we're home free. I heard Ralph's voice on the other end when you got that call. He has the balls to call you. What did he want?"

Angie took a sip of her drink. "He's trying to come to the rescue, like I need a man to defend me. I just want this evening behind us."

Lorna put her arm around Angie's shoulder. "It will be soon. You were awesome in there. I knew you had it in you."

Angie took her first deep breath of the night and sat back just as Cookie walked directly into the mayor's office. Lorna and Angie stood up and followed.

The mayor ended his call and glanced up. "Cookie, please let me see Vinnie Sortino's pension paperwork."

Angie watched as Cookie promptly took it out and handed it to the mayor.

"What is Mario's name doing here as the beneficiary? His widow is standing right here." He pointed over at Angie. "And she is the rightful recipient."

Cookie looked over at Angie and back at the mayor. "That is correct, sir."

"I don't want to know how anything happened; we can deal with that later. You need to put her name on it right now, notarize it, and hand it to Mrs. Sortino. Am I clear?"

"Clear, Mayor. I'll take care of this right now. We can settle this out front. I don't want to waste any more of your time."

"Thank you." He looked over his eyeglasses at Angie. "Are you satisfied?"

"Yes and thank you. God bless you, Mayor Borden," she added. Angie followed Cookie out.

Richie was waiting in the outer lobby as Cookie changed the paperwork, notarized it, and handed it to Angie.

"When can I expect to get my money, Cookie? I thought you were trying to help me, not help Mario steal my pension. Shame on you!" Angie exclaimed.

"I had to turn a blind eye to a lot of things here to keep my job. I just didn't know what to do about Mario. I'm so sorry that you got hurt in the process, Angie. You'll get your money by the end of the week, I promise." Cookie's shoulders slumped forward.

"I'm tired of waiting, Cookie. I'll come right back to the mayor's office if it isn't, I can promise you that. And I will keep my job here at the City Hall until I decide to leave, no questions asked." Angie drew herself up as tall as she could, standing in front of Cookie with her hands on her hips.

"This is not how I wanted things to turn out, Angie, you have to know that," Cookie said.

"Yet here we are. I had to bother the mayor and Richie just to get what I was owed." Angie glared at Cookie.

"Please accept my apology, Angie."

"I'm in no mood to forgive you or Mario right now, or likely ever," Angie said.

"I need to head back to my office. Is there anything else?" Cookie looked at Richie.

"You're good to go, but the mayor will need a full report on his desk first thing in the morning on just how this name change happened," Richie instructed.

"I will make sure that happens." Cookie left in a huff.

Angie examined the paperwork, with Lorna looking over her shoulder. "Looks like everything is in order here, Ang. Let's get out of here."

"Hold on, ladies," Richie interrupted. "I'll need those papers you showed us and also the originals. Tonight. A deal is a deal."

Angie reached in her bag and handed him the copies. "The originals are at my bank. As soon as Mario is convicted and behind bars, you have my word you will get them. Not a minute sooner, are we clear?"

"That could take some time; our court systems can be slow."

"If it's not done before the elections, then this goes public. No one is off the hook until he is behind bars, my family's safety is guaranteed, and the pension money is in my bank account. I don't care how you get it done." Angie and Lorna started to walk out of the mayor's office, leaving Richie standing there.

As they were leaving, Angie looked over at the mayor's assistant. "Please thank the mayor for his help and thank you for all you do for this fine city. Say, do you like homemade pesto sauce? It's one of my specialties."

The assistant gave Angie a perplexed look, but then said, "Actually, I do, and so does the mayor."

Angie and Lorna left the office, grabbed a cab, and headed to the Rosebud to celebrate.

"I'll call Louie Rago in the morning and straighten this thing out with Last Bite," Angie said.

"But first, my strong woman warrior, we celebrate you!" Lorna put her arm around Angie and they walked out of City Hall.

Chapter 31

Lorna and Angie enjoyed several Manhattans, pasta, and wine over the next couple of hours celebrating their victory.

"Angie, I can't tell you how proud of you I was tonight. You found your voice, and I was in awe."

"I don't think I would have found it if you weren't right there with me. I don't know where it came from, like soul rocket fuel. For the first time in my life, I was in charge. Thanks for being there for me every step of the way; this whole thing could have gone south fast."

"But it didn't, and here we are. Why don't you take tomorrow off? I think you did enough cleaning for two days."

"Are you sure? I need to keep my job until my pension checks are coming in, and I don't want Cookie trying to find reasons to fire me."

"I don't think you're going to have to worry about her. My guess is she'll be out the door tomorrow. I'm your manager, and if I say you get a day off, you get a day off."

"Thank you. I'll take it."

Lorna and Angie split the bill and made their way outside to two awaiting taxis.

Angie threw her arms around Lorna and gave her a long, strong hug. "I love you, Lorna. I'm lucky our paths crossed. You're never getting rid of me now."

Angie watched as Lorna wiped a tear from her eye. "You're the closest thing I've ever had to a sister, Ang. You're never getting rid of me either. Who knows? We may have more capers ahead."

"I'm thinking we should both take a break from caper town for now." They shared a laugh. Angie hopped in her cab and waved goodbye to Lorna.

Angie got home, satisfied to her core in ways she never felt before. She slept better than she had in weeks.

When she awoke at seven the next morning, she made a strong pot of coffee. She took her cup into the living room, sat in her chair, and put up her feet. After a few sips, she looked over at Vinnie's empty chair. "I did it, honey. Took on the mayor and won! Thanks for any help you sent. I think the old Angie is gone. Not sure you'd like the new one, but I love her."

Angie phoned Louie around eight. She knew he would be at work; death never took a vacation. Sure enough, he picked up in his gruff, baritone voice. "Rago Brothers."

"Hello there, Louie. Do you have a minute?" Angie asked.

"If it's about Last Bite, I'm in no mood."

"Please just listen to me and then you can hang up. You don't even have to respond."

He paused, then sighed. "Okay, I'm listening."

"I'll spare you all the details except that I was in the mayor's office late last night, and Mario Longetti confessed to putting syrup of ipecac in the Jell-O shots that were served at the kids' party. Oh, and by the way, he also poisoned Peggy Miggs's kitchen staff."

"Are you on drugs, Angie? This level of petty crime wouldn't make it close to the mayor's office. And I wouldn't mess with Peggy on my best day."

"That's not why Mario was there. You'll read about that in the papers soon enough. If you want to verify my facts, you can call the mayor, my friend Lorna, or Richie, the city attorney."

"I know two out of three, not that I don't trust you, Angie. I'll give Richie a call, and if he confirms this then we'll talk. I have to go; I have a body being delivered in the back."

"Just so you know, he's pretty busy today. City council starts at ten, and you know the city attorney has to be there the whole time. You may want to call him tomorrow."

"My, aren't you in the know, Angie. I'm impressed."

"You have no idea. Please call me after you speak with Richie. You take care, Louie."

Angie's soul rocket fuel was still surging as she showered, got dressed for the day, made a nice breakfast, and set herself a lovely plate with a linen napkin and placed it on her TV tray. She recalled how she always fussed over Vinnie—making everything just so—when she prepared and served his meals, and then she'd eat her meal standing up in the kitchen.

There may be something to the idea of treating yourself like your own best friend after all. Thanks, Oprah!

Angie watched her favorite local news station, relaxed, and enjoyed her breakfast. She was about to call Gina when she saw Gina was calling her. "Hello, honey, I was just about to call you. Do I have news."

"I sure hope so. Kim and I should just move out of this town. Our name is mud now."

"Oh, no, it's not. Is Kim there?" Angie asked.

"Yes, she slept over. We got home so late last night, after we cleaned every nook and cranny in our kitchen space, we both collapsed."

"You both get yourselves some strong coffee. I'm hopping a cab over to your house. I want to see your faces when I tell you my story."

"Okay. You sound different."

"I am different. See you soon."

Angie walked into Gina's apartment. Kim was sitting up on the couch in a daze. Gina was staring at her phone. A heaviness hung in the room.

Angie took one of the kitchen chairs and sat across from them in the living room. "Put your phones down and listen to me. I need your full attention."

They both sat up straight, clutching their coffee cups.

As Angie shared every detail of the prior night's caper with them, she watched their eyes widen and mouths gape as they leaned forward.

She saved the best for last. "So, I got right up in Mario's face—this is after I slugged him, by the way—and asked, 'What did you do to my niece's food?' He all but laughed in my face."

"I knew it, I had a feeling," Gina said.

"That's your gut, Gina. Trust it. It knows more than your head, believe me," Angie said.

Kim was still clutching her coffee cup, staring at Angie.

"He put syrup of ipecac in the Jell-O—that's why everyone got so sick. He wanted to destroy your business."

"He did destroy our business, Angie. Rago fired us, and our kitchen landlord is evicting us. Peggy Miggs promised to smear our names everywhere. Three strikes and we're out. We'll be lucky if we don't get sued."

Angie sat back in her chair. "Oh, ye of little faith. I got Mario to admit what he did to you in front of the mayor of Chicago and

Richie, the city attorney. Can't get better witnesses than that. I spoke with Louie this morning and he and Richie are pals from long ago; I don't think there's a person Louie Rago doesn't know."

"So, what did he say?" the stupefied Kim finally piped in.

"He's going to call Richie and check out my story. He accused me of being on drugs."

Almost on cue, Thad and Daisy walked into the apartment. "Yo, Ang—what's up?"

Angie watched as Thad looked at Gina and then Kim. "Dude, did someone die? Like you look like you took a bunch of downers, man." Daisy was by his side, humming.

"You guys stoned?" Angie asked.

"Uh, yeah, we're celebrating. We had a blast at that kids' party. I'd be down for those any time you want to throw them our way. I think I finally found my crowd," Thad said.

Angie laughed. "There's a place for everyone's special talent, Thad, and I'm glad you have found yours."

Gina looked up at him. "Thad, how did the kids enjoy the Jell-O shots?"

"I could have used twice the amount; they were downing them. I told the parents that you cut the sugar in half—they thought that was brilliant."

"No one got sick while you were there?" Kim asked.

"Well, they ate a bunch of Jell-O shots, then went right into the Jumpy Jumpy, so I wouldn't be surprised if there were some pukee lukees," Thad said.

"Those bounce houses can make anyone throw up without any help. Turns out some idiot spiked the Jell-O shots and those poor kids were so sick their parents had to take them to the doctors. It wasn't your fault. How would we have known?"

"That's bad karma right there. That idiot—whoever he is—will get his. Sorry that happened," Thad said.

"Thanks to both of you for doing that party on such short notice. You'll be the first ones we call if we ever get another chance," Gina said.

"Would you ever be down for putting me in charge of my own branch of your business, for kids' parties?" Thad asked. "I can totally up my balloon skills, and with my inside connection at the dollar store, we could rake in some serious dough. Just an idea."

Angie stood up and hugged Thad. "You're the best. Love your spirit—more people should tap into theirs."

Thad hugged her back. "Ang, you get me. Not many people your age do. So, like, I'm grateful for ya."

There was a knock at Gina's door. "UPS," a man's voice announced.

Thad opened the door; the guy handed him a sealed envelope and asked him to sign for it. He handed it to Gina. "This is for you."

Angie watched her niece's eyes narrow. "You want *me* to open it?" Angie asked.

"Nope, I'm a big girl. It's probably a letter from an attorney saying we're getting sued." Gina opened up the envelope and took out the contents. She let out a huge sigh; inside was a note wrapped around what looked like baseball tickets, best Angie could tell.

Gina removed the note and placed the tickets aside. Angie watched as Gina read it and looked up at Angie and then read it again.

"Why are you looking at me like that?" Angie knew her niece well enough to know when Gina was holding back.

"It's from Ralph . . . Do you want to hear it?" Gina was focused on Angie, waiting for a response.

"I want nothing to do with him right now. What's the

saying? Men are like streetcars; there's always another one coming along," Angie said.

"*Streetcars*, dude? You were alive when there were streetcars?" Thad asked. He snickered to himself. "Like, did you also have a horse and buggy?"

Everyone burst out laughing. Except Daisy. She had returned from the kitchen with a bag of potato chips and dip and was sitting on the floor—oblivious—crunching away. Thad sat down next to her and shared the ultimate munchie treat.

Gina began reading the note out loud. "Gina, I heard about what Mario did to you and Kim. I am so sorry that happened. Your aunt Angie saved the day; she is an amazing woman. Enclosed please find tickets for the Cubs vs. Cardinals game today. There's nothing like watching a baseball game to take your mind off your troubles. I know how much you and your uncle Vinnie enjoyed long afternoons at Wrigley Field. Enjoy. Best, Ralph."

"How sweet is that?" Kim said. "Very thoughtful."

"How many tickets did he send?" Thad asked between crunches.

Gina counted them out. "Six. Enough for all of us here, plus one. Angie, please, please come with us. You're off today. We haven't been to a game together in a long time."

Angie studied Gina's face. "Why not? At least the jerk is good for Cubs tickets. Let's all go to Murphy's, have a beer and a brat, and walk over to the field and watch our boys play."

Gina jumped off the couch and hugged Angie. "I'll take a quick shower and we'll all head over. It's a 1:10 game."

"Why not enjoy our day off? Who the hell knows what's next?" Kim chimed in.

Angie checked her watch; it was only ten thirty. "I'll call your mom and see if we can get her to play hooky too. Sound good?"

"Why not? There's nothing we can do about our business until we hear back from Rago. No use sitting around feeling sorry for ourselves. This whole thing could turn out better than we had ever hoped." Gina disappeared into the bathroom.

"That's the spirit." Angie looked down at Thad and Daisy sitting on the floor, blissfully munching away. She called Connie, who was totally in and said she'd meet them at Murphy's in an hour.

Chapter 32

Everyone convened in the back of Murphy's, sipping their beers and watching the pregame show. Angie bought rounds for everyone, including brats for those who wanted them. As always, Angie sensed the optimism and excitement of the bar crowd; it was why she and Vinnie had always come here to get into game mode. Despite the welcome distraction, she couldn't stop thinking about her time with the mayor and how she got what she wanted by being assertive, with Lorna as her backup, of course. *I can't believe Ralph sent over these tickets.* She could feel herself softening toward him. Anybody who loved the Cubs that much couldn't be all bad, could they?

The sky was blue, it was a warm late-September afternoon, and there was no better place to be as they walked across the street from Murphy's into the ballpark. They had the best bleacher seats. Center field, perfect view of the field, and an excellent place to grab a few home run balls, if the stars were aligned. As they approached their seats, Kim stopped. "Wait a minute. Gina, do you see what I'm seeing? It's Peggy's girls from the kitchen."

Gina looked past the girls and saw something that astonished her. There was Peggy sitting next to Ben, who stood up and waved.

"Uncle Ben, what the hell?"

"Hey, Gina, it's a long story, but we're all here to have fun and forget about our troubles, right, Peggy?"

Peggy growled, "Why not, can't work today, schools are closed. Ben stopped by with tickets yesterday and I figured my crew needed a break after the poisoning incident." She sat back down, grumbled some more, and took a sip of her beer. Gina walked over and hugged Ben and sat between him and Peggy.

"I am so sorry about the poisoning," Gina said. "Angie got it all straightened out. It wasn't us who did it. She can bring you up to speed after the game."

"Good to hear. Sorry I was so mean to you, but it put me behind schedule," Peggy said. "By the way, my niece is coming out from San Francisco tomorrow, loves baseball. Maybe we can take her to a Cubs game. She's a private investigator and has a case here. I think you'd like her. She's a lot of fun. She bats for Kim's team."

"What's her name?" Gina asked.

"Jackie Larsen, she's one fun-loving smart cookie. Her parents disowned her when she came out, but I told her she would always have a place in my heart and home," Peggy said, and then turned to watch the players warm up. Gina went to sit with her mom, Angie, and Kim.

"That Ralph knows how to pick good seats," Connie said.

"Vinnie and Ralph spent many a day in the bleachers," Gina leaned over and remarked. "They could afford the fancier seats, but they said this is where the real fans were."

Angie bought popcorn, peanuts, and beer for the crew, toasting, "Here's to family and the Cubs." They all raised their beers, toasted, and yelled, "Go, Cubs!"

The Cardinals took an early lead with two home runs in the top of the second, and the Cubs answered in the bottom of the fifth and tied the score. Baseball time was different for Angie. She had learned from Vinnie to put all her cares away and soak it all in, one pitch at a time, one hit at a time, one inning at a time. Today, of all days, she was doing just that, glancing at the field and then over at her family, including Thad and Daisy, knowing they would always get through anything as long as they were together. She laughed out loud when one of the lunch gals yelled at the ump, "That was a strike! Get some glasses!"

What a motley crew, Angie thought.

At the top of the sixth, one of the ushers came over to where she was sitting. "Is there an Angie Sortino here?"

They all looked up. "Who wants to know?" Angie asked.

"We have a very special surprise for Angie. Are you Angie?"

"Depends. You're not from the mayor's office, are you?" Angie asked.

"No, I work for the Cubs."

"Okay then, I'm Angie. What exactly is the surprise?"

"Not at liberty to say, but if you'd please follow me, you'll know soon enough. All I can say is it must be your lucky day." He gestured for Angie to follow him.

"Bring her back in one piece," Connie called after.

"No worries, she'll be safe and sound. Enjoy the rest of the game. Go, Cubs."

Angie followed him through the park, her mind reeling. *Where is he taking me?* They navigated through all the fans, kids in tow, lines of people waiting for beer and dogs.

He took her on an elevator up several floors, and she noticed a sign pointing to the press boxes. They walked past them.

"Would you please take a seat, Angie?" said the escort. "I'll be back to get you at the start of the seventh inning." He pointed to a small area with a live TV monitor displaying the game and several chairs. "Would you like something to drink?"

"Why not? I'll take a beer, please."

The young man returned with a draft beer and a bag of peanuts. "Enjoy."

Angie sipped her beer, cracked open peanuts, and watched the rest of the sixth inning. The game was tied. Fans were yelling as the Cubs took the field at the top of the seventh. She was deeply engaged in the game when the usher interrupted her. "How are you doing?"

"Great, but I'd like to get back to my family. Time for the seventh-inning stretch."

"You'll be enjoying that in just a few minutes. A friend of yours has arranged something for you. I hope you brought your best singing voice."

Singing voice? Angie thought, as the usher led her to a door marked "Announcer" and gently knocked. *What the hell?*

"Come in," came a voice from within.

The usher opened the door and Pat Hughes, the announcer for the Cubs, glanced over. "Angie, you're going to be singing "Take Me Out to the Ball Game" with our guest celebrity."

"What! Are you kidding me? Oh my *God*! This is a dream come true!"

"Come on in. We're on in a few minutes."

Angie stepped in and froze. There in front of her was Bill Murray—*the* Bill Murray, wearing his 2016 World Series T-shirt and hat, holding a microphone. "Hey, Angie. Nice to meet you. I was a friend of Vinnie's—so sorry he's gone." He reached over and gave her a warm embrace, saying, "He was a hell of a man, and there was no better Cubs fan."

Angie was having an out-of-body experience, thoughts flooding through her mind. *Is this real? How did this happen? I'm with Bill Murray.*

Bill brought her right up front—where you could see the

entire field—and handed her a microphone. "I know you know the words," he said, smiling.

The Cubs announcer broke in, "And today we have our very own Bill Murray with a special guest, Angie Sortino, singing "Take Me Out to the Ball Game."

Bill jumped in, "A one—A two." He glanced over at Angie and they both started singing.

"Take me out to the ball game. Take me out with the crowd. Buy me some peanuts and Cracker Jack. I don't care if I never get back!"

Angie gave it all she had, joy erupting from within her. She caught sight of her and Bill on the Jumbotron. As the camera scanned the crowd, everyone got up and sang, arm in arm. "So it's root, root, root for the Cubbies . . ." The song ended, the crowd went wild, and Angie hugged Bill, smiling ear to ear.

"This was truly a dream come true." She pointed at him with both of her index fingers. "Bill Murray. I sang with Bill Murray!"

Bill gave her a departing hug. "Take care, Angie. So nice to meet you after hearing about you from Vinnie for so many years. That man sure loved you."

The usher was standing by the door ready to escort Angie back to her seat. She couldn't even feel her legs, but she knew she was moving. Fans waved and clapped as she walked past them, and when she got to her seat, her entire section of the bleachers stood up and started to chant, "Angie, Angie, Angie!"

She was still in shock; her whole being was vibrating.

Gina embraced her. "Bill fucking Murray. Are you kidding me? You killed it! Who made that happen?"

"I'm guessing Ralph. If I died tomorrow, I'd die a happy woman." The top of the eighth inning started and then the ninth. Angie couldn't focus on the game. She was truly dazed. The Cubs barely pulled it out, getting a homer with two outs on a three-two pitch in the bottom of the ninth. The stadium exploded as everyone sang the victory song, "Go Cubs Go." A man was waving the huge *W* flag in the middle of the field and no real fan left until the song was over.

Angie's crew followed her out, fans high-fiving her along the way. Her crowd made their way back over to Murphy's for a celebratory drink. They found their usual spot in the back. Peggy bought a few pitchers of beer and they reveled in Angie's big day, and the Cubs win, of course. After about an hour, the crowd in Murphy's started to thin out and Angie excused herself to go to the ladies' room. As she got close, she felt a tap on her shoulder. Thinking it was another fan ready to give her a high five, she turned around . . . and standing in front of her was Ralph. Her heart dropped. She wanted to give him a hug, even a kiss. "It was you who arranged that, wasn't it?"

"I did." He gazed deep in her eyes and she in his. She felt sudden warmth all over like she hadn't since Vinnie died. She grabbed Ralph and kissed him with everything she had, melting right into his mouth. They stood there kissing, as if they were the only ones in the bar.

Angie gazed up at Ralph. "It's a start. Don't go getting your hopes up. We're not going steady." They laughed.

"But you're saying I have a chance, right?"

"Time will tell, Mr. Conti, time will tell. Why don't you join us in the back? I need to use the ladies' room."

As she was washing her hands, Angie was mentally pinching herself. She splashed cold water on her face. *I can't believe this is all happening. How lucky am I?* She made her way back to where Ralph was laughing with Peggy and Ben. She smiled at him and sat next to Thad. "How are you doing there?"

"Ang, this was epic. You were on the big screen with Bill Murray, dude. Like blew my mind."

"Blew my mind too," Angie said.

Gina ran over to Angie. "Louie just called. He heard back from his pal in the mayor's office who confirmed everything. Said to apologize for not trusting you. We're back in business."

Kim was standing beside Gina, glowing, and wrapped her arm around Gina's shoulders as she said, "We're going to have to get back up to speed. We have to replenish everything we threw away."

Gina looked over at Angie. "Louie said you don't have to worry about Mario; he's taken care of things, whatever that means . . . and there's something else . . ."

Gina got close to Angie and whispered in her aunt's ear, "I have to tell you something. I'm falling in love with Kim."

Angie pulled back to study her niece and smiled. "I had a feeling that was going to happen. It's so nice that your friendship came first, and now a romance. Good for you, honey."

Their hug was cut short when Angie noticed Ralph walking over toward them. "Good news, I see."

"Last Bite is back in business!" Gina yelled over the noise in the bar.

Everyone threw their arms in the air and cheered. Connie rushed over and hugged Gina. Thad put his fingers in his mouth and blew a loud whistle, and Ben gave two thumbs-up.

"Last Bite is going to be hiring, if you know anyone who's looking," Gina announced.

"Well, I'll be looking for employment soon. Seems my company has gone belly-up," Ralph said.

"Oh no, Ralph, I'm so sorry," Angie said, moving closer. "I could use some help making pesto sauce," she whispered in his ear.

"I'll have time on my hands and I can't think of anyone else I'd rather spend it with, Angie." He touched her hand gently.

"We're taking things nice and slow, Ralph. I have two jobs

and a family to take care of, so I'm not rushing into anything. I don't need a man to define me anymore."

Angie stepped away from Ralph, threw her arms up, and yelled, "Victory is mine!" Happy tears streaming down her cheeks, warmth radiated throughout her body, and with newfound confidence rising from the very depths of her soul, Angie knew that something had shifted inside her forever. She had the profound knowingness that she could stand on her own two feet and be the kind of woman she had always admired and wanted to be, deep down.

Angie's journey was just beginning at the young age of forty-five, and what an adventure it was going to be . . . an adventure of her own design.

The End

Angie Sortino's Pesto Recipe

- ½ cup of organic extra virgin olive oil (EVOO)
- 3 medium-size cloves of fresh garlic
- 3 cups fresh chopped organic basil (just leaves), chopped
- ½ cup toasted or roasted walnuts or almonds, chopped
- ¼ cup freshly grated Parmigiano Reggiano
- Salt and pepper to taste

Throw everything in the blender and mix until completely blended, and you'll have a happy day. You can use this pesto on fresh-cut or chopped vegetables, pasta, or crostini. Serves 4–6 people.

Thank you to Chef Kerry Peele for permission to share this recipe.

Hungry for more?

Yes, *Scratch, My Ass!* is a real cookbook. Order your copy (and Amy's other books) at www.amyspeele.com.

Book Club Discussion Questions

1. Angie's journey is one of reinvention in midlife. How does her past shape the woman she becomes, and what parts of her transformation did you find the most compelling?

2. Chicago comes alive in this book, from Wrigley Field to City Hall. In what ways does this setting influence the tone and themes of the story?

3. How do Angie's relationships evolve over time, and what do they reveal about friendship, loyalty, and personal growth?

4. The funeral-parlor catering concept walks a line between humor and heart. What does this unlikely business say about how we handle grief, legacy, and new beginnings?

5. Baseball is woven into Angie's world, the Cubs in particular. How does the culture of the game mirror her personal stakes and turning points?

6. Food is more than just a backdrop in this story—it's part of the plot and the emotional core. How does

cooking (and failing at it!) represent connection, comfort, or chaos for the characters?

7. What expectations—personal, cultural, or generational—does Angie confront in her forties, and how does she challenge or embrace them?

8. This book blends humor with real-life messiness. What moments made you laugh, and what deeper truths do those scenes point to?

9. Which supporting character stood out to you the most? How does their presence throughout the narrative help Angie grow or reflect something new about herself?

10. If you could ask Angie one question at the end of the novel, what would it be—and why?

Acknowledgments

First, I must thank my writing soulmate sister, Betsy Graziani Fasbinder. She has supported me through all of my creative projects with kindness, clarity, and honesty. She provided me with detailed feedback that improved this story immensely. I am so grateful for her friendship, and to Linda Joy Myers and Christie Nelson—forever in my writerly corner.

Thank you to my editor, Annie Tucker, who partnered with me as I created a book in which she finally indulged my hunger to write about food along with this wild adventure. Thank you for keeping me on track, Annie; I know it can be a challenge. I still laugh at some of our conversations as the story progressed.

Thank you to Louie Rago, who opened up his beautiful funeral parlor—yeah, that's right, I said beautiful funeral parlor. Rago Brothers was established in Chicago in 1917. Louie received a call from me, a total stranger, and when he heard that I was writing a book that featured his, ahem, profession, he invited me into his world. He offered details that I could have never known about the reality of the funeral business. This is where this story of *Last Bite* begins. Thanks, Louie. Hope I won't be needing your services any time soon.

To my agent, Kimberley Cameron, who helped me to think out of the medical murder mystery box and focus on fun and romance. She provided thoughtful feedback during a very stressful time in her life. I appreciate your support and belief in me.

To Mindy Malecki, my friend of many years and the coauthor of our cookbook, *Scratch? My Ass! Store-Bought Can Be as Good as Homemade*, published in 1984. This ridiculous collection of "recipes" is referenced in this book. We will be reprinting it for those who are challenged in the kitchen but want that wow factor when they bring a dish to potlucks.

To my friend Cindy Ostroff, who reviewed the manuscript and graciously offered her suggestions. You always make my books better and I'm grateful for your keen editorial eye.

To my sister Kerry Peele, who offered her talent in the culinary world. She created some wonderful recipes for Angie, Gina, and Kim to make. Be sure to try her pesto sauce recipe—it's outstanding.

To the trailblazer Brooke Warner, for her tireless commitment to shepherding women's stories out into the world. What a gift she is to the publishing world. I'm grateful to the She Writes team, who are committed to excellence at every step of the publishing process.

Lastly, to my soulmate and creative husband, Mark Schatz, who is always in my corner. I couldn't ask for a better partner on my writing journey.

About the Author

Photo credit: Lia Larrea

Amy S. Peele, RN, is the award-winning, best-selling author of *Cut*, *Match*, and *Hold*, medical mysteries with a mission and a side of humor. Her books have reached bestseller status and gained national recognition with such awards as the NYC Big Book Award, Chanticleer International Book Awards, IPPY Awards, Independent Press Awards, and more.

Before becoming a writer, Amy enjoyed a fascinating thirty-five-year career in the organ transplant field, which provided an authentic backdrop to her mystery series. She studied improv at Second City Players workshop for a year, which enhanced her sense of humor.

This is Amy's first venture into the world of women's fiction, lighthearted romance, and of course, lots of food. With great restraint, she did not kill anyone in this book and there are no transplants.

Amy enjoys meditating, Pilates, practicing and teaching chair and laughter yoga, swimming, and eating good food. She is and will always be a die-hard Cubs fan. You can find out more about her by going to her website: www.amyspeele.com.

Looking for your next great read?

We can help!

Visit www.shewritespress.com/next-read
or scan the QR code below for a list
of our recommended titles.

She Writes Press is an award-winning
independent publishing company founded to
serve women writers everywhere.